THE
Perfect
CRIME

BOOK SEVEN OF THE SYDNEY LEGAL SERIES

CHRIS TAYLOR

LCT Productions Pty Ltd
18364 Kamilaroi Highway, Narrabri NSW 2390

ISBN. 978-1-925119-58-9 (Paperback)

The Perfect Crime is a work of fiction. Names, characters, places, brands, media and incidents either are the product of the author's imagination or are used fictitiously. Any resemblance to actual persons, living or dead, events, or locales, is entirely coincidental.

Published in the United States of America.

BOOKS BY CHRIS TAYLOR

THE MUNRO FAMILY SERIES

The Profiler
The Investigator
The Predator
The Betrayal
The Deception
The Negotiator
The Christmas Vigil
The Ransom
The Defendant
The Shooting
The Maker
(Available in Audio)

THE SYDNEY HARBOUR HOSPITAL SERIES

The Perfect Husband
The Body Thief
The Baby Snatchers
The Final Bullet
The Debt Collector
The Lab Test
The Stolen Identity
The Cliff-top Killer
The Likeable Fraudster

THE SYDNEY LEGAL SERIES

An Accidental Murderer
At the Hand of Her Father
A Woman Scorned
Lies and Deception
Ordinary Evil
The Ties That Bind
The Perfect Crime
Malicious Love
Toxic Inheritance

THIS IS WHERE IT ENDS SERIES

Jessie's story

Ryan's story
Holly's story
Sarah's story
Veronica's story

THE CRAIGDON FAMILY SERIES
Callum
Joel
Isabella
Nicholas
Sophia
Flynn
Noah
Logan
Elizabeth

THE BARRINGTON FAMILY SERIES
Broken Lives
Broken Promises
Broken Bonds
Broken Spirits
Broken Vows
Broken Minds
Broken Dreams
Broken Hearts
Broken Homes

Get a FREE book when you sign up for Chris Taylor's newsletter at: www.christaylorauthor.com.au

Love Audiobooks? Check out Chris Taylor Books on audio on Audible.com, Amazon.com and the iBooks store.

Join Chris Taylor's Facebook reader group/fan page and be among the first to receive news of book releases, read and review books prior to release and other amazing offers. Join Now at: www.facebook.com/groups/1758023621144744/

Find out more about all of Chris Taylor's books, by visiting her website at: www.christaylorauthor.com.au/about/books

Dedication

This book is dedicated to my sisters, Nic and Donna for their love and support and extremely productive brainstorming one very memorable weekend. I love you both dearly.

*And as always, to my husband, Linden.
My best friend, my soul mate. I love you to the moon and back.*

Acknowledgments

As usual, no book comes into being without a lot of help and support by my friends and family. A world of thanks must go to my wonderful editor, Pat Thomas. Thank you for everything that you do to make my stories even more amazing than I could ever dare to dream. To former Detective Superintendent Michael Kilfoyle, thank you for lending my story credibility. Any mistakes are wholly my own.

To Damon Freeman, Alisha Moore and all of the staff at damonza.com, thank you for yet another fantastic book cover. To my sister, Nicole Guihot and to my friend, Ally Thomson, thank you for your excellent editorial comments, proof reading skills and suggestions. I hope you like the final result.

To Amy Atwell and her dedicated staff at Author E.M.S. who are so much more than book formatters. Amy, once again, thank you for your magic.

To the fantastic writer organizations such as Romance Writers of Australia, Romance Writers of

America and Romance Writers of New Zealand for all the help, support and encouragement they offer new and aspiring writers, including me.

To my readers, thank you for your support and love for my stories. Your encouragement and enjoyment make this journey all worthwhile.

And lastly, to my friends and family, especially my husband and children. Thank you for putting up with late dinners and even later conversations as I've emerged day after day from the sometimes scary but always enthralling world I've created on my computer.

PROLOGUE

Mackenzie Callaway downed the last of his whisky and set the glass on the bar with a grimace. He glanced at his watch. It was way past late. Time to stop drowning his sorrows over a woman who was unworthy of him anyway and head for home. To bed.

Melissa's confession of infidelity had taken him completely by surprise. He'd spoken without thinking when he'd told her to get out. In truth, he'd been angry and shocked. Now, seventeen days later, he wondered if he'd acted too hastily. She was the woman he thought he'd marry. Now they were done. *Could they have worked through their problems?* He guessed he'd never know.

With a sigh, he settled his bill and climbed off the barstool. Shouldering his way through the wooden entry door, he scanned the parking lot. His pickup truck was where he'd left it, but he was long gone from being able to drive it home. Instead, he pulled out his phone and dialed a cab and then moved to lean on the side wall of the building to wait.

The meaty fist came at him from the darkness. Mac ducked instinctively, but wasn't quick enough. The smack of flesh on flesh was sickening. The thin skin covering his bottom lip split under the impact. Pain shot through his mouth.

"What the hell—?" Reaching up, he gingerly touched the wound. His fingers came away wet with blood. With little time to contemplate what had happened, his attacker came at him again. With only seconds to spare, Mac got into position. This time, he was ready.

The flurry of punches from the short and stocky man who'd appeared from nowhere were met with solid deflections as Mac squared off against his attacker. The man's fists were fast, but Mac was quicker. In short order he managed to rain a series of blows to the man's head and shoulders until the thug cried out in pain. An instant later, with a muttered oath, the man turned tail and disappeared into the darkness.

Mac stumbled back against the red brick wall that ran alongside the building that housed the bar. The streets of Sydney were quiet. Everyone with any sense was in bed asleep, like he should have been on a Monday night. It was way past three the last time he checked. If it weren't for Melissa and her cheating heart, that's exactly where he would have been, still oblivious to the double life she'd led for who knew how long.

They'd been together more than two years and he never once suspected. *What kind of idiot did that make him?* He'd thought they had something together. Hell, he'd even thought about their future. Though he wasn't exactly the marrying type, he hadn't given up on the convention of marriage altogether... After all, he was thirty-seven and probably should settle down. That thought had crossed his mind. And Melissa had hinted at it often enough. And to think all that time she was having an affair. It was almost laughable the way she'd played him. Talk about gullible.

He thought drinking himself senseless night after night would help block the memories of her and their less-than-amicable parting.

What a joke.

Tonight all he'd gotten was a splitting headache from too much whisky and a sore and bloody lip. He'd be lucky if the thug hadn't chipped one of his teeth.

Gingerly, he moved his tongue around his mouth and was relieved to find his teeth were intact. He couldn't say the same for his bottom lip. Blood continued to drip in a steady stream down his chin and onto his T-shirt. He looked down at the mess and shook his head in disbelief.

Who the hell attacks a stranger like that?

It was downright weird. He wasn't in a rough part of the city and the man hadn't even asked for his wallet or phone. All he'd been doing was minding his own business, waiting for a cab. He hadn't even noticed the man until it was too late.

He considered going to the police station and reporting what happened, but he was drunk and what was there to tell, really? It wasn't as if he could identify his attacker and he'd only taken a punch or two...

He sighed. The week had been way past difficult and it had barely begun. In fact, the past seventeen days without Melissa in his life had been shit. He wanted to hate her for her cheating heart, but right now, drunk and weary beyond measure, he almost wanted her back. And to think he'd considered proposing. Ha! Now *that* was a joke!

The flash of lights from an approaching car snagged his attention. More cautious than he was before the attack, he pressed himself against the brick wall until he recognized the outline of a cab. Closing his eyes briefly in relief, he stepped out of the shadows and flagged the driver down. All he wanted to do was go home, take a shower and climb between the cool cotton sheets. Once there, he'd nurse his sore fists and cut lip and do his best to forget he'd ever known a woman called Melissa.

———————

From his place of concealment in the shadows, the man watched the taillights of the receding cab until there was nothing left but darkness and the streets returned to silence once again. His breath came fast. His chest was tight. His hands were still clenched into fists.

The hired thug had done his job, although it would have been better if he'd knocked out that bastard Callaway. Smashed his head upon the pavement. Left him for dead. It would have been fitting for a man who'd made yet another woman disappear.

A surge of determination filled him and his eyes narrowed. Fury ignited, slow and hot, in his gut. This time, Mackenzie Callaway wouldn't get away with murder. This time, Mac Callaway would pay.

CHAPTER 1

Four days later

With fierce concentration, Jessica Wolfe frowned at her computer screen. Night had descended hours earlier. The office had fallen silent. One by one, her work colleagues had headed home to their families, friends, or pets. But not Jessie.

With a surge of irritation, she pushed away from her desk and strode to the window. The night sky was as black as tar, visible in small patches between the tall buildings in downtown Sydney. The road far below was illuminated by the yellow-orange glow of street lights and the silence was disturbed only by the occasional siren or passing car.

She was alone in the office. At least, alone on her floor. There might be the odd lawyer working late in some other part of the building – some other poor sucker who didn't have a life – but she couldn't tell who else might still be working there from her lowly position on the fourth floor.

One of the senior partners had asked her to research a point of law and she was determined to find a loophole he could use which would allow his client to go free. She'd been at Sydney Legal for more than five years, but ever since her brother, Alistair's arrest and subsequent conviction for illegal trafficking in human organs, she'd been well and truly "on the outs" and her chances of being offered a partnership had taken a severe blow.

Though no one at the firm had come out and said it, she wasn't stupid. The firm had recently been forced to overcome negative publicity when Alexei Gianopoulos, one of the senior partners had been shot by his wife. The scandal had hit all the major media outlets and had gone viral on social media. It was a major embarrassment for everyone.

Suffice it to say, Alexei Gianopoulos' wife was now cooling her heels in jail, just like Jessie's brother. Under those circumstances, the firm wasn't about to promote someone like her, connected to yet another criminal, no matter that she wasn't responsible for her brother's actions. Now it felt like she had to work three times as hard as anyone else to prove her worth and remove the stigma Alistair had left behind.

Her brother had done his best to convince his family – and anyone else who'd listen – his actions had been done for the greater good, but he couldn't dispute the fact he'd made millions off the illegal deals, and with his conviction Jessie's chance at a partnership at Sydney Legal had been shot to smithereens. In the months that followed his conviction, she'd had difficulty holding her head up in the corridors of the esteemed law firm, let alone putting her name forward for a partnership. Two years down the track and she was forced to concede it might not ever happen.

Though she tried to ignore the whispers and sideways glances, as far as most of her colleagues at Sydney Legal were concerned, she was just as guilty as her brother – by association. It made things difficult for her, but she was determined to weather the storm and eventually, when the time was right, demand the secure future and the pay packet she deserved.

So there she was – a thirty-something single woman living in Sydney – still at her desk, even though it was going on for eleven on a Friday night. She should have been out kicking up her heels with her friends, meeting someone special. Instead, she was burning the midnight oil in an effort to impress her bosses and claw back some of the regard and respect she'd had before Alistair's spectacular fall from grace.

There were only a handful of lawyers at the firm who continued to treat her as if nothing had happened. She'd counted Sally-Ann Li, Daisy Green and Abby Brown as her friends before her brother's arrest and fortunately, they'd stood by her during Alistair's trial. Even after the guilty verdict, they'd been there for her and continued to offer her their support. She was beyond grateful for their efforts but even her well-regarded lawyer friends couldn't restore the damage her brother had done to her career.

The sound of her phone ringing startled her from her reverie. Bending low, she picked up her handbag from beneath her feet and hunted around for her phone. Pulling it out, she glanced at the screen and frowned. Lachlan Coleridge.

What was her brother-in-law doing, calling her so late? All of a sudden, she was filled with dread. Had something happened to her sister, Ava, or her nieces and nephew?

"Hi, Lachlan. What is it? Is everyone all right?"

"Yes, of course. Everyone's fine," Lachlan replied.

Relief flooded through her. "I'm so glad."

"I didn't mean to startle you, calling so late," Lachlan continued.

"You're right. It *is* late. I should be heading home."

"I thought I might catch you at work. That's why I called."

"What's this about?" she asked, frowning.

Lachlan sighed. "I'm at the station. Night shift. Dealing with the usual mayhem a Friday night in the city brings. I've been trying to find time to call you all evening, but didn't have a chance until now."

"What's up?" Jessie asked, curious. She and her brother-in-law got along well and regularly spoke on the phone, though not usually so late at night.

"A buddy of mine called and asked me to recommend a lawyer. I mentioned your name, but I thought I'd better check with you before I told him to proceed. He might call you."

Jessie's lips quirked upwards in a wry smile. "Shouldn't you have checked *before* you gave him my name?"

Lachlan cleared his throat and Jessie could tell he was embarrassed. "Yeah, I guess I should have. I didn't think. I'm sorry. It's just that this guy's a friend and he might be in trouble."

Jessie frowned. "Might be? How does *that* work?"

"See, his girlfriend – well, ex-girlfriend, actually – is missing. She's been gone three weeks. No one's seen or heard from her."

"Three weeks isn't all that long. Maybe she went on a holiday. Why would your buddy care? They're not even together anymore."

"Yeah, you're right and Mac felt much the same way. The missing persons report was filed by the girl's sister. The officer who took the initial report did some checks. The woman's bank account hasn't been touched since the day before she was last seen. Ditto for her credit card."

"So, you're thinking she might have met with foul play? Is that it?"

"Who knows?" Lachlan replied. "It's a possibility."

"What does your buddy have to say about it?"

"He's adamant he doesn't know where she is."

"How long ago did they part company?"

"Three weeks ago."

Jessie's brows shot up in surprise. "I can see why the police might be interested in him."

Lachlan blew out his breath on a sigh. "Yeah. Of course, I'm sure it's just a coincidence. He's a good bloke. I'd bet my life he hasn't done anything wrong, but the timing seems beyond coincidental. Doesn't look good for him."

"You're right," Jessie agreed. "I understand why he feels the need to speak with a lawyer."

"I'm sure he has nothing to hide. He's just being…careful."

"Fair enough."

"So you're happy to meet with him?"

"Sure."

"Thanks, Jess. You're a gem."

Jessie heard the relief in Lachlan's voice and smiled. "Hey, don't sweat it. This guy is a friend of yours. I'm good with that. What's his name, by the way?"

"Mackenzie Callaway. His friends call him Mac."

Jessie reeled backwards as if she'd been struck. It couldn't be… Surely it wasn't the same Mackenzie Callaway she'd known as a teenager. Perhaps she'd misheard.

"D-did you say Mackenzie C-Callaway?" she stammered.

"Yeah. He's a property developer. He's done very well for himself, too. His penthouse apartment in Vaucluse could grace the cover of magazines. If he weren't such a nice bloke, I'd hate him."

"H-how old is he?"

"He turned thirty-seven a couple of months ago. I was at the party. A posh do at his place." Lachlan chuckled. "Why do you ask? Don't tell me you're interested?"

Heat suffused Jessie's face and she was glad there wasn't anyone there to see her blush. "Of course not," she snapped. "I was just curious."

The age checked out. Mac had been a year ahead of her in school. Still, that didn't guarantee it was him.

She kept her tone light. "Has he always lived in Sydney?"

"Yeah, as far as I know. He attended the public school in North Randwick. I only know because he had some of his old school mates at the party. I got talking to a few of them. In fact, you might even know them. Ava told me you and she went to North Randwick High."

Jessie's heart skipped a beat. *It was him.* It had to be. He was the right age and he had attended her school. She shook her head slowly back and forth, stunned by the coincidence.

Mackenzie Callaway. It was a name she hadn't heard in a long, long time. Not since she was seventeen.

"I... I think you're right," she stammered. "I remember Mackenzie Callaway. He was in the year ahead of me and Ava. I'm not so sure you should have mentioned my name to him. Mackenzie and I haven't seen each other since high school and even then, we didn't exactly part on amicable terms."

"It didn't seem to tweak anything negative when I suggested he give you a call. He said he'd heard of you and wanted to meet with the best."

Once again, Jessie was filled with surprise. She hadn't been aware Mac knew she was a lawyer.

Had he kept tabs on her after high school? The thought filled her with a warmth that immediately irritated her. She and Mackenzie Callaway were truly over the night she found another woman in his bed. Especially when that woman had been dead.

"Where are the police in their investigation?" she asked.

"Mac was brought in earlier this evening for questioning. He agreed to participate in a record of interview. At the time, he declined the services of a lawyer, saying he had nothing to hide. He only called me about it afterwards. I believe his protestations of innocence, but like I said, he's being cautious. I guess he wants to speak to you about his rights; get some advice."

"So he hasn't been charged?"

"Hell, no. The investigating officers don't even have proof of any wrongdoing. All they have is a concerned family member and a bank account that hasn't been touched. Nowhere near enough to go making any claims of foul play, let alone arrests. Detective Zane Sullivan has been assigned the case. He's making preliminary enquires, speaking to anyone who might be able to shed light on the woman's whereabouts. Speaking with her recently ex-boyfriend was a natural place to start."

"How did the police find out about him?"

"I believe the missing woman's sister gave them his name."

"So he wasn't concerned that he hadn't heard from her?"

"No. Mac hadn't been the least interested in the whereabouts of his ex. From what he said, their parting was far from amicable. He was happy to have her out of his life."

Jessie compressed her lips on a frown. "*Ouch.* He *said* that? It probably won't help his case – if it comes to that."

"You're right. He didn't have to volunteer that information. But he did. It's another reason why I don't think he has anything to do with her disappearance – if, in fact, she really *has* disappeared."

Jessie pursed her lips in thought. "Still, it sounds like I need to talk to Mac sooner, rather than later. As a defense lawyer, I cringe when I think of someone volunteering information the police haven't requested and don't need... Especially information that might come back and haunt them."

"You're right. Mac might be a successful property developer, but he's way too trusting. I knew he should have kept his mouth shut. I wish he'd called me before he participated in the interview."

"Well, it's too late now, but I might be able to convince him to stem the flow of information he volunteers in the future. You don't honestly think the police view him as a suspect, do you?"

Lachlan's voice sobered. "Yeah, I think they do. I had a word with Sullivan. He's not sure what's going on, but his gut's telling him something's awry. The missing girl had a stable job as a realtor in a big agency in the city. Apart from being his girlfriend, she actually worked with Calloway on his big development projects. She had a wide circle of friends and was well thought of. Officers have spoken to her work colleagues as well as some of her friends and they all agree her disappearance is totally out of character. Though she has a reputation as a bit of a party girl, she's always turned up for work. To add to the intrigue, apparently our boy is sporting some suspicious facial injuries. He said he got into a fight but something seems off about his account. Says someone came out of nowhere, for no reason and started bashing him with their fists."

Jessie absorbed Lachlan's words in silence. All of a sudden, her mind latched onto the teenage girl that had been found murdered in Mackenzie Callaway's bed. *Janice Scott*. There had been evidence of rape. Eventually another boy from their school was found guilty of both crimes. At the time, it had been too much for Jessie. She and Mac had parted ways straight after. She'd never believed he was involved in the sexual assault of Janice Scott or her death, but the shock of it wasn't something she'd ever forget.

Now it seemed another woman in Mackenzie's Callaway's life had caught the interest of the police. Was it mere coincidence, or could there be more to it? After all, sometimes people didn't know their friends and family as well as they thought they did. Just look at her brother Alistair and what he'd done. Nobody had seen that coming, least of all Jessie.

"Are you still there, Jess?"

Lachlan's voice was tinged with concern. She

hurriedly responded. "Yes, I'm here. You took me by surprise. There was an incident in Mac's senior year. A school friend was raped and murdered. She was found in his bed."

"Shit," Lachlan murmured in surprise.

"Yes, it was awful, but in the end, it worked out all right for Mac. The police used DNA evidence to clear him and find the real killer."

"Wow, I had no idea he had something like that in his past. Like I said, he's a good mate of mine and certainly doesn't fit the profile of your typical criminal. He's made a real success of his life. He made *Forbes* magazine for the second time a couple of months ago, which is no mean feat for an Australian businessman. Still, I've been in this game long enough to know that criminals come in all shapes and sizes and from all walks of life. You never can tell."

Jessie absorbed Lachlan's information, storing it away for later consideration. Her mind snagged on the fact Mackenzie was a successful businessman, a property developer. Somehow, it jarred with her memories of the laid-back, fun-loving football jock who'd ditched the books at every opportunity in favor of a game.

Somewhere along the way, he'd changed.

Jessie sighed and glanced at her watch. It was after eleven. Her eyes were sore and gritty from endless hours staring at a computer screen. Her back and neck ached from being bent over so long at her desk. She wanted nothing more than to switch off her computer and call an end to the night.

But now Mackenzie Callaway had once again crashed into her life. He wanted to see her... *Was she ready to meet with him after all these years? What about the history between them? They hadn't exactly parted as friends...*

"I'll let Mac know you're willing to see him," Lachlan continued, unaware of the turmoil that filled her mind.

"D-does he know I'm the same Jessie Wolfe he went to school with?"

"I'm not sure. It was Ava who made the connection at the party. I didn't mention that to him. But he did know you were a lawyer."

Jessie eased her breath out on a troubled sigh. She didn't know if it was a good thing or a bad thing that Mackenzie Callaway might know he was seeking legal advice from a woman he'd briefly dated in high school – a woman who'd been in love with him for most of her life.

She wondered what he looked like now. *Was he still the same tall, broad-shouldered athlete he'd been at eighteen? Or had the years been less kind to him? Perhaps his desk job had turned muscle into fat?*

Did it matter? Probably not.

All of a sudden, she was filled with a yearning to see him, but it was way past late. She was tired and far from being at her best. The first time she came face to face with Mackenzie Callaway after nearly twenty years, she wanted to be firing on all cylinders. So, for now, he'd have to wait.

Chapter 2

The bright morning sun found its way beneath the brim of Mackenzie Callaway's hard hat and warmed his cheeks. The rain from the previous night had washed away the city smog and the winter sky was as bright and clear as any he'd seen in Sydney. It was the start of a new week and with it Mac hoped to put his previous problems behind him. Melissa was out of his life and it looked like it was for good. He hadn't seen or heard from her since she left and it was time for him to accept that they were over and get on with his life.

With the blueprints of his latest ten-story condominium development folded under his arm, he strode across the development site with purpose, taking care to avoid the puddles. He pulled open the door to the site office and spied his head foreman filling a Styrofoam cup with coffee from the machine. The overhead fluorescent light glinted off Steve Prendergast's gray buzz cut. Ex-military, Steve liked to wear his hair short.

"Morning, Mac."

Mac acknowledged the greeting with a smile. "You can pour another one of them for me, if you like. It'll be the first hit of caffeine I've had today."

Steve's lip curled upwards in a grin. "You trying to cut back?"

Mac's smile widened. He shook his head. "No. Just haven't had a minute to scratch myself since I woke. One of those days."

"How's the lip?" Steve asked.

Mac touched the wound and grimaced. "It still hurts like hell."

Steve shook his head. "I still can't believe a stranger attacked you like that. It's weird."

"Yeah. I don't know what the hell he was on or who he thought I was."

"You should have gone to the police."

Mac shrugged. "And tell them what? It was dark. I was drunk. I wouldn't be able to identify the man if they paid me. Besides, it's only a split lip. My attacker didn't fare so well. He went off limping." Mac grinned.

Steve smiled and shook his head. "You're a lucky bastard, that's for sure." He turned his attention back to the coffee machine and then handed Mac a cup of steaming black brew.

"Thanks," Mac murmured, taking the cup gratefully.

Steve Prendergast had worked for Mac for the past decade and knew Mac almost as well as Mac knew himself. Mac had come to rely on Steve's building expertise, exceptional organizational skills and dry sense of humor to get him through the many developments he'd completed. In fact, Mac had just made up his mind to offer Steve a partnership in the business. It would take a bit of the pressure off and it was something Steve had well and truly earned. He appeared to have finally gotten a handle on the PTSD that had crippled him when he'd first returned home from Afghanistan. He was also a helluva worker, a good bloke and someone Mac trusted implicitly. Besides, anyone who'd served their country deserved something extra out of life.

Steve leaned against the counter and watched Mac find a space for his cup on his crowded desk.

"So, do you want the good news, or the bad news?" Steve asked.

Mac groaned. "Surely it's too early in the week for bad news? What's the good news?"

"The good news is that the rain hasn't put us any further off schedule. The bad news is that I've just taken a call from Omer Demir and there's a delay on the concrete."

Mac cursed. "What the hell? We're supposed to do that pour today. I've just about had enough of that man. What's the problem now?"

Steve grimaced. "Who knows? It's just Demir getting up to his old tricks. You know how competitive he is. He'll do anything to throw our schedule into a spin. I hear he's having trouble with some of his workers on that development he's doing in Vaucluse. Maybe that has something to do with the delay?"

Mac shook his head in disgust. "So he takes it

out on me. Typical. Did he give you any kind of excuse for the delay?"

"Apparently three of his trucks are experiencing mechanical issues," Steve replied. "He's not sure how long it'll be before they're back on the road."

Mac tried to stem his anger. "How long? Hours? Days?"

Steve shrugged and sipped his coffee. "Who knows? Could be hours, but knowing Demir, more likely days."

Mac made a sound of disgust in the back of his throat. Omer Demir was a fierce competitor, a business rival who took perverse pleasure whenever one of Mac's projects went off course. And, more often than not, it was Demir who was responsible for the delay. He also owned most of the concrete trucks in Sydney. Basically, he had a monopoly on the concrete available to any developer in town. It was the only reason Mac continued to be civil to the man.

What he wanted to do was to tell Demir to shove his concrete where the sun didn't shine, but to do that would only hurt Mac's business. There were only a handful of independent concrete contractors in Sydney and they'd never be able to supply Mac's needs. Omer Demir knew that all too well.

Mac frowned as he thought through his options. "Have we tried Fallon's?"

Steve nodded. "Yep. They can't get us anything for a couple of weeks. Even then, they can supply less than half of what we need."

"What about Watson's?"

"Same thing."

Mac's lips tightened. "I guess there's no point in calling Jacobson's?"

Steve nodded. "You're right. Jacobson sold his business last week. I ran into a few of his workers who were talking about it in the bar a couple nights ago."

Mac grimaced. "Let me guess. He sold out to Demir."

Steve nodded again, his expression as grim as Mac felt.

"Damn!" The quiet curse escaped Mac's tight lips. Frustration surged through him. His fists clenched. "I just wish there was something we could do about that man. It's not right that he has such a monopoly on something so essential to our business."

"I'm hearing you," Steve replied, his tone laced with sympathy. He shot Mac a sideways glance. "I guess you could always buy him out."

Steve followed the suggestion with a slight chuckle but Mac knew his foreman was only half-joking. It was something Mac had thought of himself every time Demir pulled a stunt like this. It was just that Mac wasn't interested in owning concrete trucks. He was a property developer. That's what he loved to do. There was nothing like the excitement and adrenaline of watching a building he helped design and construct rise out of the ground. He'd been in the business for more than fifteen years and it still gave him a thrill. Besides, he shouldn't be forced to buy out a competitor just to ensure a regular supply of concrete for his building needs. And he sure as hell didn't have the time to put into a sideline business. Especially now, with Melissa pulling a disappearing act and the police breathing down his neck.

Of course, the only connection Melissa had to his work was that she was his realtor. The police were far more interested in the fact she was his ex-girlfriend. Now he not only had to fend off their questions, he also had to find a new realtor.

Great. Just another headache he didn't need. It was just like Melissa to do something like that. She always needed to be the center of attention. Now her disappearance had caught the interest of the police and they'd been asking Mac a whole lot of questions as if he were a criminal or something.

The truth was, he had no idea where Melissa was, but that truth didn't seem to matter to the cops. Now he was caught up in the middle of it, right when he needed to focus on getting his latest project completed. Talk about bad timing.

As if reading his mind, Steve voiced another question. "So, have you heard from Melissa?"

Mac shook his head. "No. I had a call from the police on Friday afternoon. They asked me to come in for an interview. Apparently her sister, Angela, is concerned. She hasn't heard from her, either," he said dryly.

Steve frowned. "What? She thinks something's happened to her?"

"Who knows? I guess so. She was the one who went to the police. Filed a missing persons report. I think it's all a bit extreme. Hell, maybe Melissa and her new lover are lying low, or enjoying the sunset over the Caribbean? She could be anywhere."

"How are you dealing with it?"

Mac compressed his lips. "I'm fine. As of today, I'm putting the whole sorry relationship behind me. Melissa and I are over. Period. She can sleep with whoever she wants. It's no longer any of my concern. As for her marketing skills, I'm sure we can find someone to replace her."

"Fair enough. But what's with Angela and the missing persons report? How long has it been since Melissa left?"

"Three weeks."

Steve shrugged. "Not so long. What's got her sister so concerned?"

"Apparently she hasn't seen or heard from her since then. She didn't even know we'd split until I told her."

Steve's eyebrows rose in surprise. "She called you?"

"Yeah. Angela's a nice girl. She and I always got on all right. She'd left a number of messages for Mel and she hadn't heard from her. She called me to find out what was going on."

"And when you told her you'd split up, she went to the police?" Steve guessed.

"Something like that. I spoke to her a week ago. I guess it took her a few more days to contact the police."

"I guess it is a little strange Melissa hasn't phoned her sister. Were they close?"

"Yeah. Mel called her at least once a day, sometimes more."

"I can understand why Angela's concerned. If it were my sister, I'd probably have gone to the police, too."

"Except you're forgetting this woman just admitted to her live-in boyfriend that she was having an affair and she didn't seem the least bit remorseful. After the argument we had, I can understand why she might want to lie low. I'd like to think she's feeling guilty for the way she treated me."

Steve nodded. "You're right. She treated you like shit."

"Thanks for understanding," Mac replied, mollified.

Steve took another sip from his coffee. "So what did the police have to say?"

Mac shrugged. "They asked me a whole bunch of questions about our relationship. I told them the truth."

"So they know about the break-up?"

"Yes, of course."

"Did you have a lawyer present when you spoke with them?"

Mac frowned. "Of course not. They were just asking questions. I have nothing to hide."

Steve shook his head. "You're being stupid, Mac. "You're the ex-boyfriend. You need to be careful. The woman hasn't been seen or heard from for weeks. You say the two of you had an argument right before she disappeared. It doesn't take a genius to work out that you might be a suspect."

"For Christ sake, Steve! Whose side are you on?" Mac cried.

Steve held his hands up in a conciliatory manner. *I know you didn't have anything to do with her disappearance, but the police don't know you like I do. As far as they're concerned, you had a nasty fight with your girlfriend and now she's disappeared. You need to treat this seriously. Don't bury your head in the sand. Until Melissa's found, this isn't going away. Talk to a lawyer. Get some decent legal advice and keep your mouth shut."

Mac sighed and took a sip of coffee. "If it makes you feel any better, I spoke to a buddy of mine. A cop. He gave me the name of someone I should talk to."

Steve shot him a look of exasperation. "So what the hell are you waiting for?"

Mac ground his teeth in frustration. "I didn't *do* anything, Steve. I don't know where the hell Melissa is. I sure as hell didn't have anything to do with her disappearance. Unless you count the argument we had. According to the police, that was the last time she was seen. I can only guess that's the reason they're looking at me."

Steve continued to look somber. "Well, I guess if you have nothing to hide, you should be all right."

"Exactly. And if it makes you feel any better, I intend to call a lawyer...soon."

Steve looked at him pointedly. "When?"

Mac lowered his gaze and shuffled some papers around on his desk. "As soon as I get a chance, okay? In case you hadn't noticed, we've got a hell of a lot going on right now. I don't have time to get into the nitty-gritty of whether or not I had anything to do with the disappearance of my ex-girlfriend. We both know I didn't hurt her... Besides, I intend to call the lawyer as soon as I have a spare moment. I give you my word."

Steve nodded and modified his tone. "Okay. I understand. Really, Mac. I do. I'm just looking out for you, buddy. That's all."

Some of the anger and tension that had held Mac in its grip ever since he'd heard about Demir's latest stunt eased. He blew out his breath on a sigh and tossed a grateful glance toward the man he thought of as the brother he'd never had.

"I know and I'm sorry for getting upset with you. It's not your fault I'm in this mess. It was uncalled for."

Steve looked away, embarrassed. "It's fine. I understand better than anyone the stress you're under, Mac. The things that have gone wrong with this development... They just keep piling up. I'm not just talking about the delays with the concrete. I haven't gotten around to telling you about the mess-up with the steel order. I—"

"What about the steel order?"

Steve looked grim. "I took a call from Johnstone Steel earlier. Someone gave them the wrong dimensions. The steel will all have to be cut again."

Anger and disbelief flooded through Mac. He stared at his foreman. "Who the hell was responsible for that mistake?"

"I'm still looking into it. I'm not sure if it came from our end or theirs."

"Well you do that and be sure to get back to me ASAP. I want to know what the hell happened.

Someone's going to pay. This is going to set us back weeks."

The two men fell into silence, each lost in their own thoughts. Mac was the first to break it.

"So, you've hit me with two pieces of bad news. Other than the rain not putting us back any further than we are, do you have any other good news? Please tell me you do."

Steve managed a smile. "Yes. I do, as a matter of fact. That couple who were looking at the penthouse apartment are now keen to sign. Whatever Melissa said to them must have worked."

Mac was flooded with equal parts guilt and relief. "That's great. Mel had been working hard on the couple trying to convince them to buy. I'm glad her hard work paid off. There'll be a decent commission from it for her, that's for sure."

"Let's hope she surfaces long enough to finalize the deal. They said they'd tried to call her, but she hasn't phoned them back."

Mac grimaced. "It's probably all part of her revenge, although *I'm* the aggrieved party, not her. No doubt she'd take immense satisfaction in having the sale of my most expensive condo fall apart."

"Even if it meant losing her commission?"

Mac sighed. "Who knows? I thought I knew the woman. Turns out I didn't know her very well at all."

"Well, let's hope the break-up doesn't affect our bottom line. Do you want me to look into finding another realtor? I'm sure you won't have trouble finding someone to replace Melissa. The other realtors have been desperate to get in on a piece of this. It's your biggest development yet."

Mac shot him a grateful look. "That would be great, Steve. Just one less headache for me to deal with."

Steve pushed away from the counter and tossed his empty Styrofoam cup into the trash. "No problem. Leave it with me. I'll put the realtors through their paces and come back to you with recommendations. Would that suit?"

Mac looked up at Steve with relief. "That would be great. Thanks, mate."

Steve nodded. "No problem. Consider it done." With that, Steve picked up his hard hat and headed toward the door. "Work calls. See you round."

Mac watched as Steve disappeared through the doorway. The sound of the construction site coming alive filtered through the opening and then was shut off again as the door closed. Mac needed to get out there, too. There had been enough delays. If he was going to make any money out of this project, he needed to get things back on track. But he also needed to deal with Melissa. Steve's words about the police considering him a suspect were still ringing in his ears. The fact Steve's concerns mirrored Mac's was of no comfort. The thought had already crossed Mac's mind. It was the reason he'd called Lachlan Coleridge in the first place.

With a sigh of resignation, he reached for his wallet and pulled out the scrap of paper he'd written the name and number on.

Jessica Wolfe.

It was a name he hadn't heard for a long time. It was a name that used to cause his heart to skip a beat and bring a smile to his lips. Now it just filled his belly with nerves. An image of Jessie Wolfe as she'd been nearly two decades before flashed through his mind. Glossy dark hair, eyes like rich dark chocolate. Her identical twin, Ava, was just as beautiful, but there was something about Jessie that had drawn him. And then Janice Scott had been found dead in his bed and his life hadn't been the same since.

———————

Jessie tucked an errant strand of hair behind her ear and continued with her dictation. She was in the middle of drafting a final letter to her client who'd just been found not guilty for aggravated robbery. She'd managed to persuade the jury that there were enough discrepancies in the grainy CCTV footage of the burglar outside the 7-Eleven to cast reasonable doubt on the prosecutor's story that the perpetrator was her client. They'd come back with a not guilty verdict and everyone in Jessie's team had been relieved.

All that needed to be done now was to finish her letter outlining how her client could apply for the return of his bail money and wish him luck for the future. And, of course, to include her final bill. A lawyer of her skill and experience didn't come cheap – something the partners of her law firm counted on. They'd be pleased with her success today in the courtroom, and no doubt she'd be sent a polite note of congratulation and perhaps a bottle of expensive champagne. It was too bad they didn't reward her with something more substantial, something she *really* wanted: a partnership in the firm. Like *that* would ever happen.

Jessie sighed and pushed the depressing thought away. Alistair was only two years into his jail sentence. She couldn't expect the partners to overlook her connection to him and his illegal behavior so quickly. It just made her mad that she suffered consequences for something her brother had done. Still, nobody said life was easy, or that the world played fair. She was a prime example of that.

The phone at her elbow rang and she leaned over and picked up the receiver. "What is it, Margaret?"

"Jessie, I have your sister on the phone. Line three."

"Ava or Samantha?" Jessie asked her secretary.

"Ava."

"Okay, thanks."

Jessie pressed the flashing button on the phone. "Ava! It's good to hear from you."

"I wasn't sure that you'd be in," Ava replied. "Aren't you expecting your jury to bring down their verdict today?"

"Yes. I've already been to court and back this morning. We won." With those words, Jessie was filled with pride. She worked hard at her job and it was always a bonus when she managed to obtain a favorable verdict from the jury. That was far from guaranteed.

She grinned at Ava's squeal of excitement.

"Whoo hoo! Well done, Jess! I *knew* you were going to win. You *always* win! You're the best criminal defense lawyer in the city! We all know that."

Jessie laughed at Ava's enthusiasm. She didn't share her sister's opinion of her high standing in the legal fraternity, but all the same she was pleased by her sister's continuing loyalty and support.

"Thanks, Ava. You're very sweet."

"I'm not sweet at all!" Ava quipped. "I'm merely stating a fact."

"Yes, well... I think you're forgetting about Sally-Ann Li and Daisy Green and Blake Harton Junior and the many other brilliant lawyers who work here. And let's not forget Kiesha Munro who has made it all the way to the District Court bench."

"Hey, nobody is arguing that Sydney Legal is a firm filled to the brim with exceptional legal minds," Ava teased. "It's just that it's about time you believed you're one of them," she added.

Jessie refrained from offering a reply. Instead, she asked a question of her own. "Is there a particular reason you're calling, or are you just wanting to pass the time?"

"As it turns out, I *do* have something pressing to discuss."

Jessie sat forward, her curiosity piqued. "Oh?"

"Yes. I meant to mention this to you the other week, but it totally slipped my mind. I've been so busy ferrying the kids around to various sporting

events and other school functions and then
Lachlan was down with the flu last week. I don't
have to tell you what he's like with a sore throat
and runny nose. It's like he's the only person in the
world to ever catch a virus. It's been hell in the
Coleridge household, let me tell you."

Jessie made a sympathetic sound. "Poor, Ava.
Why didn't you call me? I could have at least
taken Harry and Charlotte off your hands. You
must be run ragged."

"Yes, well, thanks for the support. At least I know
I can count on you to understand. Despite the
fact you don't have a husband or children, I'm
sure you know what it's like."

Jessie rolled her eyes and laughed. "Touché.
Now, what's this pressing thing you want to discuss?"

"Well, it's about Mackenzie Callaway. Lachie
and I were at a party last month at Mac's home.
Of course, I didn't realize it would be *that*
Mackenzie Callaway until I got there."

Jessie's heart thumped hard against her chest.
She'd already heard from Lachlan about the
party they'd attended at Mac Callaway's place.
But having this conversation with her sister put all
that in a different light. Ava knew Mac Callaway
from high school. She also knew about Jessie's
connection to the man. Jessie wondered if she
had the courage to ask Ava some of the questions
she had about him: *What did he look like? Was he
married? Did he have any kids?*

"Jess? Are you still there?" Jessie blinked and
forced the rush of thoughts aside. She cleared her
throat.

"Yes, Ava. I'm still here."

"Well, like I was saying, Lachie and I went to Mac Callaway's condo last month. I'm sure you remember him. You two were inseparable back in high school."

"We dated briefly," Jessie managed.

"That's right. You guys had only gone out for a few weeks when that awful thing with Janice Scott happened. That was terrible."

"Yes, especially for Janice," Jessie replied dryly.

"At the time, we all thought Mac must have had something to do with it. Do you remember?"

"Of course I do. She was found dead in Mac's bed a few hours after I saw them together near the bleachers, looking way more cozy than they had a right to be. He came to me that night and tried to explain, but I wasn't in the mood to listen. I'm afraid our fledgling relationship didn't survive that."

"I remember you telling the police you'd seen them together. Still, it wasn't like she and Mac were dating. I mean, he was *your* boyfriend."

Jessie's smile was devoid of humor. "Yeah, that's what I thought, too. Turns out I was wrong."

"You mean he *admitted* he'd been cheating on you with Janice Scott? You never told me that!" Ava's voice was faintly accusatory and filled with disbelief.

"No, of course he didn't admit to cheating, but earlier that day Janice had bragged she had his front door key. Then I saw him with her that afternoon. He had his arms around her, holding her close. I drew the only logical conclusion, just like you would have."

"It was a rough time, that's for sure," Ava said quietly. "I understand why you took flight."

"I didn't take flight!" Jessie protested. "It was just…too much for me. There were police officers all over the place, asking questions. Mac was in shock. We all were. Nobody knew what was going on."

"The police cleared him of any suspicion, right?" Ava persisted.

"Yes, they did. But I was seventeen. I felt betrayed and knew there had been secrets, things he hadn't told me. Even if he was cleared. What we'd had was a lie. I couldn't cope. I told him we were finished."

"They charged and convicted someone else for the rape and murder, didn't they? It's all a little vague in my mind now," Ava added.

Jessie nodded. "Yes. Wes Parker. They got his DNA from semen they recovered from inside her."

"Wes Parker. That's right. I can remember being shocked when the police made the announcement. I never suspected he'd be capable of something like that," Ava mused.

"Yes, it came as a shock to me, too. To most people, I think."

"Still, I guess it just goes to show you never can tell," Ava said. She paused and then added, "Anyway, I just wanted to let you know I ran into Mac. It was kind of weird seeing him after so long. He looks just the same, by the way. In fact, if anything, he probably looks even hotter than he did in high school."

Jessie's belly did a somersault. It was the information she'd hoped for, but even still, it came as a surprise. An image of Mac in high school flashed through her mind – all taut, lean muscled strength. Dazzling green eyes. The captain of the football team.

"Right," Jessie replied, keeping her response emotionally vague. Ava wasn't fooled.

"Don't tell me you're not the least bit interested to know what he looks like these days," she teased. "I remember how much you were in love with him. You had his picture all over the walls in our bedroom. You used to draw love hearts around his name in your notebooks. Don't think I didn't see that."

Jessie laughed. "Okay, you got me. It's true. At seventeen, I was hopelessly and completely madly in love with Mac Callaway."

"It's a shame things didn't work out," Ava said softly. "Who knows, if all that business with Janice Scott hadn't happened, you two might be married now."

Heat crept up Jessie's cheeks. She sighed softly. "There's no point in wondering about what ifs, Ava. That time came and went a long time ago."

"Of course, Jess. But you're thirty-six years old and still on your own. You haven't had a serious relationship for God knows how long. I'm worried about you. I want you to find someone special, someone to share your life. Someone to take care of you."

Jessie sighed again. "I know, Ava. I want that, too. It's not like I have anything against love, or marriage either. But I can't just ask any man to marry me. I'm not into marrying just for the sake of it. I'd rather be on my own forever than be with the wrong person."

"And I wouldn't want it any other way for you, Jess. I'm just lucky Lachlan came into my life when he did."

"He's just as lucky as you, Ava," Jess replied. "Don't forget that."

Ava laughed. "Of course not. I remind him of that every opportunity I get. Still, I can't help hoping you meet Mr Right someday soon." She paused and then her voice turned sly.

"You know, I could probably wangle an invitation to Mac's place again if you were interested in meeting with him, you know, for old times' sake."

Jessie rolled her eyes at Ava's audaciousness and laughed. "You don't give up, do you?"

"Not when it comes to my beloved sister," Ava replied. "My beloved *single* sister," she added.

"Well, it just happens that I might run into him without your help," Jess murmured.

Ava's shocked gasp filled the silence. "What do you mean?"

Jessie filled her sister in on the phone call she'd received from Lachlan the week before.

"Wow!" Ava exclaimed when Jessie had finished. "That's really weird. Does Lachie suspect foul play?"

"The police aren't sure, but Lachlan's confident Mac isn't behind his ex-girlfriend's disappearance. Still, he's asked me to give Mac some legal advice. He's concerned Mac might not be looking out for himself as well as he could be. So far he's been fully cooperative with the police. He's even participated in a record of interview and he did it without any legal representation."

"I didn't think anyone was silly enough to do that these days," Ava replied. "Doesn't he watch TV? Nobody agrees to a police interview without a lawyer present."

Jessie chuckled. "It's not exactly like that in real life, Ava; but I agree. Most people with any sense would ask for a lawyer. Even those with nothing to hide."

"So, how do you feel about seeing him again?" Ava asked quietly.

Without warning, Jessie was bombarded with images of the sexy teenage Mac. The sun-bleached blond hair, the smile that lit up his green eyes. His presence that commanded the attention of everyone in any room.

Jessie sighed. "It was a long time ago, Ava. I'm no longer seventeen. My head's no longer turned by a nice body and a pair of sexy green eyes. Besides, he's only a few years shy of forty. He's probably gone to fat."

"Jessie Wolfe! Haven't you been *listening*? I only saw him last month! He looks as good as ever! Maybe better."

Jessie sighed again. She was done with this conversation. Reminiscing about what could have been was pointless. She was kidding herself if she thought she could forget Mac Callaway so easily and force the memories of their time together from her mind, but she wasn't prepared to waste another moment discussing it, even with her sister.

"Listen, Ava, I'm gonna have to go. I've got a pile of things to do here and it's not even lunchtime."

"Sure, I understand. Maybe we can get together for dinner later in the week?"

"Yes. Fine. That sounds good. I'll call you." With that, she hung up.

Almost immediately, Margaret buzzed her again.

"Jessie, I have a Mackenzie Callaway on line five. Will you take the call?"

Jessie's heart skipped a beat and then took off at a gallop. *Mac Callaway was on the phone. Oh, my God! Was she ready to talk to him? What would she say?*

She was supposed to be offering him legal advice. She could barely think straight. It was like her mind had gone to mush. She didn't know if she could string two words together, let alone provide him with sound and intelligent advice. *Oh, hell. What was she going to do?*

"Jessie? Are you still there?"

Jess blinked hard and cleared her throat. "Yes, Margaret. I'm sorry. Um... Sure. Put him through."

Drawing in a deep breath, Jessie braced herself for the sound of a voice she hadn't heard for almost two decades.

CHAPTER 3

Mac listened to the on-hold music that sounded in his ear. He'd finally made good on his promise to call Jessie, only to be told by the woman who'd answered that she was currently on another call. He was asked if he wanted to leave a message and have Jessie return his call or if he'd care to hold. He chose to hold, but was fast regretting his decision. The music was doing his head in.

Why couldn't they have a connection to one of the popular radio stations? Something fast and loud with a good drumbeat that would take his mind off the problems that seemed to be sending him into overload. Anything would be preferable to the boring tune currently playing in his ear. And then the woman told him she was putting his call through and his heart ratcheted up a notch.

"Jessie Wolfe."

His mouth went dry and all of a sudden, he was bombarded with memories. *It was her.* The voice. *It was her.* Close to twenty years down the track and she sounded exactly the same. His palms went sweaty and he licked his parched lips. He forced himself to speak.

"Hi, Jessie. It's... It's Mac. Mac Callaway."

"Mac. It's been a long time. How are you?"

Her tone was cool and measured. He drew in a breath and managed to respond.

"I'm fine. Busy. I'm sure you know how it is." He attempted a laugh, but it fell flat. *This was such a bad idea.* He should have asked Lachlan to recommend another lawyer, someone he didn't have a history with, someone he hadn't once loved with all his heart...

"Yes, you have that right. I have a pile of cases on my desk. It seems no sooner do I finalize one and another one appears. I think they're breeding."

He laughed along with her and all of a sudden felt at ease. This was the Jessie he remembered, not the cool and distant woman who'd answered the phone.

"I received a call from Detective Lachlan Coleridge. He told me you were seeking some legal advice..."

Her tone was back to being cool and professional, as if she wasn't sure she wanted them to be at ease with each other. He respected her decision and replied in kind.

"Yes. My ex-girlfriend has disappeared. At least, the police seem to think so. I haven't seen Melissa for more than three weeks."

"I see. Lachlan filled me in on a few of the details, including the fact you've already voluntarily participated in a record of interview. He's concerned you might not be looking out for your best interests, and I agree. As a criminal defense lawyer, I'd never recommend anyone giving a formal police interview in the absence of a lawyer. Even someone with nothing to hide."

Mac sighed quietly. "Yeah, I understand. I was probably naïve to think that because I was innocent it would be enough to protect me. It was only afterwards that I started thinking I might need to speak to a lawyer, get some advice. Lachlan's a mate of mine. He recommended you. He told me you were one of the best in the business."

If she were flattered by his comments, it didn't show in her voice. Her tone remained cool and professional.

"It… It might be better if you came in and saw me. I have an opening later this afternoon. Would that suit you?"

"What time?"

"Half-past two?"

"I'll have to juggle a few things, but sure, I'll drop by your office then."

"Do you need directions?"

A surge of anticipation went through Mac at the thought of coming face to face with Jessie Wolfe after all this time.

"No. I'll find you."

Though it had been nearly twenty years and a lot had gone on since then, he couldn't wait to see her. The hours couldn't go by fast enough.

<hr>

Mac stood outside the glass-and-steel skyscraper that housed the offices of Sydney Legal and tried not to feel intimidated. He'd never been all that smart at school. He'd gotten into college on a football scholarship and had barely scraped by with his grades. It was only out of school that he'd found his place in the world and after a little bit of luck, and a lot of hard work, he'd managed to carve out a successful life. Still, he'd be lying if he didn't admit the thought of walking into a building filled with some of the best legal minds in the country scared the hell out of him.

Or maybe it was the thought of seeing Jessie Wolfe again…?

Jessie had always been as sharp as a tack. All through high school, she'd topped her class. She was in the year below him, but that didn't mean he hadn't noticed her. He'd noticed everything, including how smart she was. That was the reason why it took him so long to scrounge up the courage to ask her out. He'd been sure she'd turn him down. *What would she see in a football jock when she was the smartest girl in the school?*

He'd been shocked almost speechless when she'd accepted and he'd been even more surprised how well they got along. Despite the fact he barely scraped through his exams and she was borderline genius, they connected on a much deeper level, at a place beyond mere intelligence and academia. They had something he felt all the way to his soul. Yes, that was it. They were soul mates.

Then the awful business with Janice happened

and he and Jessie were no more. She'd come to him with her eyes red and swollen with tears and told him she didn't want to see him again. He couldn't blame her. The police were still combing his house for clues about Janice. No one knew what the hell had gone on, least of all him. He was as baffled by what had gone on in his home as anyone.

He protested his innocence to Jessie. Her opinion was the only one that mattered and though he comforted himself over the months that followed with the knowledge he was almost certain she believed him, every now and then doubt crept in.

Had she thought him capable of such violence against a woman? Against anyone, for that matter? Had he been kidding himself all that time when he thought she knew him better than anyone else ever had? Was she like all the others who looked at him with suspicion?

He'd left town the day the police charged Wes Parker with rape and murder. He'd managed the marks he needed and college football had beckoned. To be honest, he'd been more than relieved to exit the scene. His mind was still filled with so many questions about what had happened, but the cops weren't volunteering any information and Mac just wanted to be gone. He wanted to put the whole traumatic episode behind him. Knowing the truth about what had happened to Janice wouldn't bring her back.

"May I help you?"

Mac blinked in an effort to focus on the attractive young woman who looked up at him from the reception desk.

"Yes. I'm Mackenzie Callaway. I'm here to see Jessica Wolfe."

Jessica. He'd never called her by that name. It sounded so formal, so...distant. Like they were strangers.

"Do you have an appointment?"

"Yes."

"Very well. I'll call and let her know you're here."

Mac nodded his thanks and moved a short distance away. He heard the receptionist speaking quietly into the phone. A moment later, she hung up and looked at him.

"Jessie is on her way down. Please, take a seat."

Mac turned away and did his best to slow down his heart. In a few short minutes he'd come face to face with the girl who'd haunted his dreams. Women had come and gone in his life over the two decades since he'd left high school, but none had touched his heart like she had. He wondered what her life had been like over the past twenty years. *Was she married? Divorced? Separated? Was there a man in her life?* That thought made him frown.

"Mac?"

And there she was.

Steeling himself against the impact of her gaze on him, he drew in a surreptitious breath and turned to face her.

"Jessie. It's great to see you." He stepped forward and shook her outstretched hand, even managed to sound normal.

The first thing he noticed was that she no longer wore glasses. No doubt they'd been replaced with contacts, or maybe she'd had laser treatment. Her hair was also shorter. It had once hung down to the middle of her back in luscious dark brown waves. Now it was tamed into a sleek ponytail that fell over one shoulder and curled around her breast.

Noting the direction of his gaze, her eyes flared with awareness before she quickly masked the reaction with a forced smile.

"Let's go. Come with me."

With that, she turned and headed for the bank of elevators on the far side of the foyer. He followed at a comfortable distance, appreciating the view from the rear. Her tailored gray suit fit her to perfection, following the curves of her body like a lover's tender caress. She'd filled out a little since high school and was now softly rounded in all the right places. Mac's cock stirred and he looked down and steadfastly tried to focus his attention on the shiny marble tiles beneath his feet. He came to a halt beside her and waited for the elevator.

Risking a glance in her direction, he was unaccountably pleased to note the high color on her cheeks. Studying her more closely, he saw the rapid rise and fall of her chest. The gold silk of her blouse emphasized the gold flecks in her chocolate eyes and fluttered ever so slightly with her shallow breaths. He was glad she was just as affected as he was by their meeting. It gave him hope that where Jessie Wolfe was concerned, perhaps all had not been lost.

His gaze slid to her hands and he noted with relief that her fingers were bare. The only piece of jewelry she wore was an expensive gold watch around her wrist.

He remembered that watch.

He'd given it to her on the night of her seventeenth birthday. It had taken all his savings. He hadn't given a toss that it meant the second-hand pickup he'd been hoping to buy after graduation would be beyond his reach. *What was a car when he'd been with the most beautiful girl in the world?*

He couldn't believe she still wore it.

Catching the direction of his gaze, she frowned and flicked her wrist so that the watch disappeared beneath the cuff of her jacket. He looked away and remained silent, flooded with conflicting emotions. She was acting like they barely knew each other and yet she still wore his watch. Surely it must remind her of the night he'd given it to her, and everything that had happened afterwards? It had been the most amazing night of his life.

Ding!

The arrival of the elevator momentarily drew him from his reverie. He caught the relief on Jessie's face as she moved past him and stepped inside. In silence, she pressed the button for her floor.

Jessie snuck a surreptitious peek in Mac's direction and tried to slow her pulse. *Why the hell hadn't she remembered to take off the watch he'd given her?* She hadn't thought about the watch in years. It was just something she wore every day. She associated it with so many magical memories of her youth and hadn't wanted to part with it, even after she and Mac went their separate ways. It was like she had a little piece of him with her always and no matter what had happened, she liked the feeling that gave her.

Now she was mortified he'd spotted it. *What would he think? That she still had a thing for him? That after all these years, she still yearned for him?* How embarrassing.

She risked another glance in his direction...

He looked good. Better than good. He looked great. Just like Ava had said. Apart from the cut on his lip and the shadow of a fading bruise on his cheek, he looked as heartbreakingly handsome as he had in high school.

Her heart had begun hammering the moment she caught sight of him standing with his back to her, staring out through the tall windows that fronted her building. His muscular physique looked just as fit and taut as it had twenty years ago. His long legs and broad shoulders were clothed in high visibility construction clothing that stood out like a beacon amongst the conservative gray and navy-blue suits that filled the lobby.

Without even trying to, he managed to capture the attention of several female passersby, including the receptionist who'd been tossing appreciative glances in Mac's direction ever since Jessie had stepped out of the elevator.

He appeared oblivious to the woman's interest, or perhaps he was merely pretending not to notice... *Who knew?* It had been so long since she'd spent time with Mackenzie Callaway. She didn't have a clue how he thought these days, or the kind of man he'd become.

The facts were these: His ex-girlfriend was missing; the police were concerned enough to be asking questions; and even though Lachlan was adamant his friend wasn't involved in foul play, what did Jessie really know about the Mackenzie Callaway who stood a few feet away from her in the close confines of an elevator?

To her relief, they reached her floor and the doors slid quietly open. Not waiting to see if he followed her, she stepped out briskly and made her way down the corridor to her office. Pointing to the empty chair in front of her desk, she moved behind and took her seat in the power position. She drew herself in close, reached for her pen, a blank notepad and finally looked up at him again.

"What happened to your face?" she asked in a no-nonsense tone, determined to get the meeting back on track.

His gaze slid away from hers. "I got into a fight."

"When?"

"Last Monday night."

"Who did the damage?"

Mac shrugged. "I don't know."

Jessie frowned in confusion. "What do you mean, you don't know?"

"Exactly that. I was standing outside a bar in the middle of the night and I was attacked by some random stranger. He got in a good right hook before I could defend myself."

Her frown deepened. "You're telling me someone you've never met or even spoken to came up and assaulted you without provocation?"

"Yes. It sounds weird. It *is* weird. But that's exactly what happened."

She stared at him, unconvinced. "Did you call the police?"

"No. What was the point? It was late. I was drunk. I wouldn't have been able to identify him... I caught a cab home and went to bed."

"What did the police say about your wounds when they interviewed you last week?"

"They asked me how I got them. I told them. They wanted to take photos of my face and I gave them permission. Like I said, I had nothing to hide."

Jessie shook her head. Mac's account of the attack definitely sounded strange and that would tweak the interest of the police. No wonder they were suspicious, even though the timing was a little off. Mac said the assault happened a week earlier. According to Lachlan, the girlfriend had been missing three weeks. They were now into the fourth. The split lip and bruise on Mac's cheek were obviously much fresher than that. And that could be verified easily by asking people who'd spent time with him before the attack on the previous Monday night. With a sigh, she set aside the issue for later consideration and cleared her throat.

"Like I said on the phone, it's never wise to participate in a formal interview with the police without a lawyer present."

Mac glared at her. "I have nothing to hide."

She nodded. "Right. Look, don't get me wrong. I understand why you spoke to the police and that's all great in theory. And to tell you the truth, our system should work that way. Unfortunately, sometimes things go awry. Questions are asked and we answer without thinking about the consequences and all of a sudden, we can become the prime suspect without even realizing how it happened.

"That's where a good lawyer comes in. We're experienced in police strategies and interrogations. We can read between the lines. We know when a question is acceptable and when it's just being used to bait the interviewee to provide an answer he might not have intended to give. Unfortunately, once it's out there, it's there for all purposes, recorded for all time and then your lawyer has a hell of a time arguing in court that the answer given shouldn't be used." She glanced up at him. "Do you see where I'm coming from?"

Mac's shoulders slumped on a heavy sigh. He suddenly seemed so disheartened, she hastened to reassure him.

"Look, I'm not saying you've said anything to implicate yourself in a crime. I'm just saying that sometimes when we're under pressure and in an intimidating environment such as an interview room in a police station, we might say things we don't mean. The presence of a lawyer can prevent that."

He nodded in resignation. "Yes. I see that now. I should have called you before I agreed to participate. Now it's too late."

She shrugged. "Too late for the first one, but there might be others. I take it the missing girlfriend hasn't been found yet?"

Mac held her gaze. "Ex-girlfriend," he corrected. "And yes, as far as I know, she hasn't been found."

His expensive cologne wafted to her nostrils. She was immediately beset with memories. She couldn't believe he smelled the same as she remembered. Moving so that her back was pressed up against the back of her chair, she firmly resolved to ignore the memories that tantalized her.

"Let's start at the beginning. Tell me what happened."

CHAPTER 4

Mac stared off into the distance and wondered where to begin. Never in his wildest dreams had he imagined that the first time he ran into Jessie Wolfe since high school he'd be having this kind of conversation. And yet here he was, about to air his dirty laundry in front of her. He drew in a deep breath and eased it out, bracing himself before the reveal.

"I'd been dating Melissa for a couple of years. She's a realtor. I met her at an industry function and struck up a conversation. I was looking for a new agency to market my latest development. She was very interested in what I was doing and said all the right things. I left that night thinking that I might have just found my next agent." He paused for a moment and then continued.

"She delivered on all that she promised. She marketed the hell out of those condos and I made more money on that development than I'd ever made in the past. I was pleased to discover she was more than just a pretty face."

He drew in another breath and kept going. "We were a good team and we got along well. A few months after our first meeting, we started dating."

Mac was suddenly besieged by memories of those early days. The fun he and Melissa had shared. The constant rush of parties and other social engagements. Life had been a whirlwind of activity. And his business had prospered.

Under Melissa's expert marketing tutelage and her impressive industry contacts, profits in each subsequent development soared. To top things off, with her long blond hair and cool blue eyes and a figure that would put most men into a lather, he'd thought Melissa was all he could have wanted.

While she didn't touch his heart in the same way Jessie had, he'd learned a long time ago to push that magical time to the furthest recesses of his mind, never to think of it again. It wasn't so much as he was settling for second best, more like knowing that what he'd had with Jessie, he'd never find again.

"When did you ask her to move in with you?" Jessie asked.

Mac flushed and cleared his throat. He didn't know why he suddenly felt guilty about his relationship with Melissa, but there it was. He kept his gaze averted when he replied.

"We'd been seeing each other about three months when I made the suggestion. She lived in a cramped apartment on a busy road above a shop. I had a two-bedroom condo with ocean views in the eastern suburbs. It made sense that she move in with me."

"I'll bet," Jessie muttered.

Her voice dripped with sarcasm. Mac stared at her in surprise. *Did she care that he'd had a live-in girlfriend? Surely she didn't think he'd been single all this time?* He was thirty-seven years old. He'd hardly spent the last twenty years celibate.

His phone vibrated against his chest, indicating an incoming call. He'd switched it to silent on his way into Jessie's building. Ignoring the call, he continued.

"For a good while, things worked well. Melissa had her work and I had mine. We'd meet somewhere in the middle. I was busy building condos; she was flat-out getting them sold. The end result was that both of us ended up making money. Lots of money. I should've known it was too good to last."

"What happened?"

"I'm not exactly sure," Mac admitted. "Melissa started complaining I never spent enough time with her; I was always at work; I didn't send her flowers like I used to. She started finding fault with little things, like the way I hung my bath towel or left dirty dishes in the sink. It was almost like she was trying to pick a fight with me."

Jessie glanced at him. "How long ago was this?"

"About six months ago. We started arguing over silly things, things that shouldn't have mattered. She'd get really annoyed over something I'd always done. It was like she'd changed and expected me to change with her – only I didn't get the same memo. Still, I thought we were getting along all right, and I definitely thought we were both still heading in the same direction."

"What do you mean?"

Mac shrugged. "I'm thirty-seven. I've always intended to have a family… A wife and kids. I didn't want to wait forever."

Surprise flared in Jessie's eyes. She sat up straighter in her seat. "Do you mean you intended to *marry* Melissa?"

Mac avoided her gaze and squirmed uncomfortably. "Yeah, I hadn't laid it all out, but I guess so."

"Were you…in love with her?"

His gaze flew to Jessie's. She regarded him steadily, but he could see the effort it took her to contain her emotions.

"I don't think I was in love with her," he answered honestly. "But I cared about her enough to want to make things work. I thought what we had together would be enough. I thought she felt the same."

"How do you know she didn't?"

Mac grimaced. "Because nearly four weeks ago, I overheard a conversation she had with someone on the phone. I didn't know who she was talking to, but I could tell from her end of the conversation that it was a man.

"She thought I was in the shower. She didn't hear me come into the room. I heard her telling him she'd meet him at his apartment in a little over an hour. We'd intended to have an early night for a change, take some time to reconnect. I couldn't believe that while she thought I was in the shower for a few minutes, she'd made plans to meet up with someone else."

"Did you confront her about it?"

Mac sighed. "Yeah. We argued. It got loud. We were overheard by the neighbors. When the police came calling last week, those neighbors were more than happy to tell them about it. I'm sure that's another reason why they're looking at me."

Jessie frowned. "Right."

Mac hastened to reassure her. "It's not as damning as it sounds. When the police knocked and started asking questions about Melissa, I owned up to the argument before they even mentioned it."

Relief flashed across Jessie's face. "Well, that's something at least," she murmured. "You said the argument got heated. How heated?"

Mac's phone began vibrating once again. Though tempted to check the screen, he once again chose to ignore it and answered Jessie's question instead.

"I guess we got pretty loud. Right after she ended her call, I asked her if she was cheating on me. She looked me in the eye and told me she was." He shook his head in disbelief. "She didn't even bother to deny it. It was as if that was nothing. And this from the woman I thought I would marry. We'd been seeing each other for two years. Longer than anyone else I'd dated.

And despite all that, she had no qualms about telling me she was seeing someone else. I still can't believe it."

"Did she tell you who it was?"

"No. And I didn't ask her. I didn't want to know. It didn't matter who it was. The fact was, she'd been unfaithful and she didn't seem the least bit guilty. If anything, she seemed relieved, like she was glad I'd found out."

"Did she say how long it had been going on?" Jessie asked.

"No, but I figured it had been going on for a while. The way she spoke to him over the phone, there was a level of intimacy that's only gained over a period of time."

He glanced at Jessie and noted the color on her cheeks was high. She quickly turned her face away and cleared her throat.

"So, did the argument turn physical?"

Mac's mouth fell open in shock. "Hell, no! I didn't even touch her! I was angry and upset and I shouted, but I would never hurt her that way."

Jessie nodded slowly, her gaze now steady on his. He wondered if she was remembering Janice. He recalled how he'd told Jessie exactly the same thing all those years ago – that he could never physically hurt a woman. He hadn't been sure if she believed him then and he wasn't sure she believed him now. Still, there was nothing he could do about it. He'd told the truth, then and now.

"Okay, so let's get this straight." Jessie's tone was once again no nonsense. "You discover your girlfriend is having an affair and you get into a fight. Your argument is loud enough to be heard by some of the neighbors. What happened next?"

Mac sighed and ran a hand through his hair. "I told her I wanted her out of my place. I grabbed my car keys and headed for the door and told her she was to be gone by the time I got back."

Jessie regarded him steadily. "Where did you go?"

Mac shrugged. "I can't remember. I drove around for hours, thinking about what she'd told me. I was in shock. I still couldn't believe I hadn't known, hadn't seen it coming. Yes, she'd been more aloof than usual, and had been picking silly fights, but I didn't think anything of that, really. I just thought we were going through a rough patch. It happens to couples sometimes, doesn't it?"

He glanced at Jessie, but she refrained from replying. Just then, his phone started vibrating again.

It wasn't unusual for him to receive fifty or sixty calls a day, especially when he was coming to the end of a large-scale development. It seemed there was always someone who needed to talk to him. With a bit of luck, they'd give up and ring his head foreman. Steve was capable of dealing with almost anything. That was one of the reasons Mac employed him.

At last the vibrations stopped and he continued.

"I drove without any sense of purpose or direction. All I could think of was Melissa and her mystery man and how stupid I'd been. I'd had my future planned out before me, or so I thought. A wife, a couple of kids, a successful business. Everything was supposed to be perfect and yet my life was falling apart. At one point I found myself outside my latest development near Hornsby."

"You were a long way from home," Jessie murmured.

"Yes. As I said, I drove around aimlessly for hours. It wasn't until I spied the high chain-link fence around the development that I realized where I was."

"What did you do?"

"I sat there for a while. I can't remember how long. Then I dozed off. By the time I came to and looked at the clock it was close to one. It had only been a little past nine when I'd walked out of my condo, so I turned the car around and headed home. I was sure I'd given Melissa enough time to pack her bags and leave. At least, I hoped I had."

"Was she gone when you arrived home?"

"Yes. And I was relieved I didn't have to confront her again. The first time had been ugly enough. I didn't want to repeat it."

"Were her things gone?"

"I didn't even bother checking. I was just relieved she was gone. I took another shower and went to bed. I was beat. That was it."

"What about the next morning?" Jessie asked. "Did you have a look around the condo? See what she'd taken?"

"Yes. I noticed she hadn't taken much, if anything. I can remember feeling pissed that she'd have to come back and collect her things, rather than taking them at the time like I'd told her to."

"And over the ensuing days and weeks, you didn't think it was strange that she hadn't returned to get her things?"

"Yeah, it crossed my mind every now and then. To tell you the truth, I expected her to call and apologize, to beg me to take her back. I guessed that was why she'd left her things there. Because she hoped we'd work this out. During the time we'd been together, she'd acquired a lot more stuff. Much more than would fit in her cramped apartment. Besides, she'd gotten used to waking up to the sound of the surf."

"What kind of stuff did she acquire?" Jessie asked.

"Furniture, clothes, shoes." Mac laughed without humor. "She had enough shoes to fill the spare bedroom." He shook his head. "I never saw so many shoes outside of a shoe store."

Jessie leaned back against her chair again and folded her arms in front of her. "So, as the days and weeks went by, it didn't occur to you that something might be wrong?"

"No. She was a grown woman with plenty of money of her own. She still had her own place. None of that had changed in the time we were together. The longer it went on and I didn't hear from her, I slowly accepted she wasn't coming back. By then, I'd calmed down and I wasn't sure how I felt about that."

Jessie started in surprise. "Do you mean you would have taken her back, even after she was unfaithful?"

Mac shrugged. "I don't know. I don't think so, but I don't know. I spent more than two years with the woman. I thought we'd grow old together. And just like that, it was over. That took some getting used to."

Jessie nodded and made a note on the pad in front of her. "What about all the things she left behind? Didn't you think it was strange that she hadn't made arrangements to collect them?"

"Yes, I did. But then I decided she just ditched her former life altogether. That included me. I assumed she'd started a new life with her lover and didn't need or want the things she left behind. For all I know, that's exactly where she is."

"Is that why you didn't go to the police?"

"Yes. As far as I was concerned, we were just another couple who'd split up and would never see each other again. It happens all the time."

Jessie nodded. "Yes, it does, but most of the time people come back and get their things, or at the very least, send someone else to collect them. They don't just disappear, never to be heard from again and leave everything they own behind. Do you understand what I'm saying?"

Mac nodded. "Yes, of course. Now that I think about it, I guess it *is* a little strange Melissa left all that stuff behind. She spent a fortune on the clothes and shoes. I would've thought she'd want some of them back, despite the fact they reminded her of her time with me."

"Do you see now why the police were interested in talking with you?"

"Of course I do. I'm the boyfriend. Well, ex-boyfriend. I'm the number one suspect, right?" He tried to laugh, but it came out sounding more like a croak.

Jessie regarded him solemnly. "That's right. In a lot of cases involving domestic disputes where one of the people go missing, it's the other party who is involved in the disappearance. It's just the way it is. And until she's found, you're going to remain the prime suspect."

"What about the man she was seeing? Wouldn't they be interested in talking to him?"

"I'm sure they would be, if they can identify him. I assume you told them Melissa was seeing someone else?"

"Yes. They asked me what we were arguing about. I had no reason to lie."

"Good. Let's hope they find him. If anything, it gives them another person to focus on."

"That is, of course, if she met with foul play," Mac added. "That hasn't been established, yet. The police are only looking into this because Melissa's sister hasn't been able to reach her. They told me her bank account and credit cards haven't been touched since she was with me."

"Yes, well no one can go for very long without money. I understand why the police are on the alert."

"Yes, but it's always possible her new lover is funding her lifestyle. She's been gone less than a month. There's a possibility he's just paying for everything."

"Yes, I agree." Jessie paused and then gave

Mac a direct look. "What do *you* think has happened? You knew her better than most. What's your gut telling you?"

Mac compressed his lips and thought about it. So many times over the past weeks he'd thought of Melissa and wondered where she was. He hoped she was happy with her new lover, but it was strange she hadn't come by to collect her things. He knew how much she valued her expensive wardrobe and she'd also left behind a treasured painting that had been given to her by an aunt. At the very least, he expected her to want that. And yet it remained in place on the wall of his condo, a personal reminder she was gone.

He drew in a deep breath that expanded his lungs and then eased it out. "I honestly don't know," he said slowly. "There are so many possibilities."

"But what's your gut instinct?" Jessie persisted.

Mac stared at her. "My gut's telling me something's wrong. Melissa was very superficial and attached to her things. She loved to flaunt her wealth. She loved her designer clothes and shoes and handbags like they were her children. And then there was the painting. I just can't imagine her leaving all that behind. Fair enough that she didn't take it the night she left. She'd need a truck to cart it all away. But it's been nearly a month. Plenty of time to arrange for someone to collect it for her." He shook his head. "It doesn't make sense."

"Did you tell that to the police?"

"Yes."

Jessie nodded, appearing satisfied with his answer. "Good. Being upfront with them about anything and everything you know is always the best way to go." She looked down at her desk and shuffled some papers together. It looked like his appointment was coming to an end. Then she removed all doubt when she pushed back her chair and stood and stretched her hand out toward him.

"Thank you for coming in, Mac. It's been good to see you again."

He took her proffered hand and shook it, trying not to notice how soft and small and feminine... how right it felt in his.

"Thanks for seeing me. I feel better now that I've spoken with you."

"It's possible the police might contact you again for another interview. If they do, please give me a call before you talk to them. They're skilled at eliciting information you might not have intended to share – for whatever reason. It's always better to have an objective party there who is on your side."

He acknowledged her offer with a nod of gratitude. "Thank you. I really appreciate that. I promise I won't talk to them again without my lawyer present."

She smiled and when it reached her eyes, they crinkled at the corners. She looked so much like the Jessie of twenty years ago, he could scarcely believe so much time had passed. He wondered if her lips tasted as soft and sweet as they had when she was seventeen and then immediately scolded himself for allowing his mind to walk that path again. What they'd had together had been magical, but it hadn't lasted. The nightmare with Janice Scott had seen to that.

"By the way, here's my card," Jessie said and handed him a small piece of thin embossed cardboard.

He blinked to clear his head of the memories and took it from her. Their fingers touched and a spark of electricity jumped between them. Jessie pulled back sharply.

"Sorry," she muttered, averting her gaze. Her cheeks bloomed with color.

Mac smiled to put her at ease. "Don't worry about it. No doubt the carpet under our feet has generated some static electricity. No big deal."

"Yes. That must be it." She shot him a tight smile and quickly turned away.

He took the hint and, murmuring a final farewell, left the room.

CHAPTER 5

Mac stepped out of the elevator and headed straight across the foyer, in a hurry to leave Jessie's building. It had been good seeing her again – no, more than good – but being around her only stirred up old memories. They'd only dated a handful of weeks when everything fell apart, but it had been enough time for Mac to know she was his soul mate. The years since had only served to confirm that and knowing that he and Jessie were never going to be a couple again filled him with sadness.

He was glad he'd gone to see her, but it had been tough just the same. Now he knew where she worked, how close she was to his home. He lived about ten minutes' drive from the city. He could probably see her building from his balcony. Now whenever he looked across the harbor in that direction, he knew he'd think of her and it would drive him insane.

She hadn't worn any wedding rings, but that didn't mean she was single in every sense of the word. He wondered if he had the courage to ask Lachlan about her status. After all, the man was married to Jessie's twin. If anyone knew about Jessie Wolfe's love life, it would be him. But then, Lachlan would ask all kinds of questions and Mac wasn't sure he was ready to answer them. By nature, he was a private man and he wanted to keep things that way.

The vibration of his phone against his chest caught his attention and he was reminded of the calls he'd ignored. He tugged the phone out of his top pocket and glanced at the screen. There were three missed calls from his foreman and now Steve was calling again. He quickly answered it.

"Steve, what's up?"

"Oh, hell, Mac… You're not going to believe it."

The dread in Steve's voice filled Mac with alarm. His head foreman sounded on the verge of panic. Mac came to a sudden stop. He ignored the muttered curses of the pedestrians behind him who had to make a quick detour around him and focused all his attention on the phone call.

"What's happened? Don't tell me Demir's done something else. What is it this time?"

"No, Mac. This has nothing to do with Demir."

Mac frowned. "Okay, then. I guess that's good news. So, what is it then?"

"We've found a body."

If Steve had told Mac a spaceship had landed on their worksite and little green men had come pouring out, Mac couldn't have been more shocked. "What the hell are you talking about? A body?"

"Yeah. She was bundled into a suitcase and shoved into the air conditioning vent in one of our condos. The engineers were over there checking out the site. They could smell something awful. They're the ones who found her."

Icy dread poured through Mac's veins and settled into a hard lump in his gut. His chest went so tight he could barely breathe. All he could think of was Melissa.

"Are you sure it's a woman?"

"Yeah. One of them opened the suitcase. I haven't seen her, and apparently she's in a bad way, but it's definitely a woman."

Steve's words echoed in Mac's ears as if they came from a great distance. Shock and dread held him immobile. *Surely it wasn't Melissa... It couldn't be... It could be anyone...*

The thoughts rushed through his mind until he could barely think. And in his gut he knew... He drew in a deep breath and then another and tried to slow down his racing pulse. He needed to stay calm. He needed to think. He needed to call the police.

"The engineers have already called the police," Steve said, as if reading Mac's mind. "They might even be there by now. I've been trying to reach you all afternoon."

Remembering the phone calls he'd ignored in Jessie's office, Mac felt a twinge of guilt. "Yeah, I'm sorry about that. I'm outside the offices of Sydney Legal. I've been in a meeting with my lawyer."

"Well, I'm glad to hear you finally got around to

speaking with someone. Sounds like you might just need their services."

"Do you... Do you think it's Melissa?" Mac ventured, dreading the answer.

"Who knows? But it's one hell of a damn coincidence. Your ex-girlfriend's been missing for nearly a month and now a woman turns up dead in one of your buildings. It sure as hell doesn't look good."

Steve's somber tone sent a fresh wave of panic rushing through Mac's veins. What if it *was* Melissa? *What the hell would he do?* He knew damn well he wasn't responsible for her murder. Which meant someone had to be setting him up. *But who?* He couldn't think of anyone who hated him enough that they'd murder his ex-girlfriend and then try and blame it on him. He might not always see eye to eye with Omer Demir, but that was purely business. They were fierce competitors, but that was it. The truth was, they barely knew each other and Demir sure as hell didn't know Melissa.

No, this couldn't be the work of Demir. There must be someone else. Someone he didn't even know about. And then another thought struck him. Was this somehow connected to what happened with Janice in high school? No. The very idea was ludicrous. This was a different life...

Mac shook his head. Everything around him seemed surreal. It was like something out of a movie. That kind of thing didn't happen in real life, and it sure as hell couldn't happen twice.

"What are you going to do, Mac?"

Steve's quiet words broke into Mac's troubled thoughts. He compressed his lips and closed his eyes briefly, in an effort to block everything out.

"I don't know, but I guess I'd better head over there and see what's going on. I'm sure the police will want to speak to me, whether it's Melissa or not."

"Yeah. Don't forget to call your lawyer before you get there." Steve's voice was grim.

Mac looked down at his hand and slowly unclenched his fist. Jessie's business card was still caught between his fingers. He hadn't even had a chance to put it in his wallet. He wondered what she'd think when he told her his ex-girlfriend had likely just been found dead on his construction site.

He was about to find out.

Jessie strode passed her secretary's desk on her way back from the tea room and took a sip out of the mug of coffee she held wishing it was something stronger. After spending an hour in the company of Mackenzie Callaway, she needed all the strength a hit of caffeine would give.

It had been wonderful to see Mac again, and yet it had been difficult, too. His presence had stirred up so many memories – good and bad. It had left her feeling melancholy for what they'd had and what might have been.

"You have a call on line two, Jessie," her secretary said.

"Thanks, Margaret. Who is it?"

"It's that man you saw just a while ago. Mackenzie Callaway. He said it was urgent."

Jessie's heart skipped a beat. She silently scolded herself for her reaction. She had to remember that she and Mac were history. It didn't matter that her body reacted to his presence just like it had twenty years earlier or that she couldn't get him out of her mind. Simply put, they'd dated in high school and then they didn't. End of story. He'd come to her looking for legal advice at the suggestion of a friend, not to reignite an old relationship.

With a sigh, she headed back into her office and sat her coffee down on the desk. She reached over and picked up the phone.

"Jessie Wolfe."

"Jessie, it's Mac."

"Mac. Did you forget something?"

"No. I... I just took a call from my head foreman. Steve Prendergast. Some engineers were doing an inspection at my building site. They... They found a woman's body. I... I think it might be Melissa."

Jessie gasped in shock. "My God! Are you serious?"

"Yes, I'm afraid so. We don't have confirmation that it's her, but who else could it be?"

"Have you spoken to the police?

"No. The engineers made the call to emergency services as soon as they discovered the body. I'm headed over to the site now."

"The police will want to speak to you," she stated.

"Yes. That's why I'm on my way. Besides, I want to reassure my crew that everything's okay. No doubt they're all shaken up over this gruesome discovery. I sure as hell would be."

"Yes, of course. You need to get over there as soon as you can. Where are you now?"

"I'm not far from your building. I'm trying to hail a cab. I came into the city on public transport because it's difficult to find parking downtown. It's even harder with a truck."

"Let me come with you." The words fell out of Jessie's mouth without her realizing it. She bit her lip and waited for his reply.

"Would you?"

She heard the appeal in his voice and it reassured her that her offer was the right thing. She could only imagine how he was feeling. He wasn't in a calm frame of mind to talk sense to the police officers, especially ones who already had him in their sights. This discovery of a body would only increase their suspicions. She needed to be there for him.

"Of course. Give me a few minutes so I can rearrange my schedule. I'll meet you out front."

"Thank you, Jessie. That means a lot to me."

She heard the relief in his voice. "No problem. I'll see you soon."

She hung up. Staring blindly into the distance, she contemplated what she'd just learned. If it *were* Melissa, things had just taken a turn for the worse for Mac Callaway. She didn't believe he was capable of that kind of violence, but it had been twenty years since she'd last seen him and she'd had her doubts before, when it counted. A lot could happen over that time in a person's life to change them. Maybe his argument with Melissa had gotten out of control and led to way more than he'd admitted? After all, their voices had escalated enough for the neighbors to hear.

Her mind rebelled at the thought Mac could have caused his girlfriend's death, but she fought to keep an open mind. After all, it wasn't the first time a woman he'd been close to had turned up dead. It was only a matter of time before the police discovered that.

No doubt they'd sift through the evidence and come to their own conclusion. In the meantime, she'd give him her full support. It was the right thing to do. Besides, if there was one thing she believed in it was that a person was innocent until proven guilty.

With a sigh, she reached once again for her phone. "Margaret, something's come up. I need you to reschedule my last two appointments. I'll be out for the rest of the day."

Mac spotted Jessie exiting the glass doors of her building and hurried over. "Thanks again for agreeing to accompany me, Jessie. Even if it turns out not to be Melissa – and God knows, I hope it isn't – the police are going to be very interested in why a woman's body has been found on my construction site."

Jessie's expression was grim. She compressed her lips into a thin line and nodded. "You have that right."

Mac flagged down a cab and held the door open while Jessie climbed into the back. He followed suit and gave the driver the address in Hornsby.

"Did you come in from there this afternoon?" Jessie asked.

"No. I was at home doing some paperwork. I live in Vaucluse."

Jessie acknowledged his comment with a slight nod. "Ava mentioned you had a nice place on the water."

"Yes. It's...comfortable." He looked away. The fact was, he lived in a place valued at over four million dollars, but he wasn't the kind of guy to brag. He also didn't want his wealth to color Jessie's opinion of him. In that moment he realized he wanted her to like him for himself. Like she used to.

She turned to stare out the window. Mac felt the urge to explain.

"I had nothing to do with this, Jessie. Whoever the poor woman is, it had nothing to do with me. The last time I saw Melissa she was alive."

Jessie turned to stare at him. Her gaze delved into his, as if she were trying to see into his very soul. She'd looked at him in much the same way as she had twenty years earlier when he'd begged her to believe him about Janice.

"Okay."

He frowned. "Okay? What does that mean?"

She turned to face him. "It means okay. I'm your lawyer. It's not my place to believe you or disbelieve you. A good defense lawyer will never put that question to their client. It's my place to protect you. That's it."

His frown deepened. "From who or what?"

She shrugged. "From the police. From yourself."

He opened his mouth to protest. He was thirty-seven years old. He didn't need anyone looking out for him. And then he thought of the barrage of questions he'd faced in the interview he'd already given to the police. That had been tough enough. Now that a body had been discovered on his job site, the officers would go into overdrive. He'd be more than grateful for Jessie's presence.

A sigh escaped his lips. The tension that had held his body taut from the instant Steve told him about the discovery eased, and he sank back against the seat. The driver wove with casual confidence in and out of the mid-afternoon traffic. Jessie continued to stare out the window, lost in her thoughts. Every now and then a whisper of her perfume wafted across to him on the air. Rich and dark and sensual, it teased his nostrils and evoked images he knew were best left alone.

They'd never consummated their relationship all those years ago, but they'd come close enough on more than one occasion that he knew exactly how smooth her skin was along her ribcage and how soft and plump her breasts were. Even then, they'd filled his hands to overflowing. He could still remember the sweet touch of her lips as she kissed him and the little intake of breath when he pressed against her, hard and hot and needy.

Of course, he'd wanted to make love to her. He was a teenage boy in love with the most beautiful girl in the world. But she'd wanted to take things slowly. It would be her first time. He honored her wishes and maintained a tight rein on his self-control. Though it nearly killed him, they'd engaged in heavy petting and nothing more.

And then Janice came to him that fateful afternoon and his life had been turned upside down. He didn't blame Jessie for calling it quits on their fledgling relationship. His head still spun at the speed his world had disintegrated. One minute he was a senior on the eve of graduation. The next, he was being interrogated by the police.

"Do you remember Wes Parker?"

Jessie's quietly voiced question startled Mac from his memories and brought him back to the present with a jerk. *Why would she ask about Wes Parker?* It was as if she'd read his mind...

"O-of course," he stammered.

"I couldn't believe it when he was arrested for Janice Scott's rape and murder. I didn't know him very well, but I never imagined he was capable of such violence."

"Me, neither," Mac admitted. "I was as shocked as anyone."

"I wonder what made the police look at him for the crime. None of us had any clue who was responsible."

"They matched his DNA to semen found at the scene," Mac said.

"Yes, and at the time, I didn't think anything of that. But now I wonder what his DNA was doing in the police database?"

"I don't think it was. We were all asked to volunteer a sample. Every boy in the senior classes. That's how they matched it to Wes."

Jessie's eyes widened in surprise. "Did you provide a sample?"

Mac nodded. "Yes, of course. I had nothing to hide. I wanted the perpetrator found and brought to justice. Besides, we all did it."

Jessie nodded thoughtfully. "It was a good plan and it worked. The police found the person responsible. I just never thought it would be Wes."

"I guess it just goes to show how hard it is to really know another person. I walked the halls with Wes, shared classrooms and locker rooms with him for all those years I was in high school. We were even on the same football team. I never once suspected he was capable of rape and murder."

Jessie remained silent and Mac couldn't help but wonder if she was thinking the very same thing about him. And then he shook his head in irritation. If she thought him capable of murdering his ex-girlfriend, then so be it. He'd told her the truth twenty years ago and he'd told her the truth about the circumstances of his recent break-up. He was tired of proclaiming his innocence. She was his lawyer, like she'd said. That was it. He shouldn't consider or expect anything more than that.

CHAPTER 6

The cab came to a stop outside a construction site and Jessie reached for her handbag. On a sudden wave of nervousness, she pushed a strand of hair back behind her ear where it had come loose from her ponytail. Mac climbed out ahead of her and stood back while she alighted. She murmured her thanks as he shut the door behind her. His old-fashioned manners hadn't been lost on her. She was a modern, independent woman but that didn't mean she couldn't appreciate being treated with courtesy and respect by a member of the opposite sex. In her opinion, good manners were sadly lacking in the current population and that wasn't for the better.

Looking around her, she noticed a high chain link metal fence that surrounded a large construction site. The usual signage that warned people to keep out and to wear protective hats and clothing and to report to the site office littered the front gate. Police vehicles, both marked and unmarked, filled the entryway and the vacant space in front of the dark brick building. A black van from the coroner's office stood off to one side, no doubt waiting for the police to hand over the body.

"We're supposed to be only a few weeks shy of completion," Mac murmured. "Now this. Just what I needed."

Jessie remained silent. Even if the police dismissed Mac's involvement in the murder, the site was still a crime scene and would be buzzing with forensics personnel for the foreseeable future. No doubt word would also get out about what had been found and what the police were doing on site.

Dead bodies turning up in air conditioning vents tended to put off potential buyers. It didn't bode well for the profit margin on the eventual sale either. Still, that was probably the least of Mac's worries right now if the grim expression on the tall, broad-shouldered detective walking toward them was any indication.

"Mr Callaway."

Mac stepped forward. "Yes."

"I'm Detective Sergeant Zane Sullivan. You likely remember me from the last time we spoke at the station. I interviewed you about your missing girlfriend."

Jessie tensed. To her relief, Mac's expression remained neutral.

"Ex-girlfriend," he corrected.

"Right. Melissa Sorenson. She's still missing, isn't she?"

Mac shrugged. "I haven't heard from her, if that's what you mean."

The detective eyeballed Mac, blatantly revealing his dissatisfaction with his reply. "I'm in charge of this investigation. I take it you've heard about the body that's been located in one of the apartments?"

Mac nodded. "Yes. I received a call from my foreman."

"I see."

Jessie glared at the officer, but neither man paid her any attention. It was as if she didn't exist. She stepped between them and cleared her throat.

"I'm Jessica Wolfe. I represent Mr Callaway."

The detective's dark eyebrows flew up in surprise. He glanced at Jessie, gave her a quick once-over and then returned his attention to Mac.

"You brought a lawyer?" He smirked. "So you thought you might be in need of one, Mr Callaway?"

Mac's hands clenched into fists. It was the only outward sign that the detective's words had gotten to him. Understanding Mac's frustration, Jessie had had enough.

"Look, Detective Sullivan. My client happened to be outside my office when he received the call from his foreman. I offered to accompany him here. There was nothing more to it than that. Now what can you tell us about the body?"

A hint of respect gleamed in the detective's blue eyes as Jessie held his gaze. A minute later, he once again addressed Mac.

"We're lucky it's winter. The cool air and her location inside the air conditioning vent slowed down the decomposition. Whilst she's not a pretty sight, enough of her physical features are intact to enable a visual identification. Given that your girlfriend – sorry, your ex-girlfriend – is still missing, I was wondering if you'd be willing to take a look at the body and tell us whether, or not it's her.

"We could contact Melissa's sister, Angela," the detective continued, "but she lives in Wollongong. It would take at least two hours to get her here. If you were able to provide an identification, or even eliminate Melissa as a possibility, it could save us a lot of time."

Mac looked at Jessie and she immediately stepped forward.

"I'd like a moment with my client."

The detective inclined his head. "Of course."

Jessie waited until he'd moved out of earshot. "You don't have to do this, Mac. The police won't read anything into your refusal. The woman's obviously been dead for a while. It won't be pretty."

Mac stared at her, his expression torn with indecision. "I vomit at the sight of blood, but I need to know if it's Melissa. It's like I owe it to her to do this for her. If it *is* her. She and her sister were close. Melissa loved Angela. She wouldn't want her sister to go through any more uncertainty. I know she wouldn't."

Jessie regarded him steadily. "But you loved her, too."

"Yes, but not as much as I believed. Not as much as Angela did."

Jessie pursed her lips. She couldn't imagine what it would be like to identify the body of a loved one who'd died an unexpected and violent death. She looked at Mac.

"It's your decision. Do what you think best."

Mac slowly nodded. "It's not what I want to do, but it is what I think is right. I'll do it. Who knows? It might not be her."

"That's right. It might not be. We can always hope."

With his mind made up, Mac turned back toward the detective who stood a short distance away talking on the phone. Seeing they'd arrived at a decision, the officer quickly ended his call.

"So, what did you decide?" he asked.

Mac's expression turned grim. At the same time, Jessie recognized a light of determination in his eyes.

"I'll do it."

The detective nodded in satisfaction. "Good. Come with me. I'll take you to the body. She's been moved from the air conditioning vent to the floor of the unit she was found in. The move made it easier to photograph the body."

Together, the three of them made their way across the expanse of gravel fronting the building and then entered the main doors to the foyer. According to the information Mac had shared on their way to the site, there were sixty apartments altogether. The ride in the elevator was made in silence. When the doors slid open, Detective Sullivan motioned them toward unit fifty-three. A uniformed constable guarded the entrance. The detective flashed his identification and the constable stepped aside so they could enter.

The smell of fresh paint with a hint of something less pleasant hung in the air. Jessie noted the expensive fittings and fixtures: the high-end finish on the kitchen cabinets and the granite countertop. Bright, natural light coming through a wide bay window flooded the room.

"She's through here," the detective murmured, gesturing for them to follow.

Detective Sullivan led them into one of the two bedrooms. Almost immediately, the stench of rotting flesh assailed Jessie's nostrils. Her hand flew up and covered her nose. Her belly rebelled at the terrible smell and it was all she could do not to vomit. She glanced at Mac and could tell he was equally affected. Only the detective seemed unperturbed.

The suitcase lay open on the pale beige carpet. A forensics officer in blue overalls stood over the body taking pictures.

"Give us a minute, would you, Sam?" Detective Sullivan tossed the request to the cameraman.

"Sure, Zane. I'll be right outside."

The man left through the open doorway. Jessie guessed he was probably grateful for the reprieve although no doubt in his line of work, this kind of scene was commonplace. She shuddered at the thought.

"When you're ready, Mr Callaway," the detective murmured.

Mac tossed her a glance. *Was he seeking reassurance?* She gave him a shaky smile of encouragement, still struggling with the need to retch. He squared his shoulders and moved quickly toward the suitcase, as if he knew if he put it off he might change his mind.

Within seconds, it was over. With a hand over his mouth as if to hold back a surge of nausea, he looked at Jessie. His shocked and saddened expression told all. There was no doubt. It was her.

The search for Melissa Sorenson was over.

———————

Detective Zane Sullivan stared down at what was left of the young woman. Speaking quietly into his two-way radio, he requested his partner locate the forensic pathologist and meet him inside. Crouching down, he examined the body more closely.

There was no obvious wounds or other overt sign of trauma, yet the woman was dead. Pulling on a pair of latex gloves, he took a pencil from his jacket and moved several strands of blond hair off her face. Her dry, dull eyes were sunken and glazed over in death. She stared up at him almost accusingly. He compressed his lips together as sympathy flooded his veins. And then a sickening odor assailed him, one that only a dead body could emit. It took all of his self-control and years of being confronted with similar scenes for him to hold on to the contents of his stomach.

In an attempt to distract himself from the reality of being so close to the decomposing body, his gaze traveled lower over her body still bent in half inside the suitcase. She wore an expensive pair of designer jeans and a pale yellow silk blouse. Her feet were shod in knee-high leather boots and a red silk scarf had been tied intricately around her neck. Her skin, though now a mottled reddish-purple color, was stretched over a good bone structure. She'd obviously been a beautiful woman and dressed as she was, could have passed for a model on a fashion shoot.

He glanced across to where Mac Callaway and his lawyer, Jessica Wolfe, stood on the opposite side of the room. They had their backs to him and murmured together in low voices. Zane couldn't make out the words, but he guessed the lawyer was giving her client some advice.

He'd interviewed Mac when Melissa Sorenson's sister had first come to them with her concerns. He'd been impressed with the man's forthrightness and willingness to cooperate and while his gut hadn't notified him of anything amiss with the man's demeanor, he'd worked in policing long enough to know that sometimes good people lost control and did terrible things.

At that point, Mac's ex-girlfriend had only been a missing person. Now she'd turned up dead and on Mac's project site. That, in and of itself, made Zane wonder. More about Mac's innocence than guilt. Surely someone who killed their girlfriend wouldn't hide the body on their own job site, knowing they'd be the obvious suspect? Though there were no overt signs as to the cause of death, she sure as hell hadn't tucked herself up in that suitcase and then climbed inside the air conditioning vent. It was his job to find the cause and the person responsible.

As if aware of the direction of his thoughts, Jessica turned slightly sideways. He caught her grim expression that told him she was well aware of the seriousness of the discovery of her client's ex-girlfriend's body. Mac Callaway might be entirely innocent of any wrongdoing, but the fact was, statistics showed that most people were killed by someone they knew and he was definitely on their radar.

It was the reason Zane hadn't dismissed Mac as a suspect, should the investigation develop into something more than a missing persons case. He'd seen the obvious concern Mac had for Melissa's welfare and had found Mac more than cooperative. Still, that could all have been part of a ruse. It wouldn't be the first time a criminal had tried to charm their way off a suspect list.

Zane's attention was snagged by Detective Willie Whitehouse standing in the open doorway. Zane acknowledged the presence of his partner with a tilt of his head. Not far behind Willie was one of the city's forensic pathologists, Doctor Andrew Jones. Jones spied Jessica and his lips immediately turned up in a smile of recognition. The lawyer returned the greeting with equal affection. It was obvious the two knew each other.

And then Zane remembered the chief forensic pathologist was Samantha Wolfe and that one of her sisters was a lawyer. He could only assume that sister was likely Jessica. *Small world...*

He cleared his throat. "Gentlemen, can I have your attention?"

Immediately Jones and Whitehouse strode toward him and came to a halt beside the suitcase. Willie crouched down beside Zane.

"What do you think?" Willie asked a little breathlessly. His partner was only six months into his stint in homicide. He hadn't come into contact with many bodies, especially young women folded inside suitcases. The whites of his wide eyes were a stark contrast to his dark skin.

Zane grimaced and then glanced at the forensic pathologist. "It's my guess she's been dead three to four weeks, although I'll defer to your opinion on this, Andrew."

The examiner glanced across at Mac and Jessica and then looked back at the others.

"According to her ex-boyfriend, she was last seen on July sixth. That puts us back a little over three weeks. Give or take a day."

With gloved hands, the forensic pathologist moved the body gently this way and that before nodding agreement.

"I'd say your guess is about right, Zane. The cooler weather and the fact she's been stored indoors has helped to slow down decomp, but I'd say she died approximately three or four weeks ago. I'll have to take her back to the lab and do a full autopsy before I can confirm the timeline."

Zane nodded and got to his feet. Taking care not to breathe too deeply, he discarded his gloves and then looked around.

"Make sure the place is secured," he said to

Willie. "We'll need to go over this place with a fine-tooth comb and see if there are any clues or other evidence the killer left behind. We need to determine whether she was actually killed here or merely dumped at this site."

Willie looked around him. "There doesn't seem to be anything disturbed, although it's hard to tell with the room empty. I don't see any marks or bumps in the wall or any other indication there was a struggle. It's my guess she's been murdered somewhere else."

Zane nodded. "Yeah, that's what I think, too. Still, we need to do a thorough search of the area to rule out this site, at least. You never know what might be found."

Zane moved over to where Mac and Jessica still stood. "Thanks for coming out here so quickly, Mr Callaway and for identifying the body. It's spared Angela Sorenson a lot of additional grief and we've gained valuable time. We appreciate your cooperation."

Mac continued to look pale and shell-shocked. Zane studied him closely in an effort to detect whether it was genuine. Seemingly unaware of Zane's scrutiny, Mac stared at the ground and slowly shook his head.

"The last time I saw Melissa we'd had a nasty fight, but I never wanted her to turn up dead. Whoever did this needs to be caught. And quickly."

Zane nodded in agreement. "You're right. Nobody deserves to be murdered and tossed unceremoniously into a suitcase like a piece of trash. Do you remember what Melissa was wearing the night she disappeared?"

"I'm not sure what she was wearing when she disappeared," Mac responded. "All I can tell you is what she wore when I saw her last."

"And what was that?" Zane asked.

"Jeans and a blouse."

"The same clothing she has on now?" Zane asked.

He saw Jessica glance at her client. A few moments later, Mac sighed.

"Yes. Blue jeans and a yellow blouse."

"And the scarf?" Zane asked.

Mac shook his head. "No, not the scarf. She never wore scarves. She hated having things around her neck."

"What about the boots? Was she wearing boots the last time you saw her?" Zane asked.

"No," Mac replied. "It was late. Past nine o'clock. We were preparing for bed. I'd just taken a shower. I expected her to follow suit. And then we argued. The last time I saw her she had bare feet."

Zane pulled out his notebook and jotted something down. When he was finished, he looked back at Mac. "Well, thank you again for your cooperation. It can't be easy for you to see her like this. Go home. We'll be in touch."

Jessica turned and faced Zane. Now that he knew who she was, he could see the family resemblance. She was every bit as beautiful as Samantha.

"Does this mean my client is no longer a suspect, Detective?"

Zane shook his head. "You know the game better than I do, Counselor. Everyone's a suspect until we find that someone else did it. Your client's free to go, but not free to leave town." The last bit was issued to Mac with a warning tone attached.

Mac merely nodded. "You know where to find me, Detective. I'm not going anywhere."

———

The man watched from a safe distance through a pair of powerful binoculars. A chuckle of unrestrained pleasure rose from his chest and escaped through his mouth. Police swarmed Mackenzie Callaway's construction site. The strobing red and white and blue emergency lights pulsed in sync with the rapid beat of his heart.

They'd found her.

Of course, he knew they would. It was only a matter of time before the pungent odor of the rotting corpse permeated the walls enough for someone to notice. It was hard to mistake the smell of death.

The entryway to Mac's building was suddenly filled with a familiar figure and he watched as the man himself stumbled out into the late sunshine. He looked drawn and tired. Worried. Another chuckle escaped. Mac was right to feel concerned. This was just the beginning.

A smartly dressed woman in a tailored gray suit and black stilettoes followed behind his nemesis. She had a killer figure – long slim legs and curvy in all the right places. He sat up straighter on his perch. *Who was she?* There was something about her that felt familiar. Something about the way she held herself, the way she tossed her dark hair. And then it hit him.

Jessica Wolfe.

It had been a long time, but he'd recognize her anywhere. He ought to. Back in high school, they'd been friends. Kind of. That felt like a lifetime ago.

What the hell was she doing with Mac Callaway again?

Much closer, another man watched the chaos of strobe lights and police vehicles and was filled with rage. *Mac Callaway had done it again.* Murdered another innocent, unsuspecting girl. It was high school all over again. Only this time, he was here, not thousands of miles away, and this time he'd darn well make sure Callaway was forced to pay. He might have gotten away with the perfect crime the first time, but he wouldn't get away with it again. Never again.

Jessie watched as a tall broad-shouldered man in his late forties with a military short graying buzz cut and a wary look in his eyes approached them. He wore the same kind of high visibility clothing and steel-top boots the other construction workers on the site wore. He sidled up to Mac.

"You got a minute, Mac?"

Mac blew his breath out on a sigh and ran a hand threw his hair. "Sure, Steve. What's up?"

Steve flicked a glance in Jessie's direction. She could see the frank interest in his eyes, but the wariness remained. She wondered at it. Steve took a few steps away and motioned to Mac with his head. Mac remained where he was.

"This is my lawyer, Jessica Wolfe. We can talk in front of her. She accompanied me here to help me deal with the police."

Jessie stepped forward and held out her hand. "Hi. I'm Jessie Wolfe."

Mac's employee eyed her steadily. He grudgingly shook her hand. "Steve Prendergast."

"My foreman and right hand man," Mac added. "I don't know what I'd do without him. Especially now." Mac's shoulders slumped on a sigh. He looked at Steve. "I just identified Melissa's body. If this gets out, we're going to be screwed. As if anyone will want to spend a million dollars on an apartment where a dead body's been found."

Steve acknowledged Mac's grim statement with a brief nod, his expression just as somber. "Yeah, we could have done without this, that's for sure."

Jessie thought back to the discovery of Melissa's body. She was reminded of the way Janice Scott had been discovered in Mac's bed all those years ago. The similarities sent a shiver of apprehension down her spine. She forced it away.

Mac had been cleared of all suspicion back then, just as she was sure he'd be cleared now. Still, it was disconcerting, to say the least.

"What did you want to speak with me about?" Mac asked, directing the question toward Steve.

Once again, Steve flicked a glance in Jessie's direction and then focused his attention back on his boss.

"That other little problem we talked about earlier – the steel order – I found the culprit."

Mac's eyebrows rose up in surprise. "That was quick. Tell me it didn't come from our end."

Steve grimaced. "Unfortunately, yes. It was the new bloke, Jarrod Harris. I texted him the measurements and he was to give them to the ordering manager at Johnstone Steel. Somehow he screwed them up. Who knows how he did it... All he had to do was read the measurements I'd sent him. Could be he's dyslexic, but we can't afford mistakes like that."

Mac listened in silence, but the scowl on his forehead told Jessie all she needed to know. This wasn't going to end well for Harris.

"Fire him," Mac said.

"I already did."

CHAPTER 7

Mac stared down at the cup of black coffee in front of him and wondered how it got there. He remembered seeing a waitress, but couldn't recall speaking to her. Jessie must've placed the order. He glanced at her with gratitude.

"Thanks for the coffee. I'm sorry I haven't been much company since we returned from Hornsby. My thoughts are full of Melissa. I can't get her out of my mind. The fact someone murdered her... The way she looked in that suitcase..." He shuddered.

Jessie nodded with sympathy. "It's all right, Mac. I understand. She was your girlfriend. You guys dated for two years. You cared for her. Seeing her like that must have come as a shock. I'm sorry. No one deserves to die that way."

A surge of anger went through him. "You're right. She might've cheated on me, but she was a good and decent girl. I can't believe anyone would want to kill her."

Jessie's expression remained grim. "And not only murdered her, but it appears they've gone out of their way to make it appear you're the culprit. Not only were you the last person to see her alive, she's turned up dead on your construction site."

Mac's anger exploded. "Why would I hide her on my own job site if I did it? Surely the cops don't think I'm that stupid?"

Jessie shrugged. "Maybe, maybe not. They don't know you. And people do stupid things when they're in a panic. Like right after they've murdered someone. You can see why they haven't taken you off the suspect list."

Mac sighed. With all the stresses of his current development project hanging over his head, this was the last thing he needed. He sure as hell knew he was innocent, but it looked like it was going to take a gargantuan effort to convince the police he had nothing to do with her disappearance, her murder and her being placed strategically on one of his prime properties. Especially since he seemed to be the only one in their sights.

The thought made him frown. "What about the other guy? The one Mel was seeing? He could be behind all this. Have the police even spoken with him?"

Jessie shrugged. "I'm not sure that they've identified him, yet," she replied. I'll call Detective Sullivan and see." She reached for her phone.

Mac took a sip of his coffee and waited for her to complete the call. The conversation with the lead detective didn't last long. She hung up a few minutes later.

"No luck?" he asked.

Jessie shook her head. "No. The police still don't know who Melissa was seeing. Initially they believed you might not be telling them the truth about the real reason you fought. Then they began questioning her sister and her friends, and it appeared you were right. Angela admitted Melissa said she was having an affair and a couple of her work colleagues saw her get a ride with a man after work one day. The only description they were able to provide was that he was a good-looking businessman who drove a flashy sports car."

Mac cursed under his breath. "Great. So she was flaunting her infidelity at work. I must've been a laughingstock." He cursed again. "I can't believe none of her friends told me! I've met some of them a few times and I know Angela quite well. I would have thought one of them would have had the decency to tell me."

"Sometimes people just don't want to get involved," Jessie said quietly. "It's none of their business and all that kind of stuff. You know how it is."

Mac sighed heavily again and scrubbed his hands through his hair. "Yeah, I guess so. I'm not sure what I'd do if I thought a coworker's partner was having an affair. Probably keep my mouth shut and mind my own business," he said morosely.

A pensive silence fell between them. They both sipped from their coffee cups. Mac was the first one to speak.

"So, what do we do now?"

"Well, you keep your head down and do your best to get on with your life. The police will carry out their investigation. Let's hope the autopsy reveals some clues that point in a different direction – away from you. And if Detective Sullivan needs to get in contact with you, he'll call. I told him all questions need to go through me. I hope that's okay with you?"

Mac stared at her. He wasn't used to someone taking charge of his life, least of all Jessie Wolfe. He wasn't used to having her near him, period. As their gazes caught and held, a tsunami of memories bombarded him. Her brown eyes, so deep and filled with emotion. The same beauty as all those years ago. He remembered the way she looked at him the last time he'd seen her back in high school, with tears running down her cheeks; the way she'd told him she didn't want to see him again.

Suddenly he was filled with the need to know how she felt about Melissa's disappearance. Without thinking, he reached for her hands and grasped them tightly.

"I need you to tell me that you believe I had nothing to do with Melissa's murder. I know this looks bad, but I swear I had nothing to do with it. Just like I had nothing to do with the rape and murder of Janice."

Slowly but surely, Jessie pulled her hands out of his and tucked them against her sides. His heart plummeted.

She didn't believe him!

How was he going to convince the police of his innocence if his own lawyer had doubts? Then she looked up at him, her expression unguarded in that moment.

"I believe you had nothing to do with Melissa's murder," Jessie said quietly. "Just like I believe you had nothing to do with the rape and murder of Janice Scott. The police caught the perpetrator back then and they'll catch this killer now.

"You have to be patient. If they have more questions, we'll answer them, but we'll do it together. In the meantime, you need to try and put this behind you and get on with your life. You have a business to run, people who rely on you. And so do I."

He started in surprise. "A business to run? I'm sorry, though Lachlan spoke highly of you, I was under the impression you were an employee at Sydney Legal."

She blushed with embarrassment. "You're right, I *am* only an employee. After the debacle with Alistair, any hope of a partnership all but disappeared. Still, I'm doing my best to make a good impression on my bosses in the hope that one day they'll overlook Alistair's indiscretion and review my performance based on my own merits and give me the promotion I deserve."

Mac frowned. "Alistair?"

"My brother. You mean you hadn't heard...?"

His frown deepened. He remembered Jessie was an identical twin and she also had a younger sister. He couldn't recall any brother.

"I don't remember him," he admitted.

"He's nine years older than me. He'd left school long before we got there."

"That probably explains it. What does your brother have to do with holding you back in your career?"

Instead of answering, Jessie took another sip from her coffee cup. For a few moments, she stared off into the distance. At last she looked back at him, her expression grim.

"He went and got himself convicted for illegal human organ trafficking."

Mac reeled back in surprise. "Really? Was he living in Sydney?"

She nodded. "Yes. He was a doctor at Sydney Harbour Hospital. And a very good one, too. He was well thought of by his colleagues and loved by patients and staff alike. Then he decided to dabble in the dark side and it took over his life.

"It started out nobly enough...because our mother needed a kidney transplant and he saw the chasm of need to help people live better lives, but it became so much more than that. He made a lot of money out of it. Greed took over and he lost sight of his original goal – to ensure there were more human organs and tissue to use in transplants."

She sighed quietly and her expression became resigned. "Eventually the police caught on to what he was doing and he was arrested and charged. I can't believe you didn't hear about the debacle. The TV and newspapers were all over the story. It's the reason my legal career took a sudden nosedive. The firm doesn't look kindly on negative publicity, even if I wasn't directly involved. It didn't look good for them to have one of their criminal defense lawyers related to such a high-profile convicted felon."

Mac couldn't hide his indignation. "That's not fair! You're not responsible for your brother's actions! You had nothing to do with what he did. I'd guess you were as oblivious to what he was doing as everyone else."

"You're right, but the partners of Sydney Legal didn't see it that way. Fortunately or unfortunately, mine wasn't the only scandal they've had to face. They changed their name when one of the partners' wives was convicted of attempted murder – against the partner. You might recall we used to be known as Harton & Wentworth?"

Mac nodded slowly. "Yes, I remember that. The change only happened a year or so ago, right?"

"Yes. After the conviction they thought it was time for a new name and a new image. It was done with the hope we could leave all the scandal behind."

"I remember now. Alexei Gianopoulos. His wife was behind the gruesome murders of those gay men along the cliffs of Bondi. Is he still a partner at your firm?"

"Yes. You might not know that he also came out as a gay man around the same time his wife was arrested. The partners were in a spin. They had no idea where to turn. They abhorred the bad publicity and just wanted it to go away. The easiest way to do that was to get rid of Alexei, but he'd just come out of the closet. The partners didn't want people to think they'd gotten rid of him because he was gay. They were stuck in a lose/lose situation. I'm just glad it had nothing to do with me. Having Alistair tried and serving time in jail is bad enough."

"And what about the people who rely on you?" he asked softly. "Is there someone special in your life?"

He held his breath and waited for her answer. Her ring less fingers indicated she wasn't married, but that didn't mean she wasn't in a long-term relationship. She might even have a family. The thought filled him with disappointment. As a teen, he'd imagined they'd have a family together one day.

"I'm currently single, if that's what you're asking and I don't have any kids. But my mother had a kidney transplant a couple years ago and she still requires some help. The transplant went well, but she's not as young as she used to be and she's on her own. I call by her place at least a couple times a week to check in on her."

Mac barely heard anything past the fact she was single. He could hardly keep the elation out of his voice. "That's... That's very kind of you. You're a good person, Jessie Wolfe. That's one of the things I loved about you."

The air between them was suddenly charged as both of them remembered high school: falling headlong in love; spending every minute they could together. It had been an amazing, heady time and one Mac wished had never come to an end. He wondered where they might be if Janice Scott hadn't happened.

And then he dismissed the thought with a surge of impatience. They were nearly twenty years down the track, leading separate lives. There was no point in looking back. He needed to focus all his attention on getting himself removed from a murder suspect list, not getting distracted by memories of the past and inconsequential what ifs.

As if sensing his withdrawal, Jessie also pulled back. She pushed her chair away from the table and reached for her handbag as she stood. Tossing a few bills down to cover the coffee, she half-turned away.

"I'd better get going." Her voice was husky with emotion. She impatiently cleared her throat. "I need to get back to the office."

He stared up at her, accepting her hasty departure for what it was. "Of course. I need to get back to work, too. Thanks for coming out to Hornsby today. Having you there meant a lot to me."

Jessie nodded. "Take care, Mac. I mean it. You need to look out for yourself. This can't be easy and it's not going to get any better until they find the culprit responsible for Melissa's death – the same culprit who's trying to make it look like you did this. If you need me, give me a call. I'm here for you."

She blushed at her final words, as if they'd come out without her realizing it. Mac stared at her, his heart beating fast.

"Do you really mean that?"

Her flush deepened and spread across her cheeks. She turned away, flustered, and nervously fiddled with the straps on her handbag.

"O-of course I do," she stammered. "We go back a long way. We're friends, aren't we? Friends look out for one another."

His gaze remained fixed on her. "Are we? Friends now?"

"Of course we're friends. We always were. That mess with Janice... I was seventeen... What did you expect? It didn't mean I stopped caring."

Her voice had dropped to almost a whisper and Mac strained to hear every word. He pushed back his chair as if in a daze and closed the distance between them. Taking her by the shoulders, he turned her to face him.

"I never stopped caring about you either, Jessie. It's the reason my dating history over the last twenty years has been so sporadic. I guess for a long time I was searching for someone who could fill the void you left in my heart. It was only a couple of years ago when I finally realized no one could replace Jessie Wolfe.

"After I accepted that, being with other women got easier. I met Melissa. She was pretty and smart and knew how to have a good time. We moved in together. She badgered me to get married. Wanted to make it official. I didn't particularly want to settle down, but hey, time was running out. I'm thirty-seven. I want to be a father. Melissa was as good a partner as any."

Jessie shook her head, her eyes dark with

confusion. "I can't believe you were settling for just anyone. That any pretty face would do. You disappoint me, Mac Callaway. I thought you had more substance than that."

With that, she went to turn away, dismissing him but he reached out and grabbed her arm.

"Not so fast, Counselor."

She looked down at her forearm where his fingers still held her fast. Though not tight enough to hurt her, his hold was meant to keep her there.

"Let go of me," she bit out.

"Not until you tell me why you refused to listen to me that night."

"What night?" she hissed.

"You know what night. The night I've relived in my mind more times than I can count. The night Janice was raped and murdered and you told me you never wanted to see me again. The night you refused to let me in to explain."

Jessie stared at him, her chest heaving. Gradually, Mac loosened his hold. With her gaze still fixed on his, she dropped her arm to her side.

"You're convinced I think you raped and murdered Janice, aren't you?"

Mac tensed and narrowed his gaze. "You never gave me any reason to think you didn't, or any other reason for ending things that night."

Jessie slowly shook her head. "After all these years, you still don't get it. My anger at you that night had nothing to with whether I believed you responsible for what happened to Janice. The truth is, I never believed you had anything to do with her rape and murder.

"I was furious at you because I saw you together at the field, all snuggly, and I couldn't understand how she ended up in your bed if you weren't interested in her!"

Mac's jaw dropped open in shock and Jessie wasn't surprised. She'd never given him any hint, all those years ago, that she'd seen him with Janice earlier that day and had been filled with jealousy. Then when he'd dropped around to see her late that afternoon, she'd refused to see him.

"Perhaps we should go someplace where we can talk," she suggested.

The café had filled up with late-afternoon customers and the noise level had increased dramatically. If she and Mac were going to have a heart-to-heart, she preferred someplace a little more private.

"Why don't we go back to my place? I don't live far from here," she suggested.

Once again, Mac's face registered surprise. She grimaced. "We're going to talk, Mac. Nothing more. If you'd rather, I can take you back to my office. It's just that I already told Margaret I'd be gone for the rest of the day. She might wonder why I'm back and bringing you with me. Not that I care what she thinks. I'm entitled to do as I please, but..."

Mac blinked and then answered quickly, as if finally finding his senses. "That's fine. I'm happy to go to your place to talk. In fact, I'd love to see where you live."

Jessie gritted her teeth. *Perhaps her suggestion hadn't been such a good idea after all?* The more she thought about it, the more crazy it seemed to open up a very personal part of her life to the man she used to love. She was his lawyer. She ought to keep a professional distance. Never once before had she invited a client back to her home.

But this was different. This was Mac. She'd known him through high school. There was a time when she thought she'd one day become his wife. She'd loved him with every fiber of her seventeen-year-old body and then life had thrown them a curve ball and everything had been thrown off course.

She tossed him a narrow-eyed look to let him know once again that nothing more than talking would be going on at her place. He acknowledged her look with a nod and in silence followed her out of the café. The walk to her place didn't take long.

Less than ten minutes after leaving the café, they walked into the foyer of her building and Jessie pressed the button for the elevator. When it arrived, they stepped inside and she selected her floor. Mac shot her a grin that was tinged with disbelief.

"You live in a hotel?"

"I live in a private suite in a hotel," she replied.

He whistled. "I'm impressed. I had no idea lawyering paid so well."

"Unfortunately, it doesn't. At least, not for lawyers in my position. If I were a partner, I might have a chance of owning a property as nice as this somewhere else, but on my current salary, all I can afford is to rent. I guess I could live further out of the city and the prices would be cheaper, but I like being within walking distance of the office and the view from my living room's pretty darn spectacular."

Ding!

Right on cue, the elevator doors soundlessly slid open. Jessie stepped out and walked the short distance to her door. Using a keycard, she let herself in and held the door open for Mac.

"Wow! You weren't exaggerating. The view's amazing!"

Jessie grinned, filling with pride. She might only pay the monthly rent on a hotel suite, but she was still proud to call the place home. She'd replaced most of the standard hotel furnishings with pieces that better reflected her style. She'd scrimped and saved every paycheck to do so and was inordinately pleased with the result. Neutral tones in the furniture contrasted against splashes of colorful accessories. Bright cushions, artwork and other knick-knacks turned the suite into a home. *Her* home.

She watched Mac make his way over to the floor-to-ceiling plate glass window to stare out at Sydney Harbour below. Yachts and other watercraft moved between the city and the north shore. Ferries laden with commuters chugged back and forth. The late afternoon sun sent a myriad of sparkling diamonds across the water. It was a scene Jessie never tired of.

"Can I get you a drink?" she asked, making her way over to her modest supply of alcohol.

"Sure. What do you have?"

"Beer, wine and cider. That's about it," she said with a smile.

Mac grinned and her belly somersaulted. Ava was right. He looked even better than he had in high school.

"Sounds like you have the necessities covered." He winked. "I'll have a beer, thanks."

She handed him a Budweiser. Their fingers touched and she swallowed a gasp of awareness. Tingles made their way up her arm, leaving a trail of heat in their wake. Flustered, she turned away and busied herself getting a cider. The cool liquid felt like heaven against her heated lips. Taking one quick gulp and then another, she wiped her mouth with the back of her hand and cleared her throat, eager to get the meeting back on a professional footing.

"So, let's talk about the night Janice was raped and murdered," she said.

Mac regarded her somberly and then gave a brief nod of acknowledgement. Jessie sighed quietly and began to speak.

"I've already told you the reason I refused to let you explain that night was because I was mad at you."

Mac made his way over to the couch and sat down. He shot her a measured look. "Why were you mad? I'd seen you during the lunch break and everything was fine. The next thing I knew, you were giving me the cold shoulder. I went over to your place that afternoon and you wouldn't let me in. I stood on your front porch and pleaded with you to tell me what was wrong, but you refused. What the hell happened?"

CHAPTER 8

Jessie's belly swirled with nerves as she took a sip of her cider. Now that the moment was upon her, she wasn't sure she had the courage to see it through. Then she gave a mental shrug. *What did it matter?* They were talking about events that had happened nearly twenty years ago.

With a fortifying breath and another mouthful of cider, she risked a quick glance in Mac's direction and finally blurted it out.

"I saw you with Janice near the bleachers after school. You looked mighty cozy. I didn't wait around to ask questions. All I knew was the captain of the football team, *my* boyfriend, had his arms around the head cheerleader."

Mac was already frowning long before she finished. "Me and Janice Scott? What do you mean? Janice and I were friends, but she was nothing me. I was in love with *you*, remember?"

"Then why were you holding her? You had your arms around her. She had her head on your chest.

I saw you from thirty yards away. There was no mistaking you. It looked very intimate to me."

Mac sighed. "I remember now." He rubbed the bottle of Bud against his forehead, as if the memory pained him. "I can only imagine what it looked like to you. I understand why you jumped to conclusions. What you don't know is that all I was doing was offering Janice comfort."

Jessie stared at him in disbelief. "It looked like a lot more than comfort to me. She was pressed against you in her itty bitty cheerleading outfit and you didn't seem to mind it one bit. What else was I to think?"

Mac took another sip from his beer and slowly nodded. "You're right. But it wasn't what it seemed. What you didn't know was that Janice had a difficult home life. She came to me with a problem. I was only offering her a sympathetic ear."

"It didn't look so bad to me," Jessie scoffed. "You call having a daddy richer than Croesus and having everything she could ever want, *difficult*? I wish I'd had a difficult home life like that."

"Things aren't always what they seem, Jessie." Mac's quiet and somber tone gave her pause.

She hesitated. "What do you mean?"

Mac compressed his lips in a grimace. "Janice made me promise never to say anything. For all these years, I've kept my word. I guess now that she's dead, my promise no longer matters."

Jessie inched her way toward the couch and perched on the opposite end. Her heart had picked up its pace and she tensed at the thought of what Mac was about to reveal. "What are you talking about, Mac?"

Mac's jaw tightened and then a moment later, he spoke. "Janice's father was an abuser. He used to beat up on his wife. Janice and her sister were spared, but old man Scott showed no such restraint when it came to his wife."

Jessie sucked in her breath and her hand came up to cover her mouth. Shock ricocheted through her. She stared at Mac in disbelief.

"I had no idea!" She gasped.

"No one did."

"But... He was the mayor of Randwick! He was an upstanding citizen, always so polite and respectful. He dressed in expensive clothes and shoes and always drove that incredible car. I remember feeling envious that Janice got to ride in a Porsche." She shook her head slowly back and forth, still finding it hard to come to terms with the revelation of an abusive husband and the Richard Scott she'd thought she'd known of when she was young.

"I never once suspected," she murmured.

"No one did. Lenore Scott was too ashamed to tell anyone. It was their dirty little secret. That's how he got away with it."

"It's just...unbelievable."

"Yes. Anyway, the afternoon you saw Janice and me together, she'd just told me her dad had put her mother in the hospital the night before. It was all covered up of course, like it usually was and Janice knew nothing would change when her mother came home. She was upset and she came to me for comfort. It wasn't the first time."

Jessie stared at him, trying to come to terms with this new information. What he'd shared turned everything she'd believed on its head. She couldn't believe how wrong she'd read the situation. If only she'd let Mac explain...

"Did she go home with you? Is that how she ended up in your bed?"

Mac shook his head. "No. I'd given her a key to my house. I'd told her if she ever needed somewhere safe to stay, she could stay with me."

Jessie was filled with guilt. All this time she'd been half-convinced Mac had cheated on her, when all along he was being nothing more than an incredibly protective and thoughtful friend.

"I'm sorry, Mac."

"So am I. There was nothing ever between me and Janice. We were friends. Even when I saw her that final afternoon, I tried to comfort her as best as I could, but we eventually went our separate ways. I had to study for my final exams and I also wanted to spend time with you. And then you called and told me you never wanted to see me again. I went around to your house to talk to you, but you wouldn't listen. Eventually I left and drove around for a while, trying to clear my head. By the time I got home it was late. The house was dark, but my parents were away, so that didn't trigger anything in my head. I didn't even bother turning on the lights as I made my way down the hall to my bedroom. That's when I found Janice."

Jessie stared at him, aghast. She couldn't imagine how it would feel to discover a friend dead in your bed.

"She used the spare key to get in," Jessie murmured.

"Yes. Like I said, this wasn't the first time her father had been violent. I'd told her that any time she needed to get out, get away from the nightmare at home, she could come to my place. Prior to that fateful night, she'd only been there once."

Jessie shook her head, her mind still filled with the scene Mac must have been confronted with that terrible night. "How awful for you to see her like that," she murmured.

Mac nodded, his expression grim. "Yes. I'll never forget it. She looked like she was asleep, only she wasn't."

"What did you do?"

"Initially, I panicked. I didn't know what the hell to do. She was still warm, so I knew she hadn't been dead for long. I tore through the house, looking for whoever did it, but I didn't find anyone. Eventually, I called the police."

"And the nightmare continued," Jessie said softly.

Mac grimaced. "Yeah. You can say that again."

The pain and disillusionment that clouded his voice touched her deep inside. The police had turned the place upside down. Initially, their focus had been on Mac. It was only later, after DNA results cleared him, that he'd been able to leave town and put the scandal behind him. And all the time he'd battled through without her support, not knowing if she even believed him...

"I'm so sorry, Mac," she whispered. "I had no idea. I'd seen the two of you together and I immediately jumped to wild conclusions. Janice was tall and thin and beautiful. She was the head cheerleader! I overheard her bragging to some of the girls that she had your front door key. And then I saw you together and my jealousy flew out of control. Now I understand. I should have known you wouldn't cheat on me. You were so good and kind and loyal. Even though we'd only dated a short time, you gave me the beautiful watch and told me you loved me on my birthday. I should have trusted your love. I should have trusted *you*!"

Tears choked her voice and were suddenly flooding her eyes. Mac closed the distance between them and took her in his arms. It felt so good to be held by him, to take comfort from the man she'd once loved. A man, she realized, she *still* loved.

The thought came from nowhere and she tensed in his arms. Not knowing the reason, but sensing her distress, Mac released her without a word. The tears continued to course down Jessie's cheeks, but she was powerless to make them stop. So much had happened to alter the destiny of their lives and yet one thing had stayed the same. She loved Mac Callaway with all her heart and soul. Then...and now. The thought filled her with absolute panic.

———————

He watched Mac Callaway and Jessie Wolfe disappear into the ritzy hotel and wondered where they were headed. It was a strange meeting place for a lawyer and her client. Unless there was more going on with the two of them than anyone knew…?

Perhaps they'd picked things up from where they'd left off in high school? Perhaps they'd never stopped. No, not that. He'd been there when Mac Callaway left town, headed for college, though Mac had been oblivious to his presence. Jessie had made it clear to anyone who cared to ask that she and Mac Callaway were over.

He'd been glad to hear it. He wasn't interested in Jessie Wolfe for himself, but he didn't want Mac Callaway to have her, either. Mac Callaway was the reason Janice was dead and no one would convince him otherwise. It was too bad he hadn't been there to save her. He vowed there and then on Janice's freshly marked grave to make Mac Callaway pay.

And he was paying. Oh, yes, he was. One little incident at a time.

———

Mac moved away from the couch. The need to put distance between him and Jessie was as much for his benefit as it was for hers. One minute she'd been melting against him with tears pouring down her face and the next she'd stiffened in his arms and he'd seen the panic in her eyes. He knew how she felt.

His mind spun with all that had gone on between them and the revelations of the past few minutes. He'd had no idea her rejection of him all those years ago had been based on jealousy. It hadn't occurred to him that she'd seen him with Janice in what appeared to be a somewhat compromising position. Janice meant nothing to him beyond a friend. It was Jessie who was the love of his life.

But that was then. A lot of time had passed. He'd finally reached a point in his life where he was happy. He ran a multimillion-dollar company. He owned a condo near the beach. He drove a red Ferrari. Let's face it, he was living the dream. It didn't matter that he hadn't found the kind of love he'd once had with Jessie. He'd found something almost as good: fun and companionship.

Melissa hadn't been perfect, but then again, who was? Certainly not him. But she was beautiful, intelligent and exciting and – best of all – nothing about her reminded him of the girl he'd given his heart to in high school.

Now Melissa was dead. Murdered. And the police had their sights set on him.

He made a sound of frustration in the back of his throat. Jessie looked up from where she sat on the couch.

"What is it, Mac?"

He blew out his breath on a heavy sigh. "I was thinking of Melissa and the fact I'm still the number one suspect. I sure as hell know I didn't do it, which means the real killer is still walking free. If the detectives don't switch their focus, the bastard might very well get away with it."

Jessie came off the couch and moved to stand beside him. Her tears were now gone and she appeared much more in control of herself. It was as if her outburst a few moments ago had never happened.

Mac was relieved. He didn't know how he felt about Jessie's revelations and her interpretation of events. He needed time alone to process what had gone on. Now wasn't the best time to get into a discussion on the success and failure of their short-lived relationship.

"I called Lachlan Coleridge while we were at your construction site."

"What did he have to say?"

"He gave me the rundown on Zane Sullivan. According to Lachlan, Detective Sullivan is a good bloke and a thorough and reliable investigator. If anyone's going to catch the person responsible for Melissa's murder, it's him."

Mac nodded. "That's good to know. At least we have someone competent on the job. It just irks me that they're wasting time looking at me while the real killer is out there covering his tracks. We all know the longer the killer remains at large, the greater the likelihood he'll get away with this."

Jessie shot him a look. "Let the police do their job. You're innocent, right? The evidence will support that."

"How can you be so sure?" Mac fired back.

"Because I've spent every day since law school

believing that a man is innocent until proven guilty. Thankfully we don't live in a country where the police are all corrupt and take bribes to look the other way. They need evidence of guilt. If you did nothing wrong, like you say, then you have nothing to be afraid of."

Mac narrowed his eyes on a sudden surge of anger. "What do you mean, like I say? Don't you believe me?"

She sighed and shook her head. "We've had this conversation, Mac. It doesn't matter what I think. I'm your lawyer. It's my job to defend you no matter what."

His anger rose. "What you think matters to *me*."

Jessie crossed her arms over her chest and stared him down. "We're not doing this, Mac." He closed the distance between them, his heart pumping.

"Oh, yes we are. I refuse to engage a lawyer who doesn't wholeheartedly believe in my innocence. Look me in the eye and tell me if you think I had anything to do with Melissa's murder."

His gaze bored into hers. It took several seconds for her to formulate a reply. Several seconds too long, as far as Mac was concerned. He turned away in disgust.

"I don't believe it," he snarled. "My own lawyer thinks I did it."

"No, Mac! That's not fair!" Jessie protested.

"But it's true, isn't it?"

"Yes. No. I don't know." She threw up her hands. "How do you expect me to know who's responsible when the police are still clueless? The Mac I knew twenty years ago couldn't have possibly acted with such violence, but a lot can change in twenty years. People change. Do I think you're innocent? Yes, I do, but I have nothing to prove it either way except for what my gut tells me."

She turned away and moved to the far side of the room. She stared through the plate glass window. The silence stretched between them. Mac didn't know what to say. Finally, with her back still turned toward him, Jessie quietly spoke.

"Twenty years ago, I was shocked and horrified to discover Janice Scott had been found raped and murdered in your bed. It was months before DNA evidence pointed the finger at Wes Parker. All that time, there were whispers. Many people were convinced of your guilt. But not me. Though I was confused and a little bit angry, I never once thought you'd done it."

Slowly, she turned to face him. "When Lachlan called me and told me about what happened with Melissa, I was reminded of that earlier time and though the police are yet to identify another suspect, you were never on my radar. Twenty years ago, you were good and kind and loving. Though I try to keep an open mind, I don't really believe a person can change that much, no matter what has happened since."

Mac's anger dissolved. Hope slid through his veins. "So, you *do* believe I'm innocent?"

Jessie nodded. "Yes."

Relief surged through him. Without thinking, he strode forward and captured her face in his hands. He planted his mouth squarely on hers and kissed her hard. Despite the pain from his injured lip, fire flared in his veins. Blood pounded in his groin. He was hot and hard and wanting, burning with need. Only when Jessie wrenched away from him did the madness inside him ease. They were both out of breath when he finally managed to speak.

"I'm sorry, Jessie. That was uncalled for. I don't know what I was thinking."

Her chest rose and fell in time with her rapid breathing. She pressed a hand to her swollen lips and then slowly removed it, as if still trying to work out what had just happened. At last she turned to face him, her eyes wide with shock and a need that had been long buried.

"I think... I think it might be best for you to find another lawyer."

At once, he opened his mouth to protest. "No, Jessie! I want *you*! I'm sorry. I should never have kissed you. I stepped over the line. I promise it won't happen again."

She didn't look convinced.

"Mac, I'm your lawyer. I need to remain fully focused on your case. So far, you're just a suspect, but what if it goes further? What if the police find enough evidence to lay charges and you're brought before the court? I refuse to take the risk I might take my eye off the ball because I'm more concerned over whether we should take up our relationship where we left off."

Mac was filled with panic at the thought she might refuse to represent him. "I'm sorry, Jessie. I don't know what else to say. I give you my word our relationship will remain purely professional. I won't overstep the line again."

She stared at him for such a long time, searching his face for clues. Mac didn't know what convinced her, but finally she nodded and sighed.

"All right. I'll remain your lawyer, but that's all we are, okay? Call me during office hours if you need to discuss your case. Otherwise, you need to leave me alone. It's the only way this is going to work. Agreed?"

She held out her hand toward him. Though everything inside Mac rebelled at the idea of not being able to spend more time with her, he reluctantly shook her hand.

"Agreed."

CHAPTER 9

Mac punched numbers into his calculator and quietly cursed at the result displayed upon the screen. The continual delays with the concrete and steel were bad enough. Now with cops combing the site looking for clues to Melissa's murder...and the story about to break in the media at any moment, in addition to having lost his best realtor, there was a good chance any money he might make on this development was about to disintegrate before his eyes.

A brief knock on the door of the site office caught his attention. He welcomed the momentary distraction.

"Come in."

Steve's body filled the opening. "Is this a bad time?"

Mac sighed and waved him in. Steve took the seat opposite him.

"How are you holding up?" Steve asked, his expression concerned.

Mac grimaced. "I've had better days."

Steve nodded. "Yeah, me too."

Mac looked across at his friend. For the first time, he noticed the overgrown beard where usually there was none and the shadows of fatigue beneath Steve's eyes. His work shirt looked like it had been slept in. He wondered if Steve was still taking his meds.

"Are you all right, mate?" Mac asked.

Steve ran a hand tiredly through his buzz cut. "I haven't been sleeping so well lately. I guess I'm worried about the project."

Mac was warmed by his friend's concern, but hastened to reassure the man it wasn't necessary.

"None of this is your fault, Steve. You've been doing all you can to keep this development on track. It just seems like we've had more than our share of misfortunes this time round. What with Demir playing silly games with the concrete and Harris messing up the steel order and now this awful stuff with Melissa... Still, we'll be fine. And it's not for you to worry about my bottom line."

Steve nodded, his expression filling with relief. "I appreciate you saying so, Mac, but you're not in this alone. I want you to know that."

Once again, Mac was flooded with warmth and gratitude toward his friend. "You're a good man, Steve. Don't go losing sleep over this. Things will work out. You'll see."

"I hope so. I just heard from Omer Demir. There's been another delay on that concrete."

Mac cursed vehemently. "You have to be kidding!" he exploded. "Where the hell does this prick get off? This has gone beyond a joke. I'm going to call the bastard and demand an explanation."

"Yes. I agree. This has gone way past civil. Still, I do have some good news," Steve offered.

Mac's hand paused halfway to his phone. "Yeah? I could do with some of that right now."

"I've spoken to Melissa's real estate firm. They're as shocked as we are about her murder, but they're also business people. They're sending over a couple of their finest realtors for us to interview. I've also spoken to a couple of other firms. Everyone's keen to come on board."

Mac's lips twisted into a grimace. "Just wait until word gets out about where Melissa's body was located. They might not be so keen to take us on. It's not going to be easy selling condos that are now part of a violent crime scene."

"Leave that to them," Steve encouraged. "After all, they're the experts in marketing. Let them worry about how they're going to get them sold."

Mac sighed. "I wish it were that easy. Still, thanks for chasing this up. I appreciate it. We need all the help we can get."

"Just doing my job," Steve murmured. Silence fell between them. A moment later, Steve spoke again.

"Glad to see you finally got yourself a lawyer. It was good that she was able to come out to the site and help you with the police."

"Yeah."

Steve shot him a sideways glance. "She's kind of hot looking."

Mac kept his expression bland. "Really? I didn't notice."

"Bullshit." Steve grinned.

Mac reluctantly grinned back. "Okay, so maybe I did notice. So, shoot me."

"From what I saw, the feeling's reciprocated. She kept sending you glances that appeared mighty concerned. More concern than I'd guess was warranted for a mere client."

Steve's words settled comfortably in Mac's gut. He was more than pleased by his foreman's assessment of Jessie's attitude toward him. She was insistent the two of them maintain a professional distance, but it appeared she hadn't done such a good job of concealing her interest in him from Steve.

"Really?"

"Yeah. It was pretty obvious. Most lawyers see their clients from behind the security of their desks. She was accompanying you to a crime scene. No one does that for just anyone, especially not a lawyer. I hope she realizes your habit of having your girlfriends turn up dead."

Mac started in surprise and stared at Steve in shock. "What the hell is that supposed to mean?"

Steve shrugged, unperturbed by Mac's anger. "Just what I said. You don't have much of a track record when it comes to keeping your women safe."

"I had nothing to do with Melissa's death! You know that."

"But it's not just Melissa, is it?"

Steve's voice was so low Mac wasn't sure he'd heard him right. "Excuse me?"

"You heard me."

Mac shook his head in confusion. The conversation was completely bizarre. *What the hell was Steve playing at?*

He glared at his foreman. "No, I'm not sure that I did. You seem to be implying this isn't the first time a girlfriend of mine has turned up dead."

"Well, it's true, isn't it? Don't tell me you've forgotten about Janice."

Mac reeled back in shock. He stared at Steve. "How the hell do you know Janice?"

Steve's expression remained unperturbed. He shrugged. "I did some research before I came to work for you. You didn't think I'd just work for anyone, did you? It was all over the news. It wasn't hard to find on an Internet search. She was found dead in your bed, wasn't she?"

Once again, Mac stared at Steve in shock. He slowly shook his head back and forth, trying to understand what was happening. Steve was acting way past odd. The whole conversation was surreal. Beyond strange.

"Where is this coming from, Steve? Are you okay? You don't look so good. Are you still taking your meds?"

"Fuck off, Callaway. Don't put this back on me. This has nothing to do with me. Janice Scott died in *your* bed. Now Melissa has turned up on *your* job site. Two women from your past are now dead. It's freaking me out."

Mac stared at Steve a moment longer and then his shoulders slumped on a sigh. Though he was surprised Steve knew about Janice, he understood the man's concern. Steve battled with enough demons of his own. For a long time now, he'd been treated for PTSD, diagnosed after coming home from Afghanistan. No wonder he was freaking out. Two dead bodies was enough to freak out anyone.

"It's all right, Steve. I'm sorry I didn't tell you about Janice. I didn't realize you were even aware of what happened back then. I wish you'd come to me with your concerns rather than getting your information off the Internet, but please, let me assure you, the police found the guy responsible for that. I was cleared of all suspicion. Just like I will be over Melissa. Still, I'm sorry you've been dragged into it. I wish it didn't have to be this way."

Steve waved away Mac's apology. He blew out his breath. "There's no need to apologize, Mac. If anyone should be apologizing, it's me. I'm sorry. I shouldn't have gone off at you like that. It was uncalled for. I guess the stress of everything lately just got to me."

Mac regarded him kindly. "Like I said, this is on me. You don't have to worry about how I'm going to make ends meet. Just keep doing what you're doing and everything will work out all right. I promise. This is just a minor setback, a temporary roadblock. It will pass."

Steve appeared satisfied with Mac's explanation. With a brief nod, he pushed back his chair and stood. "Thanks, Mac. I'm sure you're right. You're a good bloke."

Mac smiled. "Don't mention it."

———————

The phone at Jessie's elbow rang and her heart skipped a beat. It had been three days since she'd seen Mac and it irked her that she missed him. Though she'd made the right decision about keeping their relationship purely professional, she'd still replayed every second of their heated kiss. More than once.

The familiar feel of his lips on hers had sent her mind into a frenzy. It was like the past twenty years had been stripped away and she was a teenager all over again. The warmth of his skin, the rasp of his stubble, the smell of his spicy cologne... All of it had assailed her senses and left her yearning for more.

And then she'd come back to earth with a crash and had brought the kiss to an end. She was his lawyer. They were no longer dating. So much had happened since then. They couldn't simply take up where they'd left off. Life didn't work like that. It was complicated, full of twists and turns and there were so many unanswered questions.

No, she was better off holding Mac Callaway at a distance and keeping her heart intact. She was so much older and wiser than she'd been at seventeen, and she had no doubt he still had the power to hurt. Loving someone made you vulnerable and she was just as vulnerable to Mac now as she'd been two decades ago. She'd best remember that.

Still, that didn't mean she hadn't missed him or didn't long to hear his voice. The phone continued to ring and she had a wistful thought that it was him. She leaned over to answer it.

"Jessie Wolfe."

"Ms Wolfe, it's Detective Sullivan. I want to talk to you about Mac Callaway. Are you still representing him?"

"Yes. And please, Detective, call me Jessie."

"All right, Jessie. I just wanted to let you know I have the results back from the autopsy. Melissa Sorenson was murdered by strangulation. There were telltale marks beneath the scarf around her neck, but the autopsy has confirmed it. Thankfully there's no evidence of rape, but the report also indicates she was three weeks pregnant."

Jessie sat back in surprise. Mac had mentioned his longing for a family, but he'd said nothing about the two of them actively trying. She wondered if he'd been more in love with Melissa than he'd admitted. The thought was sobering. A shaft of jealousy shot through her which immediately annoyed her. She had no right to feel jealous. She and Mac were friends. Nothing more.

Then another thought occurred to her. Melissa had admitted to an affair. The baby might not even be Mac's. That was always a possibility.

"I see," Jessie replied, finally finding her voice.

"We've taken a DNA sample from the fetus. I'll need a sample from your client for comparison reasons. Depending upon how backed up they are at the lab, it'll take a week or two for us to receive the results. I assume Callaway will prove to be the father, but you never know. He did tell us they fought over the victim having an alleged affair. Her sister and a couple of work colleagues seemed to support the suggestion she was seeing someone else. Still, it doesn't mean Callaway didn't kill her in a fit of jealous rage. It wouldn't be the first time. I guess we'll wait and see."

"I'll call Mac now and speak to him about giving you a sample. Make sure you let me know when you have the results."

"I will. Oh, by the way, we'd like to search your client's apartment."

"Do you have a warrant?"

"Do I need one?"

While Jessie firmly believed in Mac's innocence, she also believed in defending her client to the best of her ability and that meant making the police work for their money.

"I'd recommend that my client refuse you entry until you've secured one."

"You play hard ball, Counselor."

"Just doing my job, Detective."

"Fair enough. We're particularly interested in the kind of luggage your client owns. The suitcase the victim was found in is rather distinctive. It's also expensive. Not the kind of luggage your everyday Joe would own."

Jessie blinked in surprise. "I see."

"As soon as I hear back from the lab, I'll call you."

Jessie hung up the phone, deep in thought. Mac's ex-girlfriend had been pregnant. She'd been found on his construction site in a suitcase that was apparently expensive. Jessie recalled seeing the suitcase at the scene. She thought back, trying to visualize it, and realized the pattern of the fabric hadn't registered with her at the time. It hadn't seemed to matter. But the detective had specifically referred to it as something they were interested in. She closed her eyes and thought hard.

Burberry.

That's what it was. The plaid pattern on the suitcase containing the body of Mac's ex-girlfriend, found in the air conditioning vent on his construction site was Burberry. A distinctive and expensive brand of suitcase. With a sigh, she once again reached for her phone.

———————

With an angry curse, Mac punched numbers into his phone and waited for the call to Omer Demir's office to connect. Steve had not long vacated the site office. It was time to deal with Demir once and for all and this time Mac was taking no excuses. If he had to drive all the way across town and confront Omer himself, he would. The prick was an utter asshole.

"Mr Callaway, to what do I owe this pleasure?"

The measured, oily tones of Mac's competitor had Mac gritting his teeth. "Demir, I've been waiting a week for that concrete. It's holding up the whole job. What the hell is going on?"

"Now, now, now. That's no way to talk to a fellow businessman. Where are your manners?"

Mac held onto his temper with an effort. "Don't give me that bullshit, Demir. My foreman placed an order for that concrete a month ago. It should be here and it isn't. What the hell are you playing at?"

"You're very quick to make accusations, Mr Callaway. Things happen. Orders get lost. You're in business. You know how it is."

Mac clenched his fists and forced himself to count to ten. He couldn't afford to have Demir cancel his order altogether. The other suppliers weren't in a position to meet his needs. He needed Demir and the bastard knew it.

"I want that concrete by tomorrow. Make sure it arrives."

"Tut, tut, tut, Mr Callaway. You're not exactly in a position to make demands. And by the way, that order wasn't placed a month ago, so don't go making out it was. The first time I heard from your foreman about it was last week."

With that, Demir ended the call.

Mac cursed again. *What the hell was Demir talking about?* Of course the order had been placed a month ago. He'd discussed it with Steve. They'd agreed when it needed to happen. Demir was just playing games. Again. The asshole.

No sooner had Mac tossed the phone back into his pocket when it rang again. Thinking it was his nemesis, he answered the call without glancing at the screen.

"If you intend to give me any more lame-ass excuses about why my concrete hasn't arrived, Demir, you can stop right there. I don't want to hear them. All I want you to tell me is that my order will be here in the morning. Otherwise you can stick your concrete up your a—"

"Oh, I'm sorry. Have I called at a bad time?"

It took Mac a second to recognize Jessie's voice. He bit his lip in chagrin. "Jessie! Damn! I'm sorry. I thought you were someone else."

"Obviously," she replied. To his relief, he heard the humor in her voice.

"What can I do for you?" he asked.

"I've just had a call from Detective Sullivan. He has the results from Melissa's autopsy."

Mac tensed. "What did they say?"

Jessie paused for a moment. "Can we meet? I'd like to talk to you about this in person."

Mac frowned. This didn't sound good. Still, he sure as hell didn't have anything to do with Melissa's death. Whatever the autopsy report found, he was certain he could handle it.

"Sure," he replied. "When?"

"I have one more client to see before I can leave. Are you at the construction site?"

"Yes. It will take me at least an hour to get into the city, anyway."

"There's a bar on the corner just down from my building. How about we meet there?"

"The Cilento Bar?"

"Yes. That's the one."

"Sounds good. I'll see you there around five."

The traffic heading toward the city was heavier

than usual and it took Mac longer than expected to drive to the agreed destination. Finding a parking spot for his pickup was another challenge. It was closer to six when he finally opened the door to the bar and made his way inside.

The place was crowded with professionals in a mix of designer and off-the-rack suits. Men and women stood in twos and threes and fours and swapped stories about their day. The dim lighting hid the fatigue on their faces, but it also made it more difficult for him to see. Winding his way toward the bar, he finally spied Jessie seated at a small table on the other side of the room. She had a glass of white wine in front of her and he promptly ordered a beer. With beverage in hand, he wove his way back through the patrons and finally arrived at her side.

"I'm sorry, Jess. Traffic was crazy. There was an accident near the bridge. Thankfully I found out early enough to detour through the tunnel, but the traffic was all banked up. Then it was a minor miracle I found a parking spot after waiting for a bit, only a couple of blocks from here." He grinned and was relieved when she grinned back.

"It's fine, don't worry about it. My appointment ran over anyway. I only got here about twenty minutes ago."

Mac set his beer on the table and pulled out the only spare seat. Settling himself across from her, he took a mouthful of beer and braced himself for Jessie's news.

"So, the autopsy results are in. What can you tell me?"

Jessie leaned over and picked up her glass. She took a healthy sip before setting it back down. Mac's nerves ratcheted up a notch. It seemed he wasn't the only one who needed the fortifying strength of alcohol.

"Sullivan told me Melissa was strangled. The scarf had been tied in such a way as to hide the evidence of that."

Mac closed his eyes and swore quietly under his breath. "Poor, Melissa."

"Yes." Jessie sighed. "There's more."

Mac stilled. "Don't tell me she was raped."

"No. There was no evidence of that."

He blew out his breath on a sigh of relief. "Thank God for that. I couldn't bear it if she were raped."

"Because of Janice?"

"Yes, because of Janice. But also because of the fear and humiliation Mel would have gone through while it was happening. I'm so angry that she was murdered, but I'm glad she was spared the horror of a rape, too."

"Did you know she was pregnant?"

Mac's jaw dropped open in shock. He stared at Jessie, speechless. "P-pregnant?" he finally managed.

"Yes. Three weeks, according to the autopsy. I take it you didn't know."

Mac shook his head, still trying to come to grips with the news.

"No, I had no idea. As far as I knew, she was still on birth control. We'd talked about having a family one day and both of us wanted kids, but I wanted to wait until after we were married. Mel thought I was old-fashioned, but that's just the way I felt. Truth be told, I'd only recently come round to the idea of marrying."

"Do you think she did it on purpose, to hurry things along? Maybe you were taking too long to propose?"

Mac stared off into the distance. He still couldn't believe Melissa had been pregnant. *Why hadn't she told him?*

He returned his attention to Jessie and shrugged. "Maybe. I didn't think she was that kind of person, so deceitful. Then again, I never imagined she'd have an affair."

Jessie took a sip of her wine and slowly replaced the glass. She glanced across at him and then looked back down at the table. He could tell she wanted to say something more but wasn't sure if she should.

"What is it?" he asked.

"Don't take this the wrong way, but... Is it possible the baby wasn't yours?"

Mac reared back as if she'd struck him. "You mean, you think it might be...*his*?"

Jessie shrugged and glanced away, looking uncomfortable. "I don't know. Melissa admitted she was seeing someone else. There's always the possibility..."

Mac leaned his elbows on the table and rested his head in his hands. He couldn't believe Melissa might have been pregnant with someone else's baby. They'd been together for two years! They'd talked about having a baby. *His* baby! He wondered if she'd even known...

"I'm sorry," Jessie said quietly. "This has all come as a shock."

He sat back slowly and nodded. "Yes. You can say that again."

"You'll need to attend the police station and provide them with a DNA sample for comparison purposes."

"What about the one I gave twenty years ago? Would it still be on file?"

"Yes, I guess so. Detective Sullivan wouldn't know about that one. I'll call him and let him know."

Mac compressed his lips into a grim line. "I'd rather you didn't. We don't need to go out of our way to draw attention to what happened to Janice. Let him find out on his own time."

"Are you sure?"

"Yes. I'll make an appointment to see the detective and give him what he wants. After all, I have nothing to hide."

Jessie nodded and reached for her glass and took another mouthful. Mac took the time to drink his beer. Jessie broke the silence.

"Detective Sullivan spoke about something else."

"Oh?"

"What kind of luggage do you own?" she asked, avoiding his question.

Mac frowned. "Luggage? Why the hell would you care about that?"

Jessie shrugged. "The police are interested. I guess it has something to do with the fact Melissa was found in a suitcase."

Mac cursed. "You have to be kidding? You're telling me they're still wasting time trying to pin this on *me*?"

Jessie grimaced. "It sounds like it."

"I don't believe it! When will they wake up and start looking for the *real* killer?"

Jessie remained silent while he continued to rant against the inadequacies of the New South Wales Police Service. Finally, he ran out of steam. He finished his beer in silence.

"You didn't answer my question," she said quietly.

"Which one?"

"The one about your luggage."

"Right. I only have a black leather Oroton overnight bag. I like to travel light."

Jessie nodded, her face filling with relief. "Good. I'll let Detective Sullivan know."

Mac thought for a minute. "Melissa had a set of matching plaid luggage. I can't remember the name of it. It's a tan color with red and black stripes. She had three or four pieces of various sizes from a large suitcase down to an overnight bag."

Jessie's expression dimmed. "It sounds like you're describing a pattern known as Burberry. Does that sound familiar?"

Mac shook his head. "No, but that doesn't mean anything. I had no interest in Melissa's luggage. It's only because she insisted on taking every single piece of it every time we went away that I even know what it looks like. What does it matter to the detective?"

Jessie drew in a deep breath and eased it out. She ran her finger through a drop of condensation on the table and then picked up her wine glass. She seemed disappointed to discover it was empty. Her apparent reluctance to answer his question set his nerves on high alert. The fact the police were still looking at him for the killing was bad enough. It was obvious she knew more.

"What is it, Jessie?" he asked quietly.

She slowly met his gaze. The expression in her eyes was grim. "The suitcase Melissa was found in was Burberry."

Mac stared at her, his gut swirling with dread. Melissa had been murdered and placed in the same kind of suitcase she owned. The very same kind of suitcase she'd left in his condo. At least, he assumed they were still there. He hadn't checked.

"Did Melissa take her luggage with her the night she left?" Jessie asked, as if reading his mind.

Mac shook his head. "I don't know. I only had a cursory look around the condo. It didn't appear to me that she'd taken much of anything, but I didn't go through every closet. I assumed she'd be back to collect her things, or at the very least, arrange for someone else to come and get them."

Jessie nodded, her expression still grim. "Let's hope the suitcases made it out of your apartment or that the set is complete and still there."

"Even if they're no longer there, it doesn't mean the police will believe me when I tell them she must have taken them with her the night she left. I could very easily have bundled her into one after I strangled her and then got rid of the others."

Jessie nodded again. "Unfortunately, you're right."

Mac cursed and ran his hand through his hair in frustration. "So I'm damned either way."

Jessie reached across the table and briefly squeezed his hand. She was merely offering him reassurance, but he felt the warmth of her touch all the way through to his heart.

"It's not up to us to make the case for the police," she said. "If Detective Sullivan wants to know about the type of luggage you own, let him get a search warrant. I already told him as much. In the meantime, let's hope they come up with something else that will cast doubt on their presumption that you're the killer."

Mac closed his eyes briefly in an effort to block out the enormity of the situation he found himself in. He still couldn't believe Melissa was dead, let alone that he was suspected as being the man responsible. Again.

"How's your construction project coming along?" Jessie asked.

Mac shot her a look that let her know he was grateful for her attempt to change the subject.

"Slowly, I'm afraid."

"I take it you're having problems getting concrete?"

Mac was momentarily taken aback and then remembered she'd been privy to his conversation when he'd assumed he'd been speaking to Demir.

"Yes. I'm sorry for that. I thought you were Omer Demir. He's another property developer. Probably my biggest competition. We're always tendering against one another. He's also the largest concrete contractor in the city." Mac sighed. "He's been playing silly games with me for months and every time he screws up one of my orders, it sets my project back a few more weeks. Today I'd had enough. That was the conversation you weren't meant to hear."

Jessie frowned. "Omer Demir? I went to high school with a boy of that name."

"At North Randwick High?"

"Yes."

"I don't remember anyone by that name."

"He was in the class below you. He was the same age as me. What does he look like?"

Mac shrugged. "His family emigrated from Turkey. He's very dark. Dark hair, dark eyes. He often wears a beard. I guess some women would find him handsome. He gets around like he's a movie star. Perfectly groomed. He's always dressed in thousand-dollar suits and leather Ferragamos, even on a job site. He turns up in a motor vehicle worth almost as much as the building and gives orders. He never gets his hands dirty doing actual construction work, but he makes out as if the building would never have happened if it hadn't been for him. He's your typical rich and arrogant asshole who likes to throw his wealth in your face and he goes out of his way to make everyone else's life difficult. At least, that's the way he comes across to me."

"Sounds charming, not at all like the guy I knew in high school," Jessie replied dryly.

Mac grimaced. "Charming is one word I'd never use in the same sentence as Omer Demir. He's a snake. Though he also knows when to turn it on. I've seen him fronting the media on occasion and butter wouldn't melt in his mouth. On top of that, he seems to have a knack for drawing the women. They're probably more interested in his bank balance, but what the heck."

"It's funny. Despite his personality, he sounds very much like the Omer Demir I used to know in high school. Not the flashy arrogant asshole, but his physical description is much the same. And I'm sure Omer's family was Turkish. We weren't close, but we were friends."

"Well, I hope for your sake you weren't unfortunate enough to spend time with *this* Omer Demir. He's an absolute prick and goes out of his way to make my life difficult." Mac sighed. "It's been a terrible month. Even Steve's feeling the strain."

"What do you mean?"

Mac went on to explain the conversation he'd had with his foreman earlier that day. Jessie's expression filled with sympathy when Mac told her about Steve's battle with PTSD.

"He was in special forces. He served his country, was willing to give his life. The least I could do was give him a break by offering him a job. I thought it might help him recover, readjust to civilian life. He told me he'd been struggling to find work. I was just trying to give him a break. And it turned out he's been a blessing. Working as hard as anyone I've met."

Once again, Jessie reached out and squeezed his hand. Her expression was filled with sympathy and understanding and warmth.

"You're a good man, Mackenzie Callaway."

Her voice was husky with emotion. As she went to move her hand, Mac closed his over hers. Her eyes flared with emotion. Even in the dimness, he saw the brown of her irises deepen. For endless moments, they stared at each other, breathing in unison.

"Mac, we've already had this discussion."

He nodded and slowly withdrew his hand. "You're right. We have. I should apologize. Again. But I'm not going to, because I'm not sorry. I like touching you. I like having you close. Then and now. But I respect your position on this and I'd rather have you as my lawyer than not have you at all."

She smiled, but it appeared shaky. He wondered if she wasn't more affected by his touch than she appeared. And then he dismissed the thought as wishful thinking.

"Thank you, Mac. I appreciate your understanding." She glanced at her watch. "It's getting late. I think I should be going."

She pushed away from the table and stood. Mac stood with her.

"Thanks for meeting me," she said. She held out her hand. Mac shook it.

The handshake lasted no more than a few seconds. A handshake between strangers. His heart sank. Jessie turned away. Within seconds, she was gone.

———

Watching Mac and Jessie from a safe distance, deep within the shadows, he was filled with a sense of unease. For a man who'd so recently lost his lover to a violent and awful death, Mac Callaway seemed to have bounced back. Perhaps he hadn't been as deeply in love with Melissa as he'd appeared? The way he and Jessie kept touching each other and the intimate glances they shared... Was he misreading the entire scene before him, or had it been Mac's affection for Melissa that he'd misjudged?

He'd vowed a long time ago to destroy Mac Callaway and everything he held dear. That was his motivation behind killing Melissa. And yet it seemed his efforts were for nothing. Even the police were taking their sweet time to arrest the man. After all he'd done to set Mac up, the man was still walking free. It was beyond infuriating.

He watched Mac follow Jessie's progress across the room and saw the stark look of longing in the man's eyes. A slow smile crept across his face. Now he understood. Despite the two years Mac and Melissa had been together, she'd been nothing more than a smokescreen. *This* was the woman Mac Callaway really cared for.

Jessie Wolfe. She was the woman who'd captured Mac Callaway's heart. Perhaps she'd always had it?

That insight was an interesting revelation and it meant one thing: It was time for a new plan...

CHAPTER 10

Jessie stepped into the shower and reveled in the feeling of the hot spray as it coursed down her body. Lathering her loofah with soap, she rubbed the coarse sponge across her skin, neck and shoulders. A belly that was still flat. Long legs, slim and toned. She'd always had a good figure and she worked hard to maintain it. Despite the long hours she spent at work, she set aside regular time for sessions at the gym. The exercise kept her feeling fit and healthy and younger than her years. It was always nice when people expressed surprise that she was thirty-six.

Her hands traveled across her breasts and her nipples pebbled beneath the roughness of the loofah. From out of nowhere, thoughts of Mac invaded her mind. All of a sudden, he was everywhere. His laughing eyes, his teasing smile, the feel of his soft lips.

The memory of his lips touching hers was forever burned into her mind. She'd been so tempted to deepen the kiss, to invite his tongue inside her mouth. But taking things further would have been such a bad idea. For all the reasons she'd stated.

Once upon a time they'd meant everything to each other, but so much had happened in the meantime. He had his life as a successful property developer. He'd been living in a long-term relationship. Jessie had also forged out a successful career, and though she longed for someone to share her life with, it hadn't happened for her. Mac Callaway had captured her teenage heart all those years ago and she knew deep down, he still had it, whether he knew it, or not.

She'd dated men through college and had even had a relationship with one or two. She'd never gotten so far as moving in with any of them and at the time, she refused to acknowledge that Mac Callaway was the reason behind her reticence to take that next step. Now, after seeing him again, she couldn't deny it any longer. She accepted she was still in love with him and she didn't have a clue what to do about it.

From his response to her when they were together, it was obvious he was still interested. *But was interest enough? And just how far did his interest go?* Up until a month ago, he'd pretty much convinced himself the right thing to do was to head down the aisle with his girlfriend. In fact, if Melissa hadn't admitted to cheating and the fight had never occurred, they might very well still be together, celebrating the upcoming birth of their baby, making marriage plans.

The thought was sobering and it was enough to dim the hope that had begun to surface inside her that she and Mac could have a future together. Right now, he had a lot going on in his life. He was still a suspect in a murder investigation. He had difficulties at work and had now come face to face with the girl he'd once dated in high school. All of that was a lot for any man to deal with. The last thing he needed was another complication.

Sighing with resignation, Jessie set aside the loofah and reached for the shampoo. She poured a generous amount into her hand. Working the lather through her hair, she recalled another part of their recent conversation.

Omer Demir.

The name wasn't a very common one in Sydney. The age and physical description Mac had given her seemed to match. The man, Omer Demir, was very likely the same boy she'd gone to high school with. She was curious about why he seemed determined to make Mac's life difficult. She couldn't recall him and Mac ever meeting, let alone getting into an argument. In fact, Mac didn't even remember Omer.

That didn't come as a surprise. There had been more than a thousand students at their high school and Omer hadn't been in Mac's year. Jessie remembered him as a quiet and polite boy who always studied hard. He'd once confided that his family had great expectations for his future. They expected him to do well in life and make them proud. It was a lot of pressure on a young man, but he seemed to accept it as his lot. She admired him for his resilience and his loyalty to his family.

And then she remembered something else he'd told her. They'd been seated together as part of the debating team and they'd been talking about the upcoming dance. Jessie and Mac were going together and Omer had confided in her that he yearned to take Janice Scott out.

At the time, Jessie had urged him to ask Janice out, but Omer had shaken his head sadly and had admitted he was far too shy. That she was out of his league – captain of the cheerleaders.

"She's tall and blond and beautiful," he'd muttered. "She's the head cheerleader. So gorgeous, so bright. She could have her pick of boys in this high school. Why on earth would she pick me?"

The sadness and resignation in his dark eyes had touched Jessie's heart. "Don't write yourself off, Omer. You're good and kind and sweet. You might just be the type of boy she's looking for. You'll never know unless you ask her out," she'd urged him gently.

Omer had merely nodded and offered her another sad smile. Jessie had never asked him if he found the courage to approach Janice about the dance, but while she and Mac had been jiving their way across the dance floor, she'd noticed Janice in the arms of a football jock. Omer was nowhere to be seen.

Rinsing her hair and toweling off, Jessie stepped out of the shower and headed into her bedroom. She'd left early for the gym that morning and hadn't had a chance to make her bed. She chose not to pay extra to have her suite serviced by the hotel staff. The monthly rent was high enough as it was. Besides, most days she managed to pull up the covers, and kept the room reasonably tidy.

Donning a T-shirt and shorts, on impulse she opened the door to the closet. Reaching high up to the top shelf, she pulled down a cardboard box that contained memories of her childhood. Awards for debating, public speaking and excellence in academics. Clippings from articles she'd written for the school newspaper. Yearbooks, photos and other personal knickknacks.

Digging through the pile, she found the yearbook she was after. It had been published during Mac's last year of high school. Jessie had been in Year Eleven and so had Omer. Curious, she flicked through the pages until she found the photo she was looking for.

Omer Demir stared back at her. His dark hair shone under the lights of the camera. His dark eyes stared at her, deep and soulful and sad. She wished she'd noticed back then how sad he was. The photo had been taken before Janice Scott's death, which occurred only a few weeks before Mac's graduation. Jessie couldn't imagine how Janice's tragic and violent death had made Omer feel. And then she flipped back a couple of pages and found Mac.

Her heart jolted as it usually did at the sight of his familiar face. The teasing green eyes, so gentle and beautiful. The wide, white, confident smile...

His hair was a little longer than he wore it now,

but there was no mistaking it was him. He'd barely changed during the intervening years, at least not on the outside... She had yet to determine if he was still the Mac she'd known and loved all those years ago...

With a sigh, she slowly closed the yearbook and returned it to the box. Standing on tiptoes, she put the box back on the shelf and closed the doors to her closet. After cleaning her teeth and brushing her hair, she climbed into bed and as she slipped into sleep, her dreams were filled with images of Mac and Omer.

Jessie's eyes felt tired and gritty as she did her best to focus on the words on her screen. She'd slept through her alarm and had woken out of sorts. After eventually setting aside the year book, she'd done her best to fall asleep, but a light sleep had been broken with vivid dreams of Mac and Omer. The phone on her desk rang and she distractedly picked it up.

"Yes, Margaret?"

"Jessie, I have a man by the name of Omer Demir on line four. He wants to make an appointment."

Jessie stared at the phone in disbelief and then shook her head to clear it. She must be more tired than she thought. There was no way Omer Demir was calling her. She couldn't have possibly conjured him out of her dreams.

"Jessie? Did you hear me?"

Jessie blinked hard. "Yes, Margaret. Sorry, did you say Omer Demir was on the line?"

"Yes. He asked to speak with you and then said he'd like to make an appointment. You can put him back through to me when you're finished."

Jessie stared down at the phone, incredulous. *This was so strange.* Fancy having Omer call her now when she hadn't heard from him in years.

Quickly regaining her senses, she answered the call. "Jessie Wolfe."

"Jessie, it's Omer Demir. I'm not sure if you remember me? We went to North Randwick High School together. You were in my class. We were on the debating team."

"Yes, of course I remember you!" Jessie laughed. "You're not going to believe this, but I was only thinking about you last night. I met up with another old high school friend and we were talking about old times. I went home and dug out one of the yearbooks and there you were. Now you're calling me! This feels so strange!" She laughed again and was relieved when she heard his answering chuckle.

"That *is* strange," he commented. "I don't know what made me pick up the phone and call you. I'm after some legal advice and your name came up."

"Oh? Who were you talking to?" Despite herself, she was curious.

"Oh, just one of my business contacts. When I told them I needed a lawyer, they recommended you."

"You do know I'm a criminal defense lawyer? I hope you're not in trouble?" she asked cautiously.

She was relieved when Omer laughed. "Of course not! Nothing like that. I'm a model citizen, just like I was in high school."

Jessie smiled. Omer had indeed been a model student when she'd known him.

"Listen," Omer continued, "I was going to make an appointment to see you, but perhaps we could do this over coffee? It would be nice to see you again, catch up on old times. I'm free this afternoon, if you can get away."

Jessie glanced at her calendar. Apart from two client appointments before lunch, she was free for the rest of the day. She wondered what she and Omer would talk about and then dismissed her concern. Though they hadn't been close in high school, the two of them had been friends. Besides, according to Mac, Omer was stressing Mac out by not supplying concrete as promised for Mac's projects. Perhaps she could talk to Omer about it and sort that out? There was a chance Omer didn't even realize it was the same Mac Callaway. Maybe once he did, he'd change his behavior and it would be one less problem Mac would have to worry about.

When Jessie spied Omer already seated at the table in the café, she did a double take. What Mac had said was right. Omer was dressed from head to toe in Armani. His dark hair was cut short and his beard was neatly trimmed. He looked every bit the successful entrepreneur and she could see why he'd turn heads. In fact, several of the café's female patrons kept stealing glances at him. Jessie felt inordinately proud. Omer was finally getting the attention he deserved.

Upon spying her coming toward him, Omer pushed back his chair and stood. He greeted Jessie with a brief hug and a friendly kiss on the cheek. His beard was soft and tickled her skin. His expensive cologne lingered in the air. If she were the kind of girl attracted to Omer's dark looks, she'd be a goner for sure.

She seated herself at the table and Omer did the same. She smiled across at him. "It's great to see you! You look well."

He inclined his head in acknowledgement, his dark eyes shining, his teeth sparkling white. "So do you."

A blush stole up her cheeks at the approval in his eyes. She hastily steered the conversation toward less personal topics.

"So, what are you doing with yourself?"

"I'm a property developer, a businessman, a successful entrepreneur. I've worked hard to get where I am and I'm proud of what I've achieved."

"You certainly look the part," she agreed. "And you always were prepared to work hard. Your parents must be so proud."

His jaw tightened and the expression in his eyes dimmed. "I guess. I haven't talked to them in years. I no longer give a shit what they think."

She blinked in surprise at his expletive. The Omer she knew from high school would never have allowed a curse word to come from his mouth. His eyes twinkled with mirth and a knowing smile curved his lips.

"Yes, I've changed a bit since high school, haven't I?"

She grinned. "And here I was thinking you hadn't changed a bit!"

The waitress arrived and took their order for coffee. Omer also ordered a slice of pecan pie.

"Do you want some?" he asked Jessie.

She shook her head. "No, thanks. I'm watching my weight."

Omer's gaze drifted over her and he nodded approvingly. "You look pretty good to me. Then again, you always had a nice figure."

Jessie blushed under his close regard and felt a little uncomfortable. Never during their time at high school had Omer made any personal remarks to her about the way she looked. They'd been friends, nothing more. It felt strange to have him look at her the way he was looking at her now. She avoided his gaze and cleared her throat.

"So, what is it that you need to speak with me about?"

He acknowledged her change of subject with a brief nod and his tone immediately became all business. He leaned forward, his expression somber.

"I think one of my employees is stealing from me. I don't have any proof yet, but things have gone missing and all signs point to him."

"What sort of things?"

"Tools. Construction materials. A truckload full of concrete."

Jessie blinked in surprise. "Wow! A truckload full of concrete. That's not so easy to hide. What do you think he did with it?"

"I don't know. He probably sold it to competitors."

"Have you gone to the police with your suspicions?"

Omer shook his head. "No. As I said, I don't have any proof, yet. Until I do, the police won't be interested."

Jessie silently agreed with him. "Have you set up any CCTV cameras? You might be able to catch him in the act."

"Not yet, but that's my next step. I wanted to talk with you first, check that I was within my rights to film my employees."

"The law says you're allowed to do it as long as your employees are made aware that you're filming them," she replied. "Let them all know you're installing security cameras and that they will be operating twenty-four hours a day. You can also put up signs which alert people to the fact you have security cameras operating. Provided you cover those bases, you should be fine."

"That's good to know. Thanks, Jessie."

She smiled. "You're welcome."

The waitress arrived with their order and Jessie and Omer busied themselves adding sugar to their coffees. Omer bit into a piece of his pecan pie and groaned in delight.

"This is delicious. Are you sure you wouldn't like some?"

Jessie laughed and shook her head. "No, thanks. You wouldn't believe how many miles I'd have to run on the treadmill to work that off."

His laughter melded with hers. A friendly silence enveloped them. Jessie sipped her coffee and Omer continued to enjoy his pie. Thinking of Mac and her desire to help mend the fences between him and Omer, she spoke again.

"Do you remember a guy we went to school with, Mac Callaway? He was in the year ahead of us."

Omer's brow furrowed in thought. "Mac Callaway? No, I'm not sure that I do. Was he on the debating team?"

Jessie laughed and shook her head. "No, he wasn't on the debating team. In fact, he was the captain of the football team. Mac preferred to take instruction from his coach rather than learn from books." She shrugged. We're very different that way."

Recognition slowly flooded Omer's face. "Mac Callaway? That's right. I remember him. He was tall and blond and built like an ironman – a surfer type, right? He spent a lot of time at the beach."

Jessie nodded. "Yes, that's him."

Omer shot her a sly look. "You two dated for a while, didn't you?"

Heat crept across Jessie's cheeks. She nodded again. "Yes, we did. It didn't last."

Omer studied her in silence. "What happened?" he finally asked.

She shrugged, uncomfortable discussing her private life with him. "Life happened, I guess. Mac graduated from high school and left for college. I still had a year to go. I guess we just drifted apart."

Omer regarded shrewdly. "So it had nothing to do with the death of Janice Scott?"

Jessie blinked in surprise. "You remember Janice?"

"Of course, I do. There was a time when I loved her with everything I had. Don't you remember?"

"I remember you telling me you had a crush on her. You wanted to ask her to the dance."

Omer's lips twisted into a grimace. "Yes, what a foolish idea that was."

"Did you ever find the courage to ask her?"

Omer nodded slowly. "Yes. She said no."

"Oh! Omer! I'm so sorry! That must've been terrible for you!"

He stared at the table and began to shred the napkin. "It certainly wasn't the highlight of my life. I was crushed. The rejection took me weeks to get over. Not that it stopped me from loving her. I loved her until the day she died."

The sad wistfulness that filled his expression brought tears to Jessie's eyes. She shook her head, flooded with memories from that awful time.

"Her death must've been so hard on you," she said gently. "Loving her, like you did. I can't imagine how it felt to discover that she'd died."

"No, you can't," he said flatly.

Once again, there was a pause in their conversation, but the air between them was far less relaxed. Both of them took refuge in their coffees. After a while, Jessie spoke again.

"Did you know Mac Callaway is also a property developer?"

Omer frowned. "The same Mac Callaway you dated in high school?"

"Yes. In fact," Jessie continued, "I recently met up with him. We talked about old times. He mentioned you."

Omer shot her a wry look. "If it's the same Mac Callaway I do business with, I can't imagine he had anything good to say about me."

Jessie was surprised by his candor. "Why would you say that?"

"Because Mac Callaway and I don't exactly see eye to eye. We're business rivals, fierce competitors. This town isn't big enough for the two of us. It's time Mac realized that."

Jessie shook her head, aghast.

"Sydney is a city of nearly five million people. Of course it's big enough for both of you. You're talking nonsense."

"Jessie, Jessie, Jessie. There's so much you don't understand," Omer muttered.

His condescending tone irked her. Her temper stirred. "Don't treat me like an idiot, Omer. Mac said you were causing him grief, delaying an order of concrete. It sounds rather petty to me. What's going on?"

Omer's eyes flared with anger. Jessie sat back in her seat. Gone was the smiling, charming man and in his place sat a cold and calculating man with eyes of steel.

"You have no idea what you're talking about. I suggest you stick to lawyering and keep your nose out of my business. Why do you care, anyway? Don't tell me you and Mac Callaway have taken up where you left off?"

Jessie shivered at the menace in his eyes and leaned down to gather her handbag from beside her chair. She stood and made to leave.

Omer was immediately contrite. "Please don't go, Jessie. I'm sorry. I didn't mean that. It was just that, for a moment there, it was like I was back in high school. I was always treated like a second-class citizen and all the while there was Mac Callaway, the football star who could do no wrong. Even you treated him like a god."

"So you *do* remember him!" she exclaimed.

Omer shrugged and stared at the table. His air of bravado had disappeared and he was once again the insecure, shy young boy he'd been in high school.

Jessie slowly regained her seat. "Oh, Omer!" she said gently. "That was so long ago! Don't tell me you're still carrying a chip on your shoulder about that?"

Omer looked up at her with tortured eyes. "It was all right for *you*, Jessie! You weren't the one tormented and teased because of your foreign heritage. I worked harder than anyone, but it was never enough. Even for my mom and dad. I brought home A's on my report card and they wanted A pluses." He looked up at her. Tears glistened in his eyes.

Without thinking, Jessie reached out for his hand.

She squeezed it gently and then withdrew.

"You've worked so hard, Omer, and you've done so well for yourself. You should be proud of yourself. *I'm* proud of you."

He smiled sadly. "Thanks, Jessie. That means a lot."

She smiled back at him. "Any time."

They shared a look that went back to high school. Jessie was the first to look away. Once again she collected her handbag and stood.

"Look, it's been great to see you, but I'm going to have to go. I still have a few things to do at the office before the day is over."

He accepted her excuse without question and then stood and pushed back his chair. He held out his hand toward her.

"It was good to see you too, Jessie. You take care."

"You, too, Omer. Good luck catching your thief."

And with that, she turned and left.

CHAPTER 11

Detective Zane Sullivan bit back a yawn and scrubbed at his eyes with his fists in an attempt to alleviate his fatigue. He'd pulled double shifts all week in an effort to find Melissa Sorensen's killer. It had been two weeks since her body had been discovered and they were no closer to making an arrest. Despite his gut instinct that Mac Callaway was innocent, all signs kept pointing to the man and right now even though Zane didn't have any definitive evidence, he couldn't discount the possibility that Mac Callaway was the murderer.

First of all, there was the heated argument Callaway admitted to having with his girlfriend right before she disappeared. At least three of their neighbors confirmed they heard shouting that night coming from Callaway's apartment. Then there were the injuries Callaway sported on his face. Though there weren't any actual scratches and the wounds looked fresher than allowed in the timeline they'd constructed on

Melissa's disappearance, the signs he'd been in a fight couldn't be ignored.

Callaway's explanation of how he'd gotten the injuries was also strange. He'd been attacked by a stranger in the middle of the night and yet he failed to report it to the police. It didn't make sense. *What was he hiding and why?*

Then there was the fact the victim's body was found in a suitcase that matched a set of luggage found during a search of Callaway's apartment. It stood to reason if he'd killed her in that location, he would have used something close by and handy to hide the body. For someone as petite as Melissa Sorenson, a suitcase worked just fine.

And then, they had the discovery of the body at a location to which Callaway had easy access. No one would question his presence at the construction site. He could come and go as he pleased, even in the dead of night. During recent questioning, Callaway had confirmed that the work site was generally locked up overnight and that he and his foreman were the only ones with keys. It was Jessica Wolfe who'd asked him if it were possible the gates had been left open and someone else could have gained access to the site.

Callaway agreed that there had been the odd occasion in the past when someone had left the construction site and forgotten to lock up overnight. Of course, no one could confirm whether this had happened on the night Melissa Sorenson disappeared.

It was yet another piece of tantalizing evidence

that Zane hadn't been able to turn into something concrete for the investigation. The frustration was eating away at him. When he looked at the evidence in its entirety, the logical conclusion was that Mac Callaway was their man. Then again, Callaway had voluntarily provided a DNA sample and not everyone was prepared to do that. It went some way toward Zane leaning toward Callaway's innocence. If only they had something definitive, something more tangible than a suitcase full of circumstantial nothing.

A lot of investigators would come back to the fact the body was dumped at a mostly secure construction site. But why would anyone be stupid enough to leave the body of their girlfriend on their own job site? Mac Callaway didn't come across as stupid. Still, Zane knew from experience that some normal people who were panicked did stupid things that often led to them being caught. *Was this just another example? Would Callaway's panicked decision to dump Melissa's body at his construction site be his downfall?* Zane wished he knew.

The other possibility was that someone was trying to frame Mac Callaway. Zane had put the question to the man and pretty much been shot down. Callaway hadn't been able to think of anyone who had a beef against him. Certainly not to the extent that they'd murder his girlfriend and then try and lay the blame on him. He mentioned some difficulties he was having with a business rival, but Callaway said he couldn't imagine Omer Demir resorting to such shocking tactics. Taking the life of an innocent woman for the sake of coming out on top on a business deal was beyond ludicrous as far as Callaway was concerned. Besides, he said he kept his private life separate from his business. He didn't think Demir even knew Melissa existed, just like Callaway didn't have a clue about the women in Demir's life.

Zane sighed heavily. Despite the long hours he'd spent on the case, he was going around in circles. It was driving him crazy. The door to the squad room swung open and he looked up in time to see his partner enter the room. In his hand, Willie held an envelope.

"What do you have there?" Zane asked.

Willie strode across the room and propped a hip against Zane's desk. "Virginia handed it to me as I came in. It's the DNA results from Melissa Sorensen's fetus."

Zane's heart quickened with excitement.

"That was faster than I expected." He reached for the envelope and at the same time tried to get a handle on his pulse. In all likelihood, the unborn baby belonged to Mac Callaway. Melissa had been his girlfriend, after all. But there was always the chance it belonged to the other man, the one she'd been having an affair with. If that were the case, they might be able to identify him. So far, their enquires on that front had come up empty.

Quickly, he slid his finger under the flap of the envelope and pulled out a single sheet of paper. Scanning the contents, Zane's gaze snagged on a line about three quarters of the way down. He read it once and then read it again. He frowned in consternation and then slowly lifted his gaze to Willie. "Well, well, well. It appears that Mac Callaway was at least telling the truth about something."

Willie's eyebrows rose. "What do you have?"

Zane handed the piece of paper to Willie who took a moment to read the contents.

"So, the dead baby's daddy is a man by the name of Wesley Parker. Mac Callaway was telling the truth about the affair, after all."

"I guess so."

Melissa Sorenson had been pregnant at the time of her death with another man's baby. It gave credence to Callaway's account they'd argued over her affair, but what if the argument had also included the fact she was carrying another man's child? It was just as believable that instead of sending her packing as he claimed, he'd killed her in a jealous rage. Either scenario was possible. The only people who really knew what had gone on were Melissa and her killer.

With a sigh of frustration, Zane blew out his breath and leaned back against his chair. He took a moment to process what this new information meant. Melissa had been murdered five weeks ago. According to the autopsy report, the fetus was three weeks old. That made it approximately two months since the last known time that Melissa and her lover were together. It shouldn't be too hard to track down the father.

"We need to speak with Wesley Parker," Zane said.

Willie nodded. "It'll be interesting to know where he was the night Melissa Sorenson went missing. I can't wait to hear what he has to say. We know from the autopsy report that she died within hours of the time Callaway said they argued."

Zane nodded thoughtfully. "Yes. I'm also wondering why Parker didn't come forward to report Melissa missing. Callaway called it an affair. That implies fairly regular contact and let's face it, most babies aren't conceived the first time round. Wouldn't Parker have wondered where she was? Why he hadn't heard from her? This day and age, everyone lives on their phone. If it hadn't been for the victim's sister filing that missing persons report, we wouldn't have been any the wiser until the body showed up."

Willie frowned. "What about the victim's phone? It was found inside the suitcase with her, wasn't it? Did forensics find anything on that?"

"Yes, there were messages that could potentially indicate a secret liaison, but nothing definitive. And the two of them only referred to each other with nicknames. I think she was Blond bombshell and he was Loverboy. His texts all originated from prepaid, untraceable cards or phones."

"He was covering his tracks," Willie guessed.

"Yes, but he could have done that for a number of reasons. Perhaps he's also in a relationship? Just because he didn't want anyone to know he was sleeping with Melissa doesn't mean he murdered her."

He gave Willie a disheartened shrug then dragged his keyboard toward him. "Let's see if we have any luck finding Loverboy in here. I'm assuming he's in our database. It's the only way the lab would have been able to make the match with the DNA sample taken from the fetus. Let's hope he's still at the same address when we locate it."

Zane tapped his fingers on his desk impatiently as he waited for the information to load on the screen in front of him. Just as he'd suspected, Wesley James Parker was a convicted felon. It was the reason he was in their system. He'd been arrested and charged with rape and murder nearly twenty years earlier. Zane scanned the lines of text, and then cursed aloud in frustration.

"*Shit. Shit. Shit.*"

Willie moved closer and peered at the screen over Zane's shoulder. "What is it?"

Zane shook his head and cursed again. "The prick is still in jail."

Willie frowned. "That can't be right."

Zane pointed to the screen. "It says right here. Wesley Parker is still incarcerated in Long Bay. He's been there since November 1999. He got twenty years for rape and murder. I'll call the jail and make sure he's still alive and well and locked up behind bars, but all I can say is, the lab must have made a mistake with the DNA."

Willie shook his head in disbelief. "Man, that's just so weird. I know it happened in the old days, but I haven't heard of a mess-up like that happening recently. How could they get it confused like that? Maybe Wes has an identical twin?" Willie offered.

"Good thinking. They share the same DNA." Zane's fingers flew over the keyboard. He scanned the information that filled the page and shook his head. "Except in this case, the answer is no. Wesley Parker is not a twin."

"So where does that leave us?" Willie asked.

Zane compressed his lips into a thin line. "I think we have to go forward on the understanding that somewhere there's been a mistake. There's no other explanation. That baby couldn't possibly have been fathered by Wesley Parker, unless our victim was visiting him in jail and that's not exactly discrete."

Willie nodded. "It's a long shot, but I guess it's worth looking into."

"When I call the warden and confirm Parker's still in custody, I'll ask him to pull the visitor records from the past three months and see what I can find. Also, set up another meeting with Mac Callaway and his lawyer. Let's see if the name Wesley Parker means anything to him."

———————————

Mac was in his pickup driving halfway across town to inspect an order of glass when his phone rang. He glanced at the screen and saw it was Jessie. He pressed the green button to answer.

"Jessie. How are you doing?"

He hadn't seen her since their meeting at the Cilento bar. It felt like a lifetime ago. He couldn't believe how much he craved to be near her.

She'd been absent from his life for the better part of twenty years and yet, now that he'd seen her again, it was like they'd never been apart. He wished he could keep it that way.

"Hi, Mac. I'm fine. Listen, I just had a call from Detective Sullivan. He's asked for us to meet. He has a few more questions."

Mac grimaced. The last time Jessie had heard from the detective, he'd dropped the bombshell about Melissa's pregnancy. Mac could only guess what news he might bring this time. He sighed. "When does he want to get together?"

"As soon as possible. He suggested we meet at the café near my building in an hour. Does that work for you?"

Mac glanced at the clock on his dashboard. If the meeting with his glass supplier went to plan and he didn't get held up in traffic, he should make it. He told Jessie as much.

"Good," she replied. "See you then."

The call disconnected and Mac returned his attention to the road. The midmorning traffic was light and he made good time. He arrived at the window supplier with ten minutes to spare. Thankfully, the windows had been made as ordered and Mac signed off on the final paperwork.

"When can you get them to the site?" he asked Ronald Jackson, the manager.

Jackson frowned. "I had a truck ready to deliver them this afternoon. Your foreman told me you weren't ready for them."

It was Mac's turn to frown. "That can't be right. Steve knows we've been waiting for these."

"I'm sorry, Mac, but that's what he said."

Mac's mind was filled with confusion. *Why would Steve put off the delivery of glass?* It didn't make sense. This was the second time Steve's name had come up in connection with a delayed order. Demir had made reference to the foreman, too. It was true Steve had been a bit out of sorts of late. Mac had even had cause to wonder if the man had missed some medication. Steve had assured him all was well, but now Mac couldn't help but wonder.

"I could probably get that glass to you first thing in the morning. How does that sound?" Jackson asked.

Mac pushed his dark thoughts away and forced a smile. "That sounds great."

"It's been nice doing business with you, Mac," Jackson added, shaking his hand. "I wish all of our customers were as easy to deal with as you."

Mac shrugged. "Well, I guess it takes all types. I've had my share of difficult clients. It comes with the territory, I guess."

The manager shrugged. "I guess so."

Bidding the man farewell, Mac's troubled thoughts returned to his foreman. Steve had lied about the windows. According to Demir, Steve had also failed to order the concrete in the timeframe he and Mac had discussed. *Was it possible it was Steve behind the mix up with the steel, and not Jarrod Harris?* Steve had been acting a little weird. He'd turned up to work late three times this week. On top of that, Mac happened to walk past Steve's truck and had spied a military grade rifle across the seat. He'd immediately gone to Steve and demanded an explanation. Steve might hold the proper firearms license, but there was no way guns of any kind were allowed on the construction site and Steve darn well knew it.

Steve had been very apologetic and had admitted he'd gone hunting on the weekend. He'd forgotten to return it to his locked box in his home. He'd sworn it wouldn't happen again.

Mac had accepted the explanation and the incident had been forgotten, but it was just another example of Steve acting strangely. Perhaps he *had* stopped taking his medication? Mac only realized now that when he'd put that to him earlier, Steve had gone on the offensive and had failed to answer the question.

Mac blew his breath out on a heavy sigh. He didn't need this shit. Still, he had to get to the bottom of it. He made a mental note to call Jarrod Harris. Dread at what he might discover weighed heavily in his gut, but this wasn't the time. If he didn't get a move on, he'd be late for his meeting with Jessie. Just the thought of seeing her again erased the turmoil he felt about work and made him smile.

He climbed into his pickup and headed toward the city. It would be a bitch trying to find a parking spot downtown, but there was nothing he could do about it. To his relief, he arrived at the café two minutes ahead of time and grinned as he caught sight of Jessie waiting at a table.

The urge to kiss her hello was so strong he almost acted on the impulse before he pulled himself up short. He didn't have the right to greet her with that kind of familiarity. She'd made it clear she was his lawyer. Nothing more. He settled for a casual wave and a smile.

"Hi. How are you doing, Jessie?"

She returned his smile. "You made it with time to spare," she teased.

The light-heartedness of her tone settled his nerves. *Surely the detective would have given her some hint if things were about to go awry?* He ordered coffee and she followed suit. As soon as the waitress departed, Jessie spoke again.

"So, you're not going to believe this, but I had a call from Omer Demir."

Mac blinked in surprise. "Why the hell would he call *you*?"

"I don't know. It was completely out of the blue. He told me he needed some legal advice."

"There are thousands of lawyers in the city. Why would he choose you?" He caught the frown on Jessie's face and quickly added, "No offense."

She shot him a wry look. "No offense taken. In fact, your guess is as good as mine. He certainly remembered me from high school. Perhaps that was the reason behind his choice?"

"It sounds suspicious to me," Mac muttered. "In fact, it's downright weird. We were only just talking about him and suddenly he contacts you. If this were a spy movie, I'd be certain we'd been bugged."

Jessie laughed, but he could see the strain around her mouth. She wasn't entirely convinced of the innocence of Omer's phone call, either.

"So, what did you two talk about?" he asked.

"Like I said, he wanted some legal advice. I can't breach his confidence, but we also talked about high school. I mentioned your name. Initially, he didn't recall you from school. I had to tell him you were the same Mac Callaway he knew in the business world."

Mac frowned. "What did he say?"

Jessie shrugged. "Not much. He gave me the impression he felt no particular fondness toward you."

Mac grimaced. "I could have told you that. In fact, I did tell you that."

"Yes. Well, I thought I might be able to get to the bottom of his aggressive attitude toward you, but he wasn't forthcoming. We moved on to other things."

"Such as?"

"We talked about Janice," Jessie said quietly.

Mac tensed. "Janice? Why would you talk about her?"

"Omer was the one who brought her up. He told me how he loved Janice back then." Jessie paused. "He must've been devastated when she was murdered."

Mac frowned. "I had no idea Omer had a thing for Janice back then."

"To be fair, you didn't even know Omer existed," Jessie murmured.

"True," Mac conceded. And then another thought occurred to him. "If Omer had known Janice well enough to be in love with her, he must've also known where her body was found."

As he said the words, a shiver went down Mac's spine. He looked at Jessie. "You don't think all this business with Melissa could have anything to do with Omer, do you?"

Jessie's eyes widened momentarily in surprise and then she laughed shakily. "Don't be silly. What happened with Janice was a long time ago. Besides, you were cleared of all suspicion. If Omer followed the investigation right through to the end, he'd know that."

Mac nodded thoughtfully. "Yes, I guess you're right."

The waitress arrived with their coffees and they waited for her to leave before resuming their conversation.

"I don't understand why Omer would tell you something like that," Mac said. "I mean, it was twenty years ago. Why would he tell you he'd been in love with Janice Scott when both of you knew she'd been murdered? It's weird."

Jessie nodded. "I agree. It *is* a bit weird. Maybe he saw a familiar face, someone from his past, and he just wanted to get it off his chest?"

"Still, would *you* share details of such private matters with an old school friend after so many years?"

"Probably not," Jessie replied.

The door to the café opened and Mac looked up in time to see Detective Sullivan and his partner approaching them. His belly took a nosedive. "It looks like the cavalry are here," he murmured.

Jessie looked up and motioned for the detectives to join them. "Detective Sullivan,

Detective Whitehouse. It's nice to see you again."

"You, too, Jessie," Sullivan replied. Whitehouse acknowledged her greeting with a nod.

The men seated themselves at their table and got comfortable. After signaling the waitress and placing an order for two more coffees, Sullivan turned to Mac.

"So, Mr Callaway, we have the results back from the DNA on Melissa's unborn baby."

Though Mac knew the results would arrive at some time, he hadn't been expecting them yet. He tensed in anticipation and beneath the table his hands clenched involuntarily into fists. Still, he strived to remain outwardly calm.

"Oh? What did they show?" he asked in an almost casual tone.

The detective took his time replying. Mac's pulse rate continued to climb. When he didn't think he could stand it a minute longer, the detective spoke again.

"The baby was fathered by a man named Wesley Parker. Have you heard of him?"

Mac heard Jessie's indrawn breath from across the table. His body went tight with shock. *How the hell could Melissa have been sleeping with Wes Parker?* It didn't make sense.

"I can see from your reaction that Parker's name is familiar," Detective Sullivan said. "Would you care to explain?"

Mac glanced at Jessie. She looked pale. He focused his attention on the officers.

"I'm not sure if it's the same Wesley Parker, but I went to high school with someone of that name."

"I see," Detective Sullivan replied. "Did you know he was convicted of rape and murder twenty years ago?"

Mac nodded.

The detective's gaze narrowed on Mac for a moment before he continued. "How old are you, Mr Callaway?"

"I'm thirty-seven," Mac replied.

"I guessed as much. It seems to me that you were still in high school twenty years ago. Would I be right in assuming that?"

Mac kept his gaze and voice steady. "Yes, that's right."

"So this Wesley Parker was still in high school with you at the time he was charged with murder?"

The question came from Detective Whitehouse. Mac's gaze slid to the other man and he nodded. "Yes, that's right."

Jessie cleared her throat, drawing the attention of the men at the table. "Detectives, before we go any further, there's something I need to say. It didn't seem necessary earlier, but in the interest of being completely transparent, I think you need to know. I went to school with Mac Callaway and with Wesley Parker. I was in the year below them. I just wanted you to know."

Both detectives blinked in surprise and Sullivan sat back in his chair. "Well, this gets even more interesting."

Jessie hastened to reassure him. "There's nothing untoward about it, Detective, I assure you. Mac and I knew each other in high school. We'd lost touch over the years, but when he needed legal advice, he called me. End of story."

"And what about Wesley Parker?" Detective Sullivan asked. "How well did you know him in high school?"

He directed the question at Jessie and she quickly answered. "I didn't know Wesley Parker at all until he was charged with the rape and murder of a fellow student."

Both detectives moved their attention to Mac. "And how about you?" Sullivan asked. "He was in your year in high school, wasn't he?"

"Yes, he was," Mac replied. "We were on the same football team. I wouldn't say we were close friends or anything, but we'd acknowledge each other in the corridors and we shared conversation from time to time. Even so, I was beyond shocked when I found out what he'd done."

Sullivan's eyebrow rose. "Why? Because it seemed out of character?"

"Yes, of course, it seemed out of character," Mac replied. "I never imagined him capable of rape and murder. It came as a shock to everyone."

The detective turned to look at Jessie. "And what about you? Were you as shocked as everyone else?"

Jessie nodded, her expression somber. "Yes. I certainly was. I didn't know Wes like Mac did, but to know that a fellow student could have done that... It took a long time for us to get over it."

"It seems this is the day for revelations from the past," Mac muttered.

Sullivan immediately came on the alert. "Why do you say that?"

Mac looked at Jessie. "Go ahead, Jessie. Tell him about Omer."

"Who's Omer?" Whitehouse asked.

"He's my biggest business competitor and an all-round pain in the ass," Mac explained. "He's also a guy who went to our high school. He was in Jessie's year."

"Is this the same business competitor you mentioned when we discussed if you had any enemies?" Sullivan asked.

"Yes," Mac replied. "I dismissed him earlier because I couldn't imagine that he'd carry a bit of professional ill-feeling between us so far, but now I'm not so sure. Jessie met with Omer recently. He called her right out of the blue. He said he needed legal advice, but it seems what he really wanted to talk about was high school."

"Go on," Sullivan urged.

Mac looked at Jessie. "Perhaps you're the best one to tell them what happened?"

She closed her eyes briefly and nodded. "If you've read Wes Parker's case file, you'll know that Janice Scott was the girl he raped and murdered. She was in his class.

"Omer Demir invited me to coffee recently and told me he'd been in love with Janice in high school."

Surprise and confusion filled the faces of the detectives. "Why would he tell you something like that?" Whitehouse wondered aloud.

"Exactly," Mac replied. "It's downright weird."

"Yes. The other thing that concerns me," Jessie continued, "is that, like Mac pointed out, if Omer followed Janice's murder investigation closely, he'd know that Janice was found dead in Mac's bed."

Sullivan reared back against his chair and flung up his arms. "Whoa! Hold on a minute! This is getting way out of hand." He turned to Mac. "You and Jessie and Omer and Janice... You all knew each other as kids?"

Mac nodded. "Janice and I and Wes were in the same year. We were friends, but we didn't hang out. Jessie and Omer were in the year below. Jessie and I dated for a short while in my senior year. I didn't know until now that Omer had a thing for Janice."

Sullivan pursed his lips in thought. "And the victim was found in *your* bed? It's a tangled web. You've probably guessed I haven't had a chance to read Janice's file. It's in the archives. It'll take a couple days to retrieve. All I know is that Wesley Parker is doing time for her rape and murder and he's still incarcerated."

Mac shook his head in confusion. "He's still incarcerated? How can that be? You said the baby's DNA belonged to Wes... Melissa was having an affair with the bloke. There must be some mistake."

"I'm afraid not," Sullivan replied. "I've checked with the jail. Parker's still doing time. I also checked if he'd had any visitors over the past few months. The answer is no."

Once again, Mac tried to get his head around the confusion. "But...?"

"I understand," Sullivan said. "It took some working out for me, too. Initially, I thought your girlfriend must have visited him in jail, but that's not the case."

"So how could she have been carrying Wes Parker's baby?" Jessie asked.

"She wasn't. It's my guess there's been a mistake at the lab, either then or now. I'm on my way from here to the jail to interview Parker. It will be interesting to hear what he has to say. I understand he's never stopped proclaiming his innocence..."

The detective left the thought hanging. Mac tensed. He couldn't imagine what it would feel like to be convicted of a crime he didn't commit. *Is that what had happened to Wes? Had he spent almost twenty years behind bars, while all the time he was innocent?* He couldn't bear to think about it.

"What are you going to do?" he asked.

"When I speak with Parker, I'm going to ask him to provide us with another DNA sample. I'll also reorder a DNA test on the fetus. We need to find out whether the mistake was made during our investigations or whether it happened two decades ago. Either way, we need to get to the bottom of it. It's possible an innocent man's been rotting away in jail, but it's more likely the lab messed up the results from the fetus. Let's hope it's the latter."

CHAPTER 12

After making a few calls and pulling some strings with the warden, Zane managed to arrange an appointment with Wesley Parker less than two hours after his meeting with Mac and Jessie. The more Zane delved into the case, the more something seemed amiss.

On the face of it, Callaway seemed guilty. So much of the evidence pointed toward him. But there was something about Mac being a coldhearted killer that didn't sit right with Zane. Over his years as a detective, he'd learned to listen to his gut. This thing with Omer Demir definitely called for further investigation. As for the debacle with the DNA... *Who knew what that meant?*

Someone had made a major mistake somewhere. Zane only hoped it hadn't occurred two decades ago. He couldn't imagine the uproar that would cause. That an innocent man had been locked up in jail. It wouldn't be the first time it had happened, but it didn't happen often and Zane couldn't remember when it had happened last. It would only be a matter of time before the media got wind of it and then all hell would break loose.

In the early days of DNA testing, the science was far less exact. These days, people relied on it as almost gospel truth. Television shows had a lot to answer for in that regard, though Zane couldn't deny the value of DNA and its accuracy and he was continually surprised at how quickly technology progressed. There was no doubt the advances in science had made detective work a whole lot easier... But, every now and then they got it wrong. The technology was only as good as the human using it.

With a sigh, he swung the unmarked police car into the long paved driveway that led up to the high chain-link fence that surrounded the perimeter of Long Bay Correctional Center. The fence was topped with razor wire and the sharp edges glinted dangerously in the afternoon sun. Guards in the nearby watchtower patrolled with machine guns, a constant reminder that they took escape attempts seriously.

After showing his credentials to the security guard manning the gate, Zane drove up to the visitors' parking lot and pulled into a vacant spot. He glanced across at his partner.

"Let's hope we get the answer we're looking for," he murmured.

Willie nodded in agreement. "What are you going to tell Parker?"

Zane compressed his lips into a thin line. He'd spent the past hour going over his angle of attack in his mind. No matter how he looked at it, there was only one way to proceed.

"I'm going to have to come clean with him," he said grimly. "I don't have any other choice. The fact is, he couldn't have fathered Melissa Sorensen's unborn baby and yet his DNA is a match for the child. We need to get to the bottom of it. And fast."

Willie nodded, his expression equally somber. The men climbed out of the squad car and made their way toward reception. After emptying their pockets and going through the usual security checks, they were shown into a small interview room.

"The prisoner will be brought down to you shortly," the corrections officer said as he turned to leave.

Zane murmured his thanks and took a seat. Willie followed suit. The room was sparsely furnished, with only a single table and four chairs. The pale gray walls were cold and cheerless and matched the pale gray Formica table. The plastic chairs were hard and uncomfortable. There was nothing about the place that was inviting and it certainly didn't induce people to stay. Zane guessed that was the whole point.

He pulled out a blank notepad and pen from his briefcase and set them on the table. The room was one that was usually occupied by police officers and contained audiovisual equipment to enable interviews to be recorded. It was standard practice to do so, provided the interviewee consented.

The door to the interview room swung inward and the man Zane presumed to be Wesley Parker stood in the opening. He was a tall man of slight build with nondescript brown hair and brown eyes. A lot of prisoners spent their time in the gym, building themselves up. Zane didn't know how Parker had spent the last nineteen years, but it definitely hadn't been by lifting weights.

The man was thin, almost to the point of emaciation. His skin was pale and stretched tightly over his cheekbones. He gazed at the officers with disinterest. Zane pushed back his chair and got to his feet.

"Mr Parker, I'm Detective Zane Sullivan. This is my partner, Detective Willie Whitehouse. Thank you for agreeing to see us."

Parker ignored Zane's outstretched hand and shuffled his way forward. The clink of the chains around his ankles was loud in the silence of the room. Zane glanced at the corrections officer who'd followed Parker into the room.

"Any chance you can remove those handcuffs? And the chains? After nearly twenty years in here, I don't think he's going anywhere."

The corrections officer shot Zane a sour look and then shrugged.

"Suit yourself." With a clink and clatter of metal on metal, the officer retrieved a stack of keys attached to a metal ring from his belt loop. A few moments later, the handcuffs sprang free. He did the same with the chains around Parker's ankles.

"I'll be right outside the door if you need me," the corrections officer muttered, and took his leave.

Zane returned to his seat and Willie did the same. Dragging the notepad toward him, Zane indicated the empty chair in front of him.

"Would you like to take a seat?"

Parker shrugged, but pulled out a chair and threw himself down. Zane flipped through the notepad, cleared his throat and started.

"Mr Parker, I'm sure you're wondering why we're here."

Once again, Parker merely shrugged. Zane could understand his disinterest. Twenty years was a long time to be incarcerated. No doubt in the first few months – maybe even the first few years – he'd met with lawyers and anyone else he could think of to tell them he was innocent. As time went on, he'd gotten tired of it. After all, he'd been proclaiming his innocence for the best part of two decades and nobody had listened. Zane could understand how that kind of thing could wear a man down to nothing. *Perhaps that explained Parker's gaunt appearance?*

Zane eyed the prisoner. "Do you know a woman by the name of Melissa Sorenson?"

Parker shrugged. "No. Should I?"

Zane swallowed a sigh. "Look, Mr Parker, there's no easy way to say this. Detective Whitehouse and I are involved in a current murder investigation. The victim's name was Melissa Sorenson. The autopsy revealed she was three weeks pregnant."

Parker eyed them balefully. "So? Detectives, I've been a prisoner in here for nearly twenty years. What the hell has this got to do with me?"

Zane tried not to squirm. This was the difficult part. "Yes, Mr Parker. We understand. We're not saying you had anything to do with the murder. But the thing is, the forensic pathologist took DNA from the fetus. The DNA results came back to you."

The shock that exploded across Parker's face was entirely expected, as was the anger that swiftly followed. Zane understood exactly how the man felt. There was no way in hell he'd fathered a child in recent times.

Parker's eyes narrowed to angry slits. "Is this some sort of fucking joke? Is this what you guys are doing these days to get your kicks? Meeting with lifers like me and screwing with our minds?" He pushed away from the table and stood, his lip curling up in disgust. "You can shove your stupid fucking games up your ass. I'm not playing."

Parker turned on his heel and stormed across the room. He banged on the door and shouted for the corrections officer to open up. Zane got to his feet and held his hands out in an effort to placate the man.

"Mr Parker, I'm sorry. I know this has come as a shock. Believe me, it's no joke. The baby's DNA came back to you. We both know you're not the father. Somewhere, there's been a mistake. We're here to work out when and where that happened."

The door opened and revealed the corrections officer. He looked from the prisoner to the detectives and back again. "Is everything all right in here?" he asked.

"Yes, we're fine, aren't we, Mr Parker," Zane replied.

Parker's shoulders slumped. He turned back to face the table. The corrections officer nodded toward Zane and once again closed the door. Parker shook his head slowly back and forth. Though he seemed more composed than a few moments earlier, anger still burned in his eyes.

"For the past fucking twenty years I've been telling anyone who'd listen that I didn't rape and murder Janice Scott. They told me it was my DNA that was found inside her. I fucking well knew it wasn't. But nobody wanted to listen then and they sure as hell haven't been listening for the past twenty years. You sit here now after all this time and tell me there might've been a mistake? Go fuck yourself!"

Zane hastened to reassure the man. "Please, Mr Parker, all I ask is that you listen to what we have to say. Okay, I accept that a long time has passed since you were convicted and you've probably lost count of the number of people you've told you were innocent."

Zane shot Parker a look and was relieved to see the man was listening, albeit with a dark scowl still upon his face. Zane drew in a breath and continued.

"The thing is, law enforcement officers hear that kind of shit all the time. There wouldn't be a prisoner inside this jail who didn't proclaim his innocence. You know it as well as I do. If we were to reinvestigate every case of a prisoner who declared he was wrongly convicted, we'd never get anything else done.

"But the fact is, in your case, it appears a mistake *has* been made. We're just not sure whether it was made then, or now. We'd like to talk to you about what happened back then, and if you're willing, we'd like to take another DNA sample and compare it to the one taken twenty years ago. We're also checking the DNA taken from the fetus. It's possible the mistake was made there or at the lab and that this has nothing to do with your case. Until we get a sample from you and get it retested, we won't know for sure where we went wrong."

Parker stormed back toward Zane. The fury in the man's eyes gave Zane pause. He was acutely aware the man was unrestrained and the corrections officer stood behind a thick paneled wall. As if sensing the potential volatility of the situation, Willie climbed slowly to his feet.

"Don't you fucking tell me how sorry you are," Parker cried, ignoring Willie. "I've wasted twenty fucking years of my life in here! Twenty years living in a cell not even as big as your bathroom. I can already tell you the DNA test years ago was wrong. I sure as hell didn't rape and murder Janice Scott. It's not something I'm likely to forget."

With a savage thrust, Parker pushed up the sleeve of his green prison jumpsuit and stuck his arm out in front of Zane.

"Here. Take your fucking sample. Do it! And you'd best get those lab rats moving on it as quick as you can. I've spent nineteen years too many in this hellhole. Every second more I spend here is another second I've lost. Do it!" Parker shouted, when Zane remained stationery.

A vein popped out in Parker's forehead. His eyes blazed into Zane's. Forcing himself to remain calm, Zane returned to his seat and folded his arms in front of him.

"Just to confirm, Mr Parker, you consent to us taking a DNA sample for the purposes of comparing it to the one taken from you during the investigation of the rape and murder of Janice Scott. Am I correct?"

"Yes, you're correct," Parker spat. "Just do it." Once again, the man stuck out his arm in Zane's direction.

"We don't need to take blood, Mr Parker," Willie calmly explained. "A simple saliva test will do." With that Zane pulled a swab out of a sterile bag and handed it to the prisoner.

Parker stared at the swab. "What do you want me to do with it?"

Zane tore open the sterile packet and handed the open end to Parker. "Take the swab and scrape the cotton end around the inside of your mouth. Take care to get a decent saliva sample. We don't want to have to do this again."

Some of the anger eased out of the prisoner. Parker did as he was asked and then handed the swab back to Zane. "How long before the lab gets the results?"

Zane eyed him steadily. "Not as soon as you or I would like. There are thousands of requests and only a handful of labs, but I'll put in an urgent request. If we're lucky, we might have the results in a few days."

Parker nodded and more of his tension seemed to ease. "I guess after all this time, a few more days won't make much difference."

"We'll keep pressuring the lab," Willie assured him.

"I'll let you know as soon as we hear," Zane replied. He placed the swab in a plastic evidence bag and sealed it. "I'd like to ask you a few questions about the time around Janice Scott's murder."

Parker stared at him a moment and then sighed. "If you've read my file, you know everything there is. My story's never changed."

"I accept that," Zane replied, "but I haven't had a chance to read the file yet. This DNA evidence has only recently come to light. When I realized you couldn't possibly be the father of my murder victim's unborn child, I came straight out here to talk to you."

Parker regarded Zane and Willie in silence. It stretched for so long that the corrections officer once again opened the door and poked his head in.

He looked from one to the other. "Is everything all right in here?"

"Yes, thanks, we're fine," Zane replied.

The officer merely nodded and closed the door. Zane looked at Parker. "Are you willing to tell us what happened the night Janice Scott was raped and murdered?"

Parker stared down at his hands where they

rested on the table. His fingers were thin and pale, like the rest of him. His nails were short and clean. Pockets of dark hair sprouted from his knuckles. Finally, Parker spoke.

"It was a long time ago, but I remember it like yesterday. I guess I've had long enough to think about it, go over every single detail. The only evidence the police had on me was the DNA. If it weren't for that, I'd be a free man."

Zane nodded. He hoped like hell that Parker hadn't spent the better part of twenty years incarcerated for a crime he didn't commit, but there was a fair chance that was the case. One of the DNA tests had been screwed up. That much was for certain.

"If it's all right with you, I'd like to record this interview. That way, we have an accurate record of what's been said. No more misunderstandings," Zane said.

Parker gave his consent and Willie set up the recording equipment. After the initial introductions were made and background information given for the purposes of the recording, Zane urged Parker to continue.

"Janice and I were in the same year," Parker said softly. "We were both seniors at Randwick North High School. Her father was the local mayor. Mine was a janitor at the pre-school. We didn't hang out, but we knew each other."

"Tell me about the night in question. Had you seen Janice that day?"

"Yeah, I saw her. I remember because I saw her most days. Even though we lived on opposite sides of town, for the first part of the way from school we went in the same direction. I used to see her walking home, or sometimes she'd ride her bike. Once she got her driver's license, she used to drive. She had this really nice little red sports car her daddy bought for her."

"How do you know her father bought it for her?"

"She told me. Most days she'd drive to school, but there were times when she chose to walk. I asked her once why she didn't drive that nice car to school every day and she said that sometimes she just didn't feel like it."

Parker shook his head. "I never did understand that. I mean, you have a perfectly good car. Why would you want to walk?" He shrugged, not expecting an answer and continued.

"Anyway, the day she went missing, I saw her walk home. That was after I saw her with Mac Callaway down near the bleachers."

Zane sat forward. "You saw her with Mackenzie Callaway the same afternoon she was murdered?"

"Yes, I did. They were hugging each other. At least, that's what it looked like. I remember being surprised because I thought Mac was dating Jessie Wolfe." Parker glanced up at them. "Jessie was another girl from our school. She was in the year below. A real nice girl and a looker. Whew! She had everything going for her. What was even better, she had an identical twin.

"Not that Janice wasn't attractive. She most certainly was, but in a different, flashier way than

Jessie and her twin. I tell you, I was jealous of Mac that day. He had not one, but two of the prettiest girls in high school chasing after him."

"What happened after you saw Mac and Janice together?" Zane asked in an effort to steer the story back on track.

"Nothing. I turned away and headed for home. It was none of my business what Mac Callaway did with his time and who he spent it with. Like I said, I felt a bit jealous of Mac. He seemed to have everything going for him. He was the captain of the football team, smart, rich, good looking. The man had been dealt a good hand."

"Are you aware that Janice Scott's body was found in Mac Callaway's bed?" Zane asked.

"Yes. At first I thought like everyone else did, that Mac had raped and murdered her. Why else would she be in his bed?"

"Do you still think that?" Zane asked.

Parker took a long time to answer. Eventually he let out a heavy sigh. "For years, I wanted to believe that Callaway had done it. Even after I'd been convicted and put away, I was desperate to find the real culprit. I knew, sure as hell, it wasn't me. I had nothing to do with Janice Scott. I knew her, but so what? So did most of the kids in the high school. Her father was a prominent man in our suburb. He was also on the school board. Janice was a good-looking girl, a cheerleader. There wouldn't have been many people at Randwick North who didn't know her. And yet it appeared that merely knowing her was enough for the police to pin the rape and murder on me."

"I think you're forgetting about the DNA evidence," Zane dryly reminded him.

Parker's lips twisted into a sneer. "Yeah, of course. The fucking DNA evidence. The same fucking DNA evidence that's now under question. You think the mistake could have been made when they tested that baby, but I sure as hell know the truth. I didn't fucking kill Janice Scott. It was my fucking DNA sample they got wrong."

Zane didn't argue. After all, it was possible Parker was right. A mistake had definitely been made somewhere. It was equally possible the mistake had been made back when Parker had been arrested.

"Tell me about how you came to give a DNA sample? Did you give it up voluntarily, or did the police obtain a court order?"

Parker looked up at Zane. "There was no fucking court order. Of course I gave it voluntarily. We all did."

Zane frowned. "What you mean?"

Parker sighed. "I mean, every boy in Janice Scott's year gave a sample. And even the boys in the year below. The police were convinced the perpetrator was someone she knew. Someone from the high school. How they came to that conclusion, I'll never know, but that's what they told us. They asked for every boy in Year Eleven and Twelve to come forward and give a DNA sample. They said if we had nothing to hide, we wouldn't have a problem with it. That's exactly how I felt. I stepped up and gave a sample, like everyone else."

Zane's eyebrows rose in surprise. "You mean to

tell me every boy in those senior years voluntarily gave over a DNA sample?"

Parker nodded. "Yes. It might sound hard to believe, especially now, but this was twenty years ago. People were a lot more trusting of the police and they were also more prepared to help out. That poor girl had been raped and murdered. We all wanted to find out who was responsible and make them pay for their crime. It was our civic duty to aid the police in their investigation and provide a DNA sample. I sure as hell hadn't done anything wrong, and I had nothing to hide. So yes, Detective, I voluntarily gave the police a sample and I was more than happy to do it. Little did I know it would be held against me and I'd spend the next twenty fucking years in jail."

The anger that had been banked behind Parker's eyes once again flared to life. Zane paused for a moment and looked down at his notes, giving the man time to collect himself.

"Do you know if Mackenzie Callaway provided a DNA sample?" Zane asked.

"Yes. Of course he did. I just told you. Every boy in Year Eleven and Twelve provided a sample. I've mean, *everyone*. The principal had given the police our class lists. The samples were taken in the school hall. We all lined up and had our name checked off the roll."

"So Mackenzie Callaway was cleared and you were charged with rape and murder. Is that right?" Willie asked.

"Yes. That's exactly right. I was as shocked as anyone when the police came to arrest me. They dragged me away to the police station. They wouldn't let me call my parents because I was already eighteen. I was allowed one phone call and they suggested it should be to my lawyer."

"Did you go to trial?" Zane asked.

"Yes, I went to fucking trial! Do you think I was going to fucking plead guilty to a crime I didn't commit? Of *course* I went to trial! Not that it did me any good. The DNA evidence convicted me before I even opened my mouth. The police were sure they had their man and the jury saw it that way, too. I didn't stand a chance."

Parker's breath came fast and hard. Once again, Zane paused a moment and gave the man time to recover. After a while, Zane spoke again.

"Okay, Mr Parker, you're adamant you didn't do this to Janice Scott. Then tell me, who did? You've had plenty of time to think about it. What's your theory? Who do *you* think raped and murdered her?"

Parker sighed. "Like I said, for a long time, I assumed it was Mac Callaway, like everyone else did. After all, I'd seen her with him earlier that afternoon and then she was found dead in his bed. It seemed a logical conclusion to think he had something to do with it.

"I told Janice's step-brother as much when he posed the same question. He came to see me, demanding to know why I'd murdered his step-sister. I told him in no uncertain terms it wasn't me."

"When did he speak with you?"

"It must have been at least ten years ago now. I remember thinking it was strange that he'd waited so long to seek out answers. Then he told me he'd been overseas on deployment. He was in the military. He'd not long arrived back home."

"What's his name?" Willie asked.

"Steve Prendergast."

Zane made a note of the name on the pad in front of him. Something stirred in his memory, but the hazy thought remained just out of reach. Determinably, he continued with the interview.

"You said for a long while you thought the person responsible for Janice's murder was Mackenzie Callaway. Do you still feel that way?" Zane asked.

Parker let out a heavy sigh. "I knew Mac pretty well. We were both on the same football team. You might find that hard to believe looking at me now, but I didn't always look like this. Of course, I was never as good a player as Mac was, but I held my own. Mac was always good to me. He didn't have any attitude like some blokes did. He had everything going for him, every reason in the world to feel superior, but he didn't. He treated everyone the same, and I liked that."

"Okay, so you don't think it was Mac Callaway. Who do you think it was?" Willie asked.

Parker slowly shook his head. "You're right. I've had a lot of time to think about this. I have no proof, all I have is my gut instinct. But there was a guy in the year below us by the name of Omer Demir. I didn't know him very well, but he was someone I never warmed up to. He always seemed the secretive type, darting here, darting there. He never looked you in the eye. On the days Janice walked or rode her bike, I'd see him following her home. They lived in the same part of Randwick, so his behavior wasn't entirely suspicious, but it was odd how he used to follow her like that, always the same distance behind.

"I could tell he really liked her, but she wouldn't have given him the time of day. He wasn't her type. Not rich enough or good-looking enough for Janice. Of course, his family had money, but they were hard-working immigrants. Not like Mac Callaway's family."

Zane stilled, his senses on high alert. It was the second time the name Omer Demir had come up in relation to Janice Scott. First, he was someone Jessie Wolfe had described as being in love with Janice. Apparently she'd gotten this information directly from Omer himself. Then there was the business rivalry between Demir and Mac. *Was there a link between the two, or was he grasping at straws?*

A surge of frustration went through him. This case was hard on his head. It was like there were so many essential details hovering just out of reach. Things that were floating around in the periphery of his mind, too flimsy for him to grasp and yet imperative for him to understand.

It was clear there was a link between all the players in his case and that link might even go as far back as twenty years. Mac and Jessie and Omer and Wesley.... *How did they all fit in?*

Swallowing a sigh, Zane looked back at Parker. "Thanks for answering our questions, Mr Parker. We appreciate it. And thank you also for being willing to give us another DNA sample. Like I said, we'll rush this through the lab. As soon as I have the results, I'll let you know. Let's hope it provides the answers you're looking for."

Parker nodded, his expression resigned. "I've had your so-called lab experts fail me once before. I'm not holding my breath they'll see it my way this time around. I'll believe it when I see it."

With that, the prisoner pushed away from the table and turned and pounded on the door.

"Officer! Open up! We're done here."

CHAPTER 13

Steve squinted against the late afternoon sunlight that burned into his retinas and tried to ignore the pain in his head. Ever since that piece of shrapnel had lodged itself in the side of his skull, he'd had headaches. Of course, the field doctors had removed the twisted shard and had declared him lucky to be alive, but the persistent agony behind his eyes flared up with monotonous regularity and was enough to remind him of the hellhole he wished he could forget.

The medication prescribed by his doctor usually kept the worst of it at bay, but sometimes, like now, it felt like a jackhammer had taken residence in his head. Coupled with the escalating hatred he felt toward Mackenzie Callaway and it was no wonder his head felt like it was about to explode.

He hadn't been there when his step-sister, Janice, had been brutally raped and murdered. Instead, he'd been stuck in a nightmare of his own. He'd done a total of four tours in Afghanistan and probably would have done more if he hadn't been wounded and sent home. It was then he learned of Janice's death.

Okay, so they weren't actually blood relations, but that didn't matter. She was the only sister he had. And now she was gone and the man responsible had gotten away with it.

Mackenzie Callaway.

When Steve had arrived to discover Janice had been murdered, the police had already put someone behind bars. Wesley Parker's DNA proved he was the killer. Steve had been disappointed to discover Parker was out of reach, but he still paid him a visit in jail. He wanted the bastard to know Janice had family who loved her and who missed her every day. He wanted Parker to stare into his eyes and know that one day, Steve would exact his revenge.

Parker had been given twenty years for the rape and murder of Steve's little step-sister. One day Parker would be a free man. And Steve would be waiting. If Afghanistan had taught him anything it was the art of immeasurable patience...and how to make a person die...

Only, it hadn't worked out that way. Wesley Parker had denied being the one responsible for the heinous crimes committed against Janice. At first, Steve refused to believe him. After all, Parker wasn't the first criminal to protest his innocence. But something about Parker's manner spoke to Steve. He gradually, reluctantly came to accept the truth: Wes Parker hadn't killed his step-sister.

It was then Parker told him about Mackenzie Callaway. Steve had already accessed all the information he could via the Internet. He was aware Janice had been found dead in Mackenzie Callaway's bed. He'd been immediately suspicious of the good-looking, wealthy football jock who'd been born with the proverbial silver spoon in his mouth. But then the news reports he found spoke about Wesley Parker and the positive DNA test and Steve had shelved his suspicions of Callaway.

After his meeting with Parker in the visitor's room of Long Bay Correctional Facility, he'd reconsidered. What if Parker was telling the truth? What if the DNA test was wrong? What if the real killer had gotten away scot-free? It was beyond thinking about. After many more weeks of indecision, he'd finally reached a conclusion: Mackenzie Callaway had raped and murdered his step-sister. Somehow the DNA results were switched. Callaway's family had enough money to make anything go away. And all the while, the bastard paraded around the streets of Sydney a free man, getting rich.

Steve's blood boiled at the very thought. His anger was so immense, the pain in his head had been almost too much to bear, but he welcomed the agony, embraced it. One day he'd need that anger to see his mission through.

He'd purposefully set out to find Callaway and befriend him. He became his right hand man. He became indispensable. And then he started putting his plan in action. Just little things at first, like orders for steel and glass and concrete that somehow went astray. Like leaving the gates unlocked at the close of the day in the hope vandals would enter and cause carnage. Like not looking for a realtor when he assured Mac he was. Without a solid marketing plan and an enthusiastic and expert team behind it, Mac would be hard-pressed to move those condos. Especially now.

Steve never had much to do with Melissa and he sure as hell hadn't killed her, but he was more than pleased with the way things had worked out in that regard. He couldn't have planned it better himself. Mac was under police suspicion and his multimillion dollar development was headed up shit creek. It was almost funny. It would be funny if it wasn't so serious.

It was too bad Mac had caught the eye of his hot-looking lawyer. From what Steve had seen, the lady was way past interested. Some men caught all the breaks. Life wasn't fair. Still, slowly but surely, Steve would sneak under Callaway's defenses and when he did, everything would be over. He could hardly wait.

Jessie hitched the plastic shopping basket higher on her forearm and continued her way up and down the aisles of her local supermarket doing her best to remember what was on the grocery list she'd left on her fridge. Ever since her meeting with Mac and the detectives, she hadn't been able to stop thinking about high school. It seemed ridiculous that Omer could have had anything to do with Janice's death and even more ludicrous that he'd murdered Melissa, but it was strange how his name kept cropping up and even stranger that the DNA taken from Melissa's unborn baby had been matched to the sample given by Wes Parker all those years ago. The coincidence was almost too much to believe and from the look on Detective Sullivan's face when he discovered the connections, he thought so, too. Quite a conundrum…

She wondered what Wes had said when the detective confronted him with what they now knew about the DNA results. It must have come as a shock. The police would have told him a mistake had been made somewhere. They just had to figure out where. She could imagine the elation Wes was feeling.

According to the detective, Wes had spent almost twenty years proclaiming his innocence. In fact, she could recall him doing just that when he was first arrested. She'd been away at college by the time the case came to trial, but she'd caught snatches of it in the newspaper and was kept up to date by various friends. Wes had continued to tell anyone who'd listen that he was innocent. Perhaps he was finally going to be able to prove to the rest of the world that he was right.

Then again, it could be a recent mistake made at the lab. That was always a possibility. She understood the detective's hope that the mistake came from the baby. She shuddered at the thought of the legal nightmare that would ensue if it were discovered that an innocent man had spent the past twenty years in jail. Or the tsunami of cases from other prisoners claiming the same thing.

Or that the real murderer had not been brought to justice and still roamed the streets. Possibly still doing harm to people like Janice and Melissa...

Still, no matter where the fault lay, as far as she was concerned, discovering Mac's girlfriend was pregnant to another man helped Mac's credibility. He'd told the police during his initial interview that he and Melissa got into an argument over her admission she was having an affair. At the time, the police had no reason to believe there was an actual affair other than Mac's say so, but now they had proof. The existence of another man in Melissa's life also raised another suspect, provided they could identify him. Regardless of who that was, they all knew now that it sure as hell wasn't Wes Parker.

Caught up in her thoughts, Jessie turned into the next aisle and ran straight into another shopper. Their baskets collided. She flushed with embarrassment.

"Oh, I'm so sorry! I wasn't looking—"

Mac's teasing green eyes smiled down at her. She blinked in surprise.

"W-what are you doing here? I thought you said you lived in Vaucluse? Surely there's a supermarket closer than this?"

He laughed and her belly did a flip-flop. His usual high-visibility construction clothing had been replaced with tan chinos and an emerald-green polo shirt, the seams of which stretched taut across his muscular shoulders.

Realizing she'd spent way too much time checking him out, she quickly averted her gaze.

"You're right. I have a well-stocked deli right around the corner from my condo, but I had a meeting in the city with my architect. We just finished. I thought I'd pop in and pick up something for dinner."

She reflexively looked into his basket. Sure enough, a nice-looking piece of sirloin steak, baby potatoes and a small pack of green beans already filled the bottom. There was also a carton of milk, a loaf of crusty bread, some soft cheese and a box of crackers.

"Looks like you have it covered," she said a little wistfully.

Her suite at the hotel had a small fridge and a modest kitchenette, but nothing that allowed her to cook extravagant meals that required more than the use of a cooktop. Sometimes she wished for a house with a backyard where she could have a BBQ, or at least a balcony with one.

His gaze slid to her basket. "A microwave meal? That's it?"

A blush stole across her cheeks. "Hey, don't judge me. I live in a hotel. It might be glitzy and glamorous and close to work, but it also comes with...restrictions."

He nodded somberly, but his eyes were full of laughter. She found herself smiling back.

"Right. So you'd rather give up home cooking for sleeping in until just before nine."

"I'll have you know, most mornings I'm at work before eight o'clock!" she replied with mock outrage.

He stepped back, pretending shock, and pressed

a hand against his chest. "Oh my goodness! At work before eight? What is this lunacy?"

She couldn't help herself. She burst out laughing. "All right, Mr Smarty Pants. What time do you start your day?"

"Well, I'm usually up by five. I do an hour in the gym, come home, shower, breakfast and hit the road. Depending on traffic, I'm at the job site by seven."

She shook her head, impressed. "Wow. You must go to bed with the birds."

Jessie was suddenly bombarded with images of Mac's naked body sprawled amongst the sheets. Heat scalded her cheeks. She snuck a peek at him and noticed his eyes had darkened to a deep green. A sexy smile played around his full lips.

The air around them was suddenly charged with awareness. With that, she remembered the time twenty years earlier when they'd snuck away from everyone and spent all night under the stars. Back then, they'd done nothing more than heavy petting – kissing and touching and wanting – but now she wished they'd done so much more.

His gaze moved slowly over her, pausing at her mouth a moment before dropping to her pale pink silk blouse with the two top buttons undone. Her breasts seemed to swell and press against the soft fabric. Her nipples hardened involuntarily. His gaze moved lower, glancing over her hips and down her legs. She shivered at the fire left in the wake of his heated gaze.

"Not always," he finally responded. "Sometimes I stay up late. Very late."

His voice had dropped to a sexy growl and a strong shaft of desire flooded through her and centered between her legs. Her clit tingled with need. She pressed her thighs together.

This was ridiculous! They were in the supermarket! And yet all she wanted to do was rip his clothes off and roll around naked with him on the floor. *Madness!* This is what happened when she went without sex for so long. It turned her into a desperate idiot!

Hoping he hadn't noticed the flush of desire on her face, she cleared her throat and changed the subject.

"Well, I guess I'd better let you get on with it... Dinner, I mean." She blushed again and cursed silently under her breath.

He chuckled, slow, sexy and low. Shivers of desire melted their way up her spine. She remembered that chuckle. Oh, God, did she remember that chuckle. Usually when he teased her about something – like the glasses she used to wear in high school that always slipped down over her nose. He loved to push them gently upwards with his finger and then steal a kiss. He usually followed it with a chuckle like the one he'd just given.

"Why don't you join me?"

His husky-voiced invitation took a moment to register. She blinked and was once again enveloped in heat.

"I-I... Thank you, that's very nice of you, but I—"

"Already have your dinner planned. Yes, I see." He took a peek into her trolley. "Butter chicken.

Three minutes in the microwave. I bet it tastes great."

She wanted to take offense. After all, who was he to judge her eating habits? But the fact was, he was right. Quick and easy maybe, but microwave dinners were far from satisfying or tasty. She knew that all too well. She looked at Mac and saw he was waiting for an answer. She dug around in her mind for her arsenal of excuses and came up empty.

"So? Is it a yes, or a no?"

Jessie bit her lip in indecision. The truth was, she wanted to accept his invitation. She was curious about where he lived and in the short time they'd dated years before, he'd never had her over to his place for a meal. The fact he'd offered to cook for her now was endearing and so very tempting.

"Come on, Jess. You know you want to say yes."

It was his teasing, cajoling tone that did her in, as well as the laughter in his eyes. Being around Mac Callaway used to be so much fun. He'd never taken life too seriously. At least, not back then. She guessed life had a way of knocking some of the fun out of all of them, but every now and then she saw it in Mac again. Like now.

She peeked at him again and opened her mouth. "Okay, it's a yes."

His *whoop* of joy immediately had her wondering if she'd done the right thing. She was his lawyer, after all. She'd set boundaries. Now she'd accepted an invitation to dinner. And not just to dinner, but to his house. It made things way more personal.

But she couldn't bring herself to regret the decision. She wanted to see Mac in his home, on his own turf...and she wanted to enjoy his presence. She didn't expect it to go anywhere, but she wanted it just the same. And that was that.

———

Mac glanced across at Jessie, still unable to believe she'd accepted his invitation to dinner. It was surreal having her seated next to him after all these years. Once it had been in a second-hand pickup. Now they rode in his Ferrari, but the impact of having her there beside him in the close confines of his vehicle was just the same.

After initially expressing surprise and delight when she saw his mode of transport, Jessie had been mostly quiet on the drive over and he wondered if she was already regretting her decision to come home with him. He risked another glance in her direction, but her neutral expression gave him no clue.

Swallowing a sigh, he pressed the button on the remote device that triggered the opening of the black cast iron gates that were part of the high fence that surrounded the property. The Ferrari purred softly as it moved smoothly down the short paved drive. He pulled in beside his pickup. There were a few perks to living in the penthouse suite. One of them was an additional parking space.

"It must be nice to have the extra parking space," she murmured, as if reading his mind.

He grinned. "When you design and construct the building you live in, you make sure it meets your needs." He winked.

She blushed. The pink color that stained her cheeks helped ease his nerves. For all her protesting that she was nothing more than his lawyer and he was her client, her reaction to his nearness and gentle teasing definitely indicated otherwise. It gave him heart that all was not lost. Their short-lived relationship might not have ended on a high, but if the rapid rise and fall of her chest and the flutter of the pulse in her neck were any indication, she was definitely aware of him in a way that spoke far more than a mere professional relationship or interest.

He opened the door and climbed out of the Ferrari. Leaning over, he collected the supermarket purchases from the small space behind the front seat. Jessie grabbed her handbag and followed him toward the elevator.

"What floor are you on?" she asked.

"The top one, of course." He winked again.

She rolled her eyes, but a smile tugged at her lips. "Of course."

"Hey, like I said, when you're the one putting up all the money, you get to choose from the best. I regard it as my due, my bonus for coming in not only on time, but on budget."

Jessie's eyebrows rose. "Wow! I'm impressed. I know absolutely nothing about the practical construction of buildings, but I know achieving

even one of those is no small feat. To do both..."
She smiled and shook her head. "You must be
very good."

His belly tightened on a knot of desire at the
glint of teasing laughter in her eyes. A surge of
heat rushed through his veins and centered in his
groin. He suppressed a groan. Only Jessie Wolfe
had been able to turn him on with nothing more
than a look. He didn't know how she did it. It had
happened in high school and it was happening
again now. He hadn't even touched her and he
was hard as a rock. It was ridiculous!

The *ding* of the elevator doors registered a few
seconds before they slid open. He swallowed
another groan. Sharing the close confines of the
elevator with Jessie, surrounded by her warmth,
her presence, her smell was doing his head in. He
needed to get a grip – and fast – before he did
something stupid. Like try and kiss her again.

Swapping the grocery bags to his left hand, he
fished his key out of his pocket and inserted it in
the lock. He opened the door and stood back to
allow her to enter. She brushed by him and kept
on walking across the wide foyer that opened up
into an open concept kitchen and living room. All
the while, his heart pounded.

Jessie set her handbag down on the burnt
orange leather modular sofa that took up most of
the space in the living room. Like the suite at her
hotel, one wall of his condo was floor to ceiling
glass that framed a spectacular view of Sydney
Harbour. Right now, the sky was black and the
only thing visible were the myriad of lights from the

houses and apartment buildings below him and those on the other side of the harbor.

"You have a nice place," Jessie murmured, looking around.

"Thanks." Mac dropped the sacks of groceries on the kitchen counter and then gave the room a quick once-over. Although he had a housekeeper who took care of the cleaning, she only came in once a week. He wasn't exactly the tidiest person. Quite often he left dirty dishes in the sink. He risked a glance in that direction and swallowed a sigh of relief. For once, the sink was empty.

And then he spied a pair of dirty socks lying on the floor beside the couch. He'd taken them off the night before while he was stretched out watching television. Jessie remained standing with her back to him, taking in the view. As stealthily as he could, he made his way over to the offending items and kicked them under the sofa. Sensing his presence, she turned back to face him and offered him a smile, seemingly oblivious.

Phew!

He'd been to her suite. The place was spotless. It had hardly looked as though anyone lived there. It wouldn't do for her to think he was a slob. And then he noticed the trash can that stood at the end of the counter. It overflowed with rubbish. He'd meant to take it with him on his way out to work that morning, but he'd been running late and had forgotten. Now the evidence was there for all to see. There was no hiding *that* under the couch.

As discretely as he could, he opened the cupboard door beneath the sink and pulled out a new garbage bag. Tugging the one that overflowed out of the trash can, he quickly tied a knot around the top and set it aside.

"I'm sorry. I meant to take the garbage out this morning. It slipped my mind."

Jessie waved away his embarrassment. "Who cares? It's your place. You can keep it any way you like."

"No, I really mean it. I usually like things neat and tidy."

She gazed at him, her eyes brimming with good humor. "What are you saying? You don't like mess?"

He squirmed, not sure where she was coming from. It was obvious she was a neat freak. There hadn't been a single thing out of place in her hotel suite. Did she want him to agree with her question, or not? Damn it, he was so confused.

"I'm not a clean freak, but I do my best to keep the place tidy," he replied, hedging his bets.

"Same here," she said.

He looked at her in surprise. "You mean to tell me you're not a neat freak?"

Jessie laughed. "Good God, no! I hate to tell you, but sometimes I don't even make my bed!"

"No!" he exclaimed in mock horror. "I mean, who does that?"

"I know. It's so naughty of me, isn't it?"

She giggled and the delightful sound of it sent warmth surging to his cock once again. It reminded him so much of the girl she used to be. In an effort to distract himself, he sought clarification of his earlier confusion.

"When I went to your room it was as neat as a pin. Nothing was out of place. I take it the hotel staff service your room on a daily basis."

She shook her head. "I wish. My budget doesn't stretch to having my room serviced. I take care of the cleaning myself."

Mac's eyebrows rose in surprise. "You're a top notch lawyer at the most prestigious firm in the city. They mustn't be paying you enough."

She blushed at the compliment. "Thanks. That's really sweet of you." She sighed and looked away. "The truth is, I should have made partner by now. If it hadn't been for Alistair's conviction, I would have."

Mac nodded in understanding, even though he hated the thought that Jessie might have been overlooked for a partnership because of the actions of her stupid brother.

Pulling out groceries from the bags, he set the items on the counter and then opened the packet of beans. He rinsed them in the sink. Slicing them up, he placed them in a microwave dish. Jessie reached for the baby potatoes.

"There's a peeler in the drawer to your right," he said.

Together, they worked in companionable silence. Mac tried not to think about how good it felt having her there in his private space, doing something as intimate as preparing dinner.

"So, how are your parents?" Jessie finally asked. "Do they still live in Randwick?"

Mac nodded. "Yes. Dad retired a few years ago and he and Mom spend most of their time overseas. It seems they barely return from a trip and they're off on the next one."

Jessie smiled wistfully. "Good for them. I'm glad they're well enough to be able to travel."

"Yes, they've been lucky. Dad's sixty-nine this year and mom's not far behind. They used to talk about traveling the world when they retired. Now they do."

"I wish my dad had lived long enough to go traveling with my mom. She's spent most of her life alone."

"He died when you were very young, didn't he? The four of you were raised by your mom."

She smiled sadly. "Yes. Dad died when Ava and I were only two. I barely remember him. In fact, it's unlikely I'd remember him at all if not for all the photos Mom kept."

"How is she? You mentioned something about a kidney transplant."

Jessie sighed and hunted around in his cupboard for a saucepan.

"The next drawer across," he told her, instinctively knowing what she was looking for.

She pulled out a saucepan and dropped the potatoes into it. "Mom's doing great. Better than great. She managed to get a transplant and everything went well. It's been two years now and she's back to robust good health. She'd like to travel overseas, but she has no one to go with and she doesn't want to do it alone. That's why your parents are so lucky they still have each other and are in good health. Not everyone's that lucky."

Her voice had dropped to a husky whisper. She looked at him and their gazes caught. He couldn't look away. The pupils of her eyes dilated and the color turned a tumultuous chocolate. Her chest rose and fell beneath her pink silk blouse. Time stood still as they stared at each other. Mac fought to catch his breath. All he wanted to do was to take her in his arms and kiss her like he had all those years ago.

Before his brain could catch up to what was going on, his feet had closed the distance between them and he pulled her into his embrace. She melted against him and it was as good as it always had been. He kissed her with all the passion that had been pent-up for so many years and when she began to respond, his brain exploded like firecrackers, hot and full of need.

He pressed his throbbing erection against her at the same time he cupped her ass. Her butt was firm and rounded and fit snugly in his hand. Her lips moved under his, so soft and so alluring. When her hardened nipples scraped across his shirt, it was all he could do not to gather her up and find the nearest flat surface.

And then she was gently pulling away and disengaging her arms from around his neck. Embarrassment, coupled with confusion and desire warred for dominance across her face.

"I-I'm sorry, Mac. We need to slow down. I didn't come here for this."

Breathing hard, Mac did all he could to regain his control. A moment ago he'd been canvassing options where he could make love to her all night long. Now she was asking him to stop. It took him a moment to get his head around it.

"Don't look at me like that," she said with a frown.

"Like what?"

"Like you don't know if you want to kiss me or spank me. I'm sorry. I shouldn't have led you on like that. I won't deny that I've thought about kissing you ever since... Well, ever since that day in the café. But you and I...being together... It isn't as easy as that under the circumstances."

He grimaced. "Yeah, I get it. You're my lawyer. We need to keep a professional distance. I've heard it all before. And it's bullshit."

She gasped. Whether it was from his words or their vehemence, he didn't know. Still, he wasn't about to apologize. What he'd said was true.

"It's not bullshit," she said quietly. "I am your lawyer. There's something...unethical about me sleeping with my client."

"Don't tell me it's a conflict of interest. We're on the same side. Besides, I haven't been charged with anything. All you've done is provide me with a little advice. Big deal. Why does that mean we can't see each other?"

She shrugged helplessly. "When you put it like that, it sounds like I'm making this into something it's not. I swear, I'm not trying to make this a big deal. I like you, Mac. I like you a lot and I like our kisses way too much. I'm no saint. I just want to do the right thing."

He eyed her steadily. "All right, tell me this, would sleeping with me affect the quality of your work? The advice you might offer me?"

She looked appalled. "No! Of course not! I'd continue to give you my very best work, no matter what."

"Then what does it matter what we do?"

She stared at him a long time and he saw the battle going on in her head through her tumultuous, expressive eyes. Finally, she sighed.

"You're right. What does it matter if I sleep with my client? I'm turning this into something it's not. It won't affect the quality of my work – or anything else for that matter."

She drew in a deep breath as if fortifying herself for what was to come.

"Okay, let's do it," she said as if they'd been discussing going out for dinner or eating in.

His eyes widened in surprise. "Let's do it?"

She continued to hold his gaze. Hers was now filled with hunger and determination. "I want you to make love to me, Mackenzie Callaway."

Twenty years earlier, they'd never made it all the way. What she offered him now was so amazing, so precious, he could hardly believe what she was suggesting. Setting aside the beans, he once again closed the distance between them.

"Are you sure?" he whispered, his face only inches from hers.

"Yes."

"If it makes you feel any better, I could fire you right now. Then you wouldn't be my lawyer and I wouldn't be your client."

She laughed and he felt the full-throated sound of it deep inside. His stomach clenched with need.

Of all the women who'd come in and out of his life since high school, none had touched him the way Jessie Wolfe had. She was his soul mate. Then and now. He just hoped he could convince her of it.

CHAPTER 14

Jessie stared down at Mac's outstretched hand and her heart began to pound. This was the moment she wanted more than anything and yet, just for the tiniest second, she wondered if it was the right thing to do.

"You're fired, remember?" he murmured, his voice husky and low.

A flash of desire rushed through her and she nodded. "You're right. I never imagined losing a client would feel so good."

With that, she placed her hand in his. He squeezed her fingers reassuringly and all at once, everything felt right. More than right. *Perfect.* Twenty years earlier they'd been madly in love, but they'd never taken that final step. Now, as he led her down the hallway with its thick plush carpet that silenced their footsteps, she was filled with a mix of anticipation and apprehension.

He was such a good-looking, virile man. He must have slept with scores of women. She, on the other hand, had very little experience when it came to the opposite sex. She wasn't a virgin, but she wasn't far off it. All of a sudden, she wondered if she'd measure up.

What if she didn't know how to please him? She was thirty-six years old. He'd never imagine a woman of such mature years to be relatively inexperienced.

As if sensing her growing anxiety, he pulled up short and drew her close. "What is it, Jessie?" he asked softly.

She blushed, appalled at the thought of confessing her insecurities. "N-nothing," she stammered and blushed again.

"Are you having second thoughts? It's fine if you are. We don't have to do anything."

"No, I'm not having second thoughts." She realized that was true. She wanted to kiss and touch and taste him. She wanted to know him in every way there was. She'd waited twenty years to consummate their relationship and all of a sudden, she couldn't wait another moment. She stood on her tiptoes and pressed her lips against his.

He responded instantly to her kiss. His lips were warm and pliant and slanted over hers. He tasted and sipped and loved her mouth until she cried out at the sheer sweetness of it. He tasted every bit as delicious as she'd imagined.

Slowly, he drew back. He stared down at her with eyes that were backlit with desire. "We'll take it slow. I promise. Well, as slow as I'm able. We won't do anything you're not comfortable with."

"It's okay, Mac," she hastened to reassure him. "I want this. I want *you*."

Overwhelmed with emotion, he swept her into his arms and covered the short distance to his bedroom. Pushing the door open with his shoulder, he entered the room. Inch by inch, she pressed against him as he lowered her until her shoes once again touched the floor. With his arms still around her, he bent his head and kissed her again.

The kiss was as warm and passionate as the first one and within moments, Jessie was mindless with need. Her pulse beat a staccato rhythm in her chest and at her temples. Heat ignited inside her, rushing through her veins. When Mac pulled away, she was breathless and pleased to see that he was panting, too.

He reached for the buttons on her blouse and slowly undid them one by one. When he was finished, he spread the fabric open. Her white lacy bra peeked out from beneath and his hands reached out and cupped her breasts. His expression was one of wonder. His eyes were wide with awe.

"You can't imagine how many nights I dreamed of doing this. Our feverish groping in high school was all I had to remember of you. I wanted you naked and proud before me, giving all of yourself without restraint. And here you are. Am I dreaming?"

She smiled hesitantly and reached out to cradle his cheek in her hand. "You're not dreaming. I'm here. I'm real. Touch me."

She took his hand and once again lay it against her breast. The soft mound swelled against his fingers. He scraped her nipple beneath her bra and the little nub immediately pebbled.

"You're so beautiful," he whispered, his voice hoarse with need.

"So are you," she replied.

He ducked his head, but she would have none of it. She framed his face in her hands. She looked him in the eye and then kissed him long and thoroughly.

"Okay, you're doing a good job of convincing me," he gasped.

She smiled and shucked off her blouse, taking enjoyment in the way his gaze followed her every move. Next, she undid the button on her skirt and shimmied it down her hips. Her white lace panties were mostly concealed by her black stockings, but it wasn't long before they were gone and she stood before him in nothing but her underwear.

The heat in his look seared right through her. She felt his desire right down to her toes. It gave her the confidence she needed to step forward and tug at the hem of his polo shirt until it came free of his pants. He lifted his arms and helped her get rid of his shirt. And then it was her turn to gasp.

He'd always had a muscular physique in high school, but now he was a full-grown man. He'd broadened and lengthened in all kinds of places and his chest and shoulders now looked like silken steel. Tanned in spite of the winter weather, his pectorals stood out against his hairless chest. Unable to help herself, she ran her fingers across them, loving the feel of the taut flesh underneath.

Her fingernails scraped across his nipples and she heard his sharp intake of breath. Her hand skimmed lower, across a washboard flat stomach...

and lower still, to the top of his pants. The bulge behind his zipper was unmistakable and she longed to see it revealed. Sliding the button through the hole and then tending to the zipper, she slid her hand under the waistband of his underwear and took hold.

Thick and hard and throbbing, his cock felt alive in her hand. Wanton heat pooled between her thighs at the thought of him inside her. Even as a seventeen-year-old, she'd longed to make love with him, but she was a good girl raised in a good home and they hadn't been dating long. Perhaps if fate hadn't intervened and they'd dated into college, they would have consummated their relationship to the fullest. Only, things hadn't turned out that way.

Now here they were, almost two decades later, with a lot of water under the bridge. She had a past and so did he, but somehow, when they were together like this, all of that faded away. They were just Mac and Jessie, two kids in love, two kids with the world at their feet. Anything was possible and tonight, she was more than willing to believe.

Stepping slightly away, Mac took off his pants and underwear. He hadn't gotten round to switching on the light, but the moonlight that streamed through the floor-to-ceiling bedroom window illuminated all of him that mattered.

His legs were long and muscular and sculptured to perfection, like his chest. His thick cock stood out from a nest of brown curls, darker than the golden blond on his head. She could have stood there looking at him for hours, such was the beauty of this man… But he had other ideas.

Closing the distance between them, he reached around and unclasped and removed her bra. Kissing his way across her breasts, he kneeled before her and tugged at the waistband of her panties. Still on his knees, he slid the lace down over her hips and down her legs. She stepped out of them and just stood there, transfixed by the look on his face.

He stared at her with eyes that were wide with wonder, trailing heat in the wake of his gaze. He leaned forward and buried his face against her belly and breathed.

"You're so soft and warm and silky. You smell like peaches and cream. Lovely."

His voice, muffled against her skin, was thick with longing and need. He kissed his way down her belly and then pressed his face against her mound. She sucked in a breath at the intimacy of it and buried her fingers in his hair.

His mouth found the soft lips of her sex and his tongue slowly stole inside. Stroke by stroke, he set her on fire until she was sure she would explode.

"Please, Mac. I want to touch you," she moaned and urged him to his feet.

Slowly, he stood and kissed her again. "Come."

He led her to the king-sized bed that dominated the room. The cool, dark satin bedspread felt like heaven against her flushed and naked skin. Mac lay her back gently and followed her down, pressing his body against hers.

She touched his face, his biceps, his taut belly and once again, closed her fist around his cock.

Slowly, she stroked him in a firm rhythm, clenching and releasing her fist. The thick hard length of him pulsed against her fingers, warm and alive with need. And then he gently removed her hand and rolled her onto her back.

Reaching into the drawer of his nightstand, he pulled out a condom and sheathed himself. She was glad he was prepared because she hadn't even given it a thought.

Moving over her, he positioned himself at her entrance. She felt the hard probe of his cock. She tensed momentarily – it had been so long – and then forced herself to relax. This was Mac, the man she loved. The only man she'd loved. Now and always.

Though the knowledge of how deep her feelings were for him still had the power to fill her with panic, right now she wanted to revel in those feelings and give everything she had to him. Relaxed now and impatient, she opened her legs and urged him inside. With one sharp thrust, he did just that and almost drove the wind out of her.

He was so thick and hard, he stretched her wide until she almost couldn't bear it. And then he started to move and the need began building deep inside her once again. Stroke after stroke, he moved inside her, each one longer than the last. Tension built as she climbed higher and higher. Closer and closer to the peak until at last, she was finally there.

With a cry, she reached her climax and slowly toppled back down to earth.

Opening her eyes, she found Mac smiling down at her, his eyes filled with love and satisfaction.

"Was it good?" he asked almost shyly.

"It was better than good."

He bent down and kissed her on the lips, the tenderness in his touch almost bringing tears to her eyes.

"I'm glad. I've dreamed of this moment for so long. I wanted it to be perfect."

"It was everything I wanted it to be," she assured him. "Only twenty years too late."

Regret briefly shadowed his expression. "You're right. But the best part is, now we have years to make up for time apart."

With that, he plunged into her again and in short order he found his release. She held him as he cried out in an agony of relief.

It was a long time later, after they'd caught their breath that Mac whispered against her ear. "I love you."

Jessie froze in shock and then slowly smiled from ear to ear.

Omer's legs were stiff and his neck had a crick in it from sitting in a cramped position in his Lamborghini for so long. He didn't know what impulse had propelled him to Mac's condo in the exclusive seaside suburb, but he was glad he had followed his instincts. He'd come away with a wealth of information that would help him move forward with the next step in his plan.

He'd been surprised to see Jessie alight from Mac's car. Mac had fetched grocery bags from the back and together, they'd walked inside. It was such a scene of domesticity, it had taken him aback. After seeing them together in the café, it had become obvious there was more than a professional relationship going on, but he'd had no idea things had escalated to this.

He'd waited for Jessie to reappear, but hours passed and nothing. *Surely they couldn't still be having dinner?* Even if those grocery sacks had held enough for three courses, they must be finished now.

Another hour passed and then another. It was now a long way past late. The penthouse remained well-lit, like it had when the two lovebirds had arrived, but the back of the place was dark.

Had they escaped to the bedroom? Had their relationship gone that far? But why hadn't he seen any lights come on? Perhaps they preferred to do it in the dark. One thing was for sure, it didn't look like Jessie was leaving any time soon. It was already past one in the morning. Tomorrow was a working day. Unless she intended to call in sick, she was leaving it late to be getting home for a decent sleep.

No, there was only one logical explanation. They were fucking with the lights off. By now, they were probably sleeping a relaxed and contented sleep. Unlike him, who was tense and tired and frustrated and angry...

Why should Mac Callaway be allowed even a smidgen of happiness? The man had destroyed Omer's life. And yet here was his nemesis, spending the night with a beautiful woman, a successful criminal defense lawyer, no less.

It seemed that no matter what Omer did, Mac Callaway's star just continued to shine. Well, he was determined to put an end to that. He thought it would happen with Janice, but the cops found someone else to blame. Then he pulled some strings and sent some of Mac's building projects haywire, but even that hadn't been enough to slow the man down. When Omer latched onto Melissa, he was sure he'd finally found Mac's Achilles heel.

The plan had been perfect. He'd snatch the love of Mac's life right from under his nose. The pair were living together, planning on getting married. That's what Melissa had said. When he asked why she was fucking him if she was so in love with Mac, she'd merely laughed that tinkling laugh of hers and had told him she was getting tired of waiting and a girl needed some kind of distraction in the meantime.

Omer had laughed along with her, but inside he'd burned with hate. She was another Janice all over again. It made him so mad to be so blithely discounted as a contender for her heart. Just like Janice. Damn Mackenzie Callaway. It was all his fault. And now it seemed like he was about to get away with it again.

A surge of determination went through him. He'd be damned if he'd let Mac Callaway get away with anything. Omer had managed to pull off the perfect crime once before. He sure as hell could do it again. Just watch him.

CHAPTER 15

"Hey, Sullivan, I'm doing a coffee and doughnut run. Do you want anything?"

Zane looked up from the papers spread all over his desk. "A black coffee would be great, thanks Willie. Are you going to Krispy Kreme?"

Willie rolled his eyes. "Is there any other kind?"

Zane chuckled. "I'll have a cinnamon apple doughnut. And maybe a double dark chocolate one." Reaching into his pocket, he pulled out his wallet and handed Willie a couple bills. Willie waved the money away.

"You got it the last time. This one's on me."

Once again, Zane murmured his thanks and as Willie disappeared through the squad room door, he returned his attention to the file and the crime scene photos in his hand.

The file from Janice Scott's rape and murder had finally made its way out of archives and had arrived on his desk. He'd been poring over the contents all morning. It was interesting reading.

Eighteen-year-old Janice Marie Scott had been

241

found murdered by Mackenzie Callaway on the night of October fifth. At nine-ten pm, the emergency call had come in. While Zane didn't have the actual recorded phone call, the transcript had been included in the file. Mackenzie Callaway had called the murder in. Though it was impossible to gage his tone or demeanor, his words indicated shock and panic. Several times he begged the emergency services operator to send the police. She assured him just as often the police were on their way.

Zane tried to imagine what it would feel like to Mac to suddenly discover a dead body in his house – and not just in his house – in his bed. To make matters worse, the body was someone Callaway knew. The shock and panic made sense...but had it all been an act?

Zane looked down at the crime scene photos. As far as crime scenes went, it was almost clinically clean. There was no blood spatter on the walls, the headboard, the covers. The victim lay on top of the bedspread as if she were asleep. Not even her clothing was disturbed, even though Zane knew she'd been raped. The killer had taken the time to rearrange her clothing back to the way it had been. The only telltale sign of violence was that her eyes were wide open and glazed over with death. She stared blindly across the room.

Zane's gaze moved lower, taking note of the white knit crop top that exposed a smooth, taut stomach and designer jeans that hugged her long, slim legs. Janice Scott had been a good-looking girl. In fact, with her long blond hair, high cheekbones and generous mouth, she'd been an outright stunner. The red scarf around her neck highlighted the paleness of her skin – pale in death, but also pale in life, if her high school year book photo was anything to go by.

The year book had been included in the case file. The names of the Year Eleven and Year Twelve male students corresponded with those who'd provided their DNA. Zane flipped through the pages and then checked the list of donors. It was as Callaway had said. Every single male student in the senior years at Randwick North High School had provided a sample of their DNA.

It was an extraordinary example of a community coming together for the better good. Early in the investigation, the police were convinced the perpetrator was someone the victim had known. Zane hadn't read through the file from top to bottom so he hadn't yet pieced together how the police had come to that conclusion, but it was obvious as time went on, they'd narrowed their suspicions even further to the young men with whom the victim had gone to school.

In an ordered and systematic way, each senior student had fronted up and provided a sample to the police officers who'd set up in the school hall. Each donor was duly crossed off the list. The samples were tested and only one out of the two hundred and thirty-six samples came back a positive match to DNA found on the victim. The perpetrator was identified as Wesley Parker.

Only, now, almost twenty years later, it was obvious to Zane that an error had been made and Wesley wasn't guilty.

Zane had put a rush on having the DNA of Melissa's fetus retested. It had taken forty-eight hours, but he now had the results in his hands. He'd sent the sample to a different lab, but the outcome had been the same. Once again, the tests indicated a 99.9% chance that Wesley Parker, their convict, was the father of Melissa's unborn child.

And there was no way in hell that could be right.

The DNA of the fetus had been compared to Wesley Parker's DNA, already held on file. It was found to be a match. The only explanation was that the DNA the police had for Wesley Parker was wrong. A mistake had been made and it hadn't been made recently. Somehow, somewhere a mistake had been made twenty years ago when Wesley Parker had voluntarily offered his DNA.

The most likely error was that the sample had been mislabeled. Parker's name had been applied to it, but it hadn't been his sample. It was a fairly simple mistake to make and one that had happened in the past, but right now that one simple mistake reverberated with massive repercussions. Not the least was that an innocent man had spent the better part of twenty years in jail, if Zane's theory was correct.

The door to the squad room swung inward and Willie appeared in the opening. "I come bearing gifts. Coffee and fresh doughnuts. What more could you want?"

Zane managed a half-hearted smile, pleased for the distraction. When he considered all that was to come, his gut churned with dread. A hot coffee and a doughnut was just the kind of thing he needed. He sat up straighter in his chair and reached for the Styrofoam cup his partner offered.

"Thanks, Willie. You couldn't have arrived at a better time." Willie set the bag of doughnuts on top of a pile of paperwork on Zane's desk.

"What's up?" he asked and then bit into a Krispy Kreme.

Zane grimaced. "You don't want to know. At least, not until after you've finished your doughnut. Let's just say, it isn't good."

Willie's eyebrows rose, but he merely took another bite from his doughnut. Zane sipped at his coffee and then did the same thing. Of all the wonderful flavors offered by Krispy Kreme, cinnamon apple was his favorite. He didn't indulge very often, but when he did, he enjoyed it like a young child enjoyed Christmas. Pure delight. Unadulterated pleasure. One fritter was never enough. It was a good thing he worked out as often as he did or his cholesterol would be through the roof.

After Willie had taken his final bite and Zane had wiped the sugar and cinnamon from his hands, the two men gathered around Zane's desk.

"Okay, partner. Hit me with it," Willie said.

"The results from the second DNA test on Melissa Sorenson's baby have come back the same. They matched the sample to Wesley Parker. We both know that can't be right, so it's now obvious there was a mistake during the collection of Parker's sample. Incidentally, the results on the sample Parker provided us with the day we visited him in Long Bay have also come back. There's no surprise this DNA profile is completely different from the one that is on the record as provided by him while he was at high school."

"Shit," Willie muttered. "That's not good news, on either score."

Zane compressed his lips into a thin line. "You're right. So, I've been going through Janice Scott's case file, trying to find where the mistake was made. It had to have happened then, as part of that investigation. Somehow Parker's sample was mixed up with someone else's."

"How many samples are we talking about?"

"Two hundred and thirty-six."

Willie nodded. "Okay, that's quite a lot for someone to keep track of, especially when the samples were all taken at once. I can see how a mistake might have occurred."

Zane grimaced. "Yeah, so can I. Unfortunately, it doesn't make things any easier. A mistake was made and it looks likely an innocent man has spent almost twenty years of his life in jail."

Willie looked at Zane, his expression grim. "That is a monumental fuckup."

"You won't get any argument from me. Fortunately for us, that's not our problem. Once we notify the correct authorities that will become someone else's headache. Right now, I want to find out who murdered Melissa Sorenson. We have two possible suspects: Mackenzie Callaway or the father of the victim's unborn child. It's clear she was having an affair. That's corroborated by Callaway's story. We need to identify the man so we can gage whether he's guilty of murdering Melissa, or whether he's as much a victim as she was. And what we find could impact on a twenty-year-old case, too."

"Do you have anyone in mind?"

Zane shook his head. "No one concrete, and unfortunately, the DNA evidence of the baby is now worth shit. We need to go back to good old-fashioned policing, the way we used to do things before we got so reliant on technology."

Willie blew out his breath on a sigh. "Where do we start?"

"Funny you should ask that. Remember that conversation with Callaway and his lawyer the other day? She told us they'd known each other in high school, along with a man by the name of Omer Demir."

"Yeah. Is that the same Omer Demir who owns half this city?"

"Yes. He's done well for himself. He emigrated to Australia with his family when he was only eight years old. They settled in the eastern suburbs. He attended Randwick North High School. His father is a construction worker. His mother is a nurse. Both of them are still alive and living in a very expensive condominium right on the beach in Bondi."

Willie's eyebrows rose. "They sure did well for themselves."

"Yes, though it's interesting that Omer Demir Senior still works in construction, but not with his son. You'd think if your boy owned a successful business in your industry, you'd be on his payroll. Apparently not."

"What's your theory?" Willie asked.

Zane shrugged. "Who knows? Perhaps 'Papa' is too proud to work for his son? Maybe they just don't get along? Could be any number of reasons. I'm not sure that it's relevant."

"Right," Willie agreed. "Well, it's something to keep in mind." He reached down and picked up the crime scene photos spread across Zane's desk.

"They were taken from Janice Scott's murder scene twenty years ago," Zane offered.

Willie flicked through the colored 10 x 8's. He came to one and paused. A frown creased his forehead.

"This one here, the one with the scarf. Didn't Melissa Sorenson also have a scarf around her neck?"

Zane sat up, at once on high alert. "You're right. Shit. I should have remembered that." He shuffled files and papers around on his desk and finally laid his hands on the file he was after. Opening the folder, he pulled out an envelope that contained the photos of Melissa's crime scene. Impatiently, he flicked through them.

"Here it is. You're dead right, Willie. There's a scarf around her neck. It was hiding the strangulation wounds."

"How did Scott die?"

"By strangulation," Zane replied slowly. "And it says here the scarf around her neck initially hid the evidence." A shiver of excitement slid down his spine. His gut churned. He looked up at Willie, whose expression revealed he'd also made the connection.

"That's a fair coincidence and with the DNA mix-up…?" Willie muttered.

"Yes. Too bad I don't believe in coincidences."

"Give me a look at the names of the boys who volunteered samples in high school," Willie said.

Zane found the list and handed it over to him. "Every boy enrolled at that high school in Years Eleven and Twelve voluntarily provided DNA samples," Zane said. "I can't believe the police pulled it off, but somehow they did."

"Is there any connection between any boys on the list and those who had contact with Melissa Sorensen?"

"Yes, in fact, there is," Zane replied. "Mackenzie Callaway and Omer Demir. Both of them knew Janice Scott. They went to high school with her. Both of them provided DNA samples shortly after her death. And then there's Wesley Parker."

"Right, the one who was put away for Janice Scott's rape and murder and who we've now discovered is likely innocent of the crime."

"Right," Zane agreed, his tone somber.

Willie nodded. "Okay, so we have Mackenzie Callaway and Omer Demir. Both men have a connection to our dead teenager. I get that. But what about now? Callaway and Sorenson were in a relationship, but what's Demir's connection to Sorensen?"

Zane bit down a surge of frustration. "At this stage, we haven't identified one. What we do have is a connection between Demir and Callaway."

"So they continued their friendship past high school?" Willie asked.

Zane shook his head. "I wouldn't call it a friendship. According to Callaway, Demir was in the class below him in high school. He didn't have anything to do with the man back then. It's only as adults that they've crossed paths again. They're both in the construction industry, both high rollers dealing with large-scale developments."

Zane paused a moment before continuing. "Remember, when we asked Callaway in the initial interview whether he had any enemies or whether he could think of anyone who might want to hurt Melissa?"

Willie nodded thoughtfully. "Yeah, I remember that now. He couldn't think of anyone who had a beef against him and then he mentioned Omer Demir. I remember making a note of the name, but it didn't set off any alarm bells. I guess because the way Callaway talked about the guy, it didn't seem such a big deal. There definitely didn't seem enough bad blood between them to warrant us looking at Demir as a possible murder suspect trying to put suspicion on Callaway. Perhaps we were wrong."

"Who knows?" Zane muttered. "At the time, I remember thinking Callaway was kidding himself if he didn't think he had any enemies. A successful businessman like him: wealthy, good looking, easy going, full of charm... There must be someone jealous of all that."

Willie looked at Zane. "So, what do we do now?"

"Go and talk to Demir. We need to know if he knew Melissa Sorensen and see what he says about his mate, Mackenzie Callaway. There are always two sides to a story, as you know. It's time we heard his."

Determination glinted in Willie's dark eyes. He liked nothing better than to question potential suspects and do his best to punch holes in their stories. "Let's do it."

A quick phone call to the office of Demir Construction confirmed that Omer was in. Arming themselves with another cup of coffee, Zane and Willie left.

The drive from police headquarters to Omer's building took less than five minutes and along the way the detectives planned their strategy.

The offices were located in a prestigious part of the city, close to the harbor, the botanical gardens and a million-dollar view. Zane couldn't imagine the cost of the rent on such a place. It was obvious Demir had done well for himself and that the construction business was booming.

Inside the marble-lined foyer, the pretty receptionist directed them to the tenth floor. Willie and Zane were whisked upwards in the elevator and within seconds, had stepped out into another world. No expense had been spared on the decor for the extravagant office suite. Plush carpet, priceless artwork and furniture that cost more than what Zane made in years filled the generous reception space. Another attractive young woman sat behind a desk. She greeted them with a smile.

"Detective Sullivan?"

Zane walked up to where she sat. "Yes. I'm Detective Zane Sullivan and this is my partner, Detective Willie Whitehouse. We're here to see Omer Demir."

The girl nodded. "Yes, Jenny phoned ahead from downstairs to let me know you were on your way. Mr Demir's on the phone at the moment, but as soon as he's finished, I'll let him know you're here."

"Thanks," Zane murmured.

"Please, take a seat," the girl offered. "Can I get you some coffee?"

Zane lifted the Styrofoam cup that was still in his hand and shook his head. "No, thanks. We're good."

The girl simply nodded and then returned her attention to the computer screen that stood on the desk in front of her. Zane and Willie turned away and took a seat on the dark leather couch that sat against one wall. A scattering of architectural design magazines were spread artfully across a glass-topped coffee table. Zane reached out and picked one up and began to browse through it.

An article three pages in caught his eye. It was an interview Demir had given to *Architectural Digest* about his latest design project. The female interviewee gushed over every single element of Omer's design and gushed just as effusively over the man himself. The article included a picture of

Demir – and Zane could see there was a lot for any woman to like.

In the photograph, Omer was dressed to kill in what Zane guessed to be a five-thousand-dollar Armani suit. He wore a cravat that had been tied so intricately, Zane couldn't help but wonder how he'd done it. Cravats were no longer in fashion and he couldn't think of anyone who knew how to tie one, let alone was able to tie one with such finesse. Perhaps Demir hired an old-fashioned man servant who did that for him? Most likely he had a battalion of staffers.

And then the significance of the cravat struck him. The intricate knots at Demir's neck were reminiscent of the knots on the scarves around the necks of Janice Scott and Melissa Sorenson.

Was Zane merely clutching at straws, or was he onto something? It irritated him that he wasn't sure. He showed the article to Willie.

His partner scanned over the writing and came to rest on the photograph of Demir. "The man sure has nice taste in suits," Willie murmured. And then his eyes widened in surprise. "Holy shit! Get a look at that thing around his neck!"

"It's a cravat," Zane murmured.

"Look at the way it's tied. It reminds me of the scarf we found around that poor girl's neck."

Zane felt a burst of satisfaction. At least he wasn't the only one who felt there might be a connection.

"And Janice Scott wore a scarf around her neck, too."

CHAPTER 16

Before Willie could reply, the man he and Zane were there to meet came striding toward them. Zane quickly set the magazine aside and stood.

"Omer Demir? I'm Detective Sullivan. This is Detective Whitehouse. Thank you for seeing us."

Demir looked every bit as impressive in the flesh as he had in the magazine. He inclined his head slightly in acknowledgment of Zane's greeting and then offered them a wide smile. The man's straight teeth were dazzling and gleamed in the overhead light. His thick dark hair was groomed to perfection, along with his neatly trimmed beard. The arrogant magnetism in his dark eyes drew Zane in and he had to blink to break the powerful connection.

What the hell just happened? He shook his head to clear it and vowed silently to remain on guard against Omer Demir. He could see why the female journalist had come across all aflutter in the magazine article. The man was so charismatic he was downright dangerous, and not just to women.

"Welcome, Detectives. Please, follow me."

With that, Omer turned on the heels of his shiny black Ferragamos and led the way down a short corridor. They followed him into an office that was one of the most extravagant Zane had ever seen.

Floor-to-ceiling glass wrapped around two walls of the spacious corner office. Spectacular views of Sydney Harbour, the botanical gardens and Circular Quay filled the room. It was almost as if Zane was out there, on the harbor, or strolling across the promenade, enjoying all that Sydney had to offer.

"Nice view," Willie murmured behind him.

Once again, Omer dazzled them with an arrogant grin. "Thank you. I worked hard to get here. It's nice to be rewarded with a view like this every day."

Omer tugged at the cuffs of his designer suit and then seated himself behind an enormous hand-carved red cedar desk. The few loose papers that were on the surface were lined up with military precision. Two Mont Blanc pens lay perpendicular to a pristine white blotter pad. An enormous computer screen and a phone were the only other things to adorn the desk.

Omer pointed to the two empty chairs opposite him. "Please, Detectives. Take a seat. I'll have Kelly bring in some coffee."

"Don't bother for me," Zane replied. He held up his half-empty Styrofoam cup. "I'm all good for coffee."

"Me, too," Willie replied. "But thanks, anyway."

Omer merely nodded and then sat back against his chair, looking the epitome of relaxed. If he was nervous about being in the company of two detectives, he certainly didn't show it.

"So, Detectives. I must admit, your visit has come as a surprise. What can I do for you?"

Zane cleared his throat. "Do you know a woman by the name of Melissa Sorensen?" He watched the man closely. Omer's expression remained pleasant and relaxed.

"No, I don't think I do. Should I?"

Willie pulled out a photo that had been taken while Melissa was still alive. It had been provided by Mackenzie Callaway at the request of the police.

"Take a look at this picture," Willie said.

Omer obligingly reached for the photo and took his time studying it. Eventually, he shook his head. "Pretty girl, that's for sure. But I'm afraid I've never seen her before. Who is she?"

"Melissa Sorenson. She was murdered about seven weeks ago."

Omer frowned. "Murdered? Hell! That's awful! But what does that have to do with me?"

Zane eyed the man who sat across from him coolly. "You tell us."

When the tiniest flicker of movement caught Zane's attention he tensed and focused all his concentration on Demir. He studied the man for any other sign of discomfort or guilt, but caught nothing more. Omer faced him with another irritatingly pleasant smile.

"I've already told you, Detectives. I've never heard of Melissa Sorensen. I don't have a clue who she is. As for who and why she was murdered, I don't know what you want me to say. I've never met the woman. She's a stranger to me."

Zane kept his gaze steady on Demir. "What about Mackenzie Callaway? Do you know him?"

At last, Zane managed to elicit strong emotion from the slick-looking businessman. Omer's jaw tightened and his face filled with anger. A moment later, as if by magic, the tension in the man's expression disappeared and was replaced with its previous pleasant countenance, leaving Zane to wonder if he'd imagined the dark emotion from seconds before.

"Mac Callaway? Well, that's a blast from the past. We went to high school together. Randwick North. But I'm sure you know all this. That's why you're here, isn't it? You've already spoken to Mac Callaway about me."

Zane nodded. "Yes, along with Jessica Wolfe. You remember her, don't you?"

Omer smiled fondly. "Jessie Wolfe and I were friends in high school. We were in the same year. We lost touch after we graduated. How is she?"

"You should know better than we do. You met with her a couple of weeks ago, didn't you?"

Omer nodded slowly. "Yes, that's right. So I did. The meeting slipped my mind."

Willie sat forward and frowned. "You mean to tell me you haven't seen this woman since high school and suddenly you meet up again and the meeting completely slips your mind? What's wrong with you, man? Don't you have eyes? She's the hottest thing I've seen outside of the catwalk. It's a meeting I sure as hell wouldn't forget."

A faint blush stained the high cheekbones on Demir's face. Reference to Jessie Wolfe or being called out by Whitehouse made him uncomfortable. *Interesting.* Zane tucked the information away for further consideration.

"You're right," Demir conceded, and an embarrassed expression filled his face. "Of course I remember Jessie. She's a hard woman to forget. Like you said, Detective. Sizzling hot."

"Were you two an item in high school?" Zane asked.

Omer shook his head, his expression now filled with regret. "No, there was nothing like that between us. We were just friends who happened to spend time together while we were on the debating team."

"So you weren't interested in her?" Willie asked.

"God, yes! Of course I was interested, along with other every other boy I knew. It was just that she had eyes only for Mac Callaway. No one else stood a chance."

"That must've been hard," Zane persisted.

Omer shrugged. "It was high school. It was what it was. Don't tell me you never had a crush on a girl in high school, one that wasn't returned?"

Zane nodded. "Of course I did."

"And how did *you* deal with it?" Omer challenged.

Zane kept his gaze steady on Omer's face. "I

eventually got over the girl in question and moved on. I fell in love with someone else."

Demir nodded approvingly. "There you go. The same thing happened to me."

Zane nodded. "Yes, so we heard. Jessie told us about your crush on Janice Scott. In fact, the way Jessie tells it, you were in love with the girl."

A shadow passed across Demir's face along with anger and pain. *Interesting.* After all these years, something told Zane this powerful and charismatic man was still in love with her – a dead woman.

Omer ran a hand across his face. "I'm not sure why I told Jessie that. She must have caught me in a weak moment. Not that it matters. It's true. I was in love with Janice Scott in high school, even though she was way out of my league. I guess a boy can't help dreaming, right?"

Zane nodded and pretended to understand. "Of course. It was like that with me. There's no fun in loving someone who doesn't love you back."

He and Omer shared a look. Zane felt a burst of satisfaction. The man believed he had found common ground with him, like they were kindred spirits. Omer might just let down his guard. Zane pressed home his advantage.

"That's an interesting cravat you're wearing," Zane commented. "I saw your picture in the *Architectural Digest* magazine in the waiting area. Is it your thing, wearing cravats?"

Omer glanced down at his neck cloth with a half-embarrassed smile. He touched the soft fabric almost reflexively and nodded. "I guess so. My father is a Shia Muslim. Wearing a turban is a religious observance. He wears one even now, in Australia. I prefer something less...divisive and let's admit, a whole lot fancier. I've found a cravat serves my purposes better. Besides, it goes with my suit, don't you think?"

Omer the proud peacock had surfaced and Zane played right along. "Yes, of course it does. It's totally unique and gives you the air of a wealthy and debonair gentlemen. I like it. I also like your suit. I wish I could afford a suit like that."

Omer preened. "This suit set me back several thousand dollars, but it was worth it, don't you think?" He brushed away an imaginary piece of lint and then offered Zane a smile.

Zane smiled back enthusiastically. "Absolutely. It suits you. Tell me more about your penchant for cravats. Do you tie them yourself, or does someone else do it for you?"

Omer's smile widened. "My manservant tried hard to learn the technique, but he was absolutely hopeless. Eventually, I gave up on him. I tie them all myself."

He said it with such pride. Zane nodded in approval. "You're very good at it."

Omer continued. "My father drummed it into me from a very young age... About working hard to get somewhere in life. He was convinced that if you worked hard enough, you'd get everything you wanted. Of course, it doesn't always work out that way."

"Not a bad philosophy to live by, though" Zane commented. "How did it turn out for your father?"

"I don't know. I haven't spoken to him for years. You'd have to ask him."

"Why doesn't he work for you?" Zane asked casually.

Omer shrugged. "The whole father-son thing is overrated. Besides, he'd rather work on his own."

"With someone else, you mean," Zane added.

Anger flashed in Omer's eyes. "If you say so," he replied through the slightest of clenched teeth.

"I don't have to say so. I did a bit of a background check. It was easy to discover your father works for another company. Blackwood Stone Construction, right? Some might call them your competition."

The anger that had glinted in Omer's eyes now flashed across his face. "Competition?" he sneered. "Not likely. They're tiny tadpoles in a large pond. No one can get close to me. I own the show. I own the majority of concrete trucks in the city. Anyone who wants to build anything in this city must come to me."

Zane regarded the man steadily. "It must be very gratifying to know you have so much control over other people's lives," he said softly, baiting Omer.

Omer leaned forward with a menacing glint in his eyes. "You have no idea."

With an effort, Zane held the other man's gaze. It was as if the slick and charming businessman had been replaced by a hardened street fighter who meant business. As if nothing and no one would stand in the way of getting what he wanted.

Still, Zane hadn't gotten to where he was in the

police service by being intimidated by every thug who came along. When he spoke again, his voice was laced with steel. "Where were you on the night of July sixth?"

Once again, anger flared to life behind Omer's eyes. The man did an admirable job of hiding it beneath a casual voice.

"I have no idea. I'd have to consult my diary. What day of the week was it?"

"A Thursday," Willie replied.

Omer made a show of reaching for a leather-bound diary that sat in one corner of his desk. He flicked back pages until he came to the one he sought. "Thursday, July sixth. I had a meeting with a fellow businessman. We talked about the state of Sydney's building industry."

"What's his name?" Zane asked.

"Joe DeMarco."

Zane wrote down the name in his notepad. He looked back at Omer. "Do you have a number where he can be reached?"

Omer rattled off a cell phone number and Zane recorded the details. He then looked back at Omer. "What time did you finish your meeting?"

Omer paused. "I think we left the restaurant about eight o'clock. I'm not exactly sure. I didn't realize it would be important."

"Where did you go then?" Willie asked.

"I went home. It had been a long day. I wanted an early night."

"Where do you live?" Zane asked.

"I have a condo in the city, within walking distance from here," Omer replied.

"Address?" Zane pressed.

Omer supplied it in a bored tone, as if the information was of no consequence.

"What time did you get home?" Zane asked.

"We had met at Fat Tony's – a bar and pizza place on Bathurst Street. Instead of taking a cab, I chose to walk there and back. The night was cold, but the wind had died down when I headed home. The air was refreshing. Besides, I needed the time to think. I guess it was close to half-past eight when I arrived home."

"Can anyone verify that?" Zane asked.

"I'm not sure. There might've been people walking past."

"Do you live alone?" Zane asked.

Omer nodded. "Yes."

"Did you speak to anyone else that night?" Willie asked.

"No. I came home, took a shower and went to bed. That was it."

"We'll need to speak to Joe DeMarco," Willie said.

Omer nodded. "By all means," he murmured. "I have nothing to hide."

"Let's talk about Janice Scott again," Zane said, watching Omer closely.

Omer merely shrugged that time. "What about her?"

"You said you were in love with her, but that it wasn't reciprocated. That must've been tough."

"Yes, Detective. I thought we already established that. Haven't you also been involved with someone who didn't love you back?" A derisive grin tugged at the corners of Omer's lips. Zane remained silent, refusing to be riled by the knowing look in Demir's gaze.

Instead, he cleared his throat and continued. "Did you ever approach Janice and tell her how you felt?"

The tiniest narrowing of Demir's eyes was the only indication that he'd even heard the question. Zane waited for the man to reply. When he didn't, he prompted him again.

"Did you ever tell Janice Scott that you were in love with her?"

Demir's eyes now flashed with anger. "Yes, Detective. I did. Did you ever get the courage to tell *your* girl how you felt?"

Zane stared at Demir. "This isn't about me, Omer. So, you told Janice you were in love with her. What did she say?"

Omer made a sound of irritation in his throat. "Where are we going with this, Detective? We both know Janice was raped and murdered and that I had nothing to do with it. The police found the man who was responsible. He was another boy in her class. He was tried and convicted and as far as I know he's still warming his ass in jail. What does any of this have to do with me?"

Zane nodded. "You're right. Wesley Parker was convicted of those crimes. But here's the thing, Omer. Recent evidence has come to light. It's clear a mistake was made with the DNA sample submitted by Parker all those years ago. It turns out he's innocent of any wrongdoing." Zane's gaze drilled into Omer's. "Do you understand what I'm saying? He didn't rape and murder Janice Scott. Someone else did."

Zane hoped to get a reaction out of Demir, and he was in luck. Underneath the fake tan, Demir paled. The tiniest frisson of fear crept across his face and then disappeared, artfully replaced by a tight smile.

"My sympathies to Wesley Parker," Omer replied. "That poor bastard has spent the past twenty years in jail. I wouldn't like to be you guys, explaining that fuckup to the powers that be." His lip curled up in a sneer.

Zane's fists clenched beneath the desk, but he kept his voice steady as he replied.

"If it turns out there's been an injustice, you're right. And then we'd expect there'll be hell to pay when Parker finds out. Nothing can bring back those twenty years, but I'm sure his lawyers will do their best to see that he's adequately compensated – as he should be if he's innocent. In the meantime, we have another unsolved murder on our hands." He paused and then continued in a quiet conversational voice.

"Tell me more about you and Mac Callaway."

Anger flared once again in Omer's eyes. "Mac Callaway is a dreamer. He's kidding himself. He sees himself as a true competitor, as if we're on the same level. Ha! What a joke! He has no idea! I could crush his little business over breakfast if I wanted to."

"I don't know about that, Omer," Zane replied in a casual voice. "I did a little background research on Callaway, too. He's headed Forbes list of most successful businessmen two years in a row. That has to mean something. How many times have you made the list?"

Omer's jaw clenched and his eyes turned dark. Zane's comment had hit a raw nerve.

"What the hell would I care about that?" Omer snarled.

Zane offered a nonchalant shrug. "I don't know, Omer. You tell me. I just figured a man such as you who takes such pride in his achievements might want to receive some public recognition. There's no better way than being recognized in *Forbes*. According to the magazine, Mackenzie Callaway was the most exciting, successful, up-and-coming entrepreneur in the Asia-Pacific. That's a fair accolade, isn't it?"

A muscle at the side of Omer's mouth began to tick. Zane continued to eye the man, hoping for an unguarded moment when Omer's anger got the better of him. He didn't have to wait long.

"Mackenzie Callaway was born with the proverbial silver spoon in his mouth," Omer spat. "He never knew what it was like to struggle. To come to a new country, unable to speak English, not to have a single friend. To have parents who wanted the best for me and worked sixteen hours a day to make that happen. Mine were never there when I got home from school because they were always at work.

"Mac Callaway's father inherited his wealth from a father who inherited it from his father. Old money that's been handed down, all the way down to Mac. He makes out that he's a self-made man." Omer's lips twisted into a sneer. "Self-made, my ass."

"So his father handed him the construction company that bears his name? I thought his father was a doctor?"

"I didn't say old man Callaway handed Mac the company, but by helping him to finance his way in, he might as well have."

"How do you know Callaway Senior financed his son into business?"

"It's an educated guess, Detective."

"Any proof?" Zane pressed.

Omer gave him the death stare. A lesser man might have felt intimidated. Zane stared blandly right back.

"No, Detective. Only what I know up here." Omer tapped the side of his head and his derision was there for all to see. So... It was obvious Demir suffered from an acute case of jealousy as far as Zane was concerned. He decided to put his theory to the test.

"You're jealous of Mac Callaway, aren't you? You're jealous that he came from a wealthy family, that life came easy for him. He's good-looking, fit and athletic and he was captain of the football team. No doubt he had his pick of girlfriends. Is that where all this animosity stems from? Was Janice in love with him? Is that why she turned you down?"

Fury erupted on Omer's face and he pushed back his chair and leaped to his feet. He leaned over his desk threateningly. A pulse was visible in his neck. His face was red and his breath came fast. He glared at Zane and opened his mouth, as if he were about to speak.

Then, with what seemed a mammoth effort, he checked himself, got himself back under control. Slowly, his breathing returned to normal and he returned to his seat.

Zane unclenched his fists from beneath the desk and breathed a sigh of his own. Though he could have taken Omer down if he had to, it was better that he hadn't been forced to act. It was obvious there was bad blood between Callaway and Demir. Callaway had made mention of it, but it appeared to run a whole lot deeper than even he'd mentioned.

"You provided a DNA sample to the police way back in high school," Zane commented in a deliberately casual voice.

"Yes." Omer's reply was far more cautious.

"Would you mind providing us with another? We're retesting everyone who provided samples in the Janice Scott case."

Omer eyed him distrustfully. "Why?"

"I already told you. We're now sure Wesley Parker didn't do it. We need to find out who did."

Omer looked away. "I'd rather not."

Zane frowned. "Why not? What difference does it make? You already provided us with a sample and you were cleared. Are you afraid it might not work out that way a second time? We can seek a court order, if you like."

Icy anger sparked in Demir's eyes. He stared hard at Zane. "You know, Detective, I'm about done with your questions. This interview has come to an end. If you have any more questions, you'll have to speak to my lawyer. He'll be handling anything you need to know from here on. Okay?"

Zane nodded and slowly got to his feet. Willie did the same. "Fair enough. Well, thanks for taking the time to meet with us, Mr Demir. We sure appreciate it."

Omer growled an unintelligible response.

Zane and Willie let themselves out.

CHAPTER 17

From his position on his wide balcony, Mac stared across the harbor at the sparkling Pacific Ocean. It was another beautiful winter's day. The sun had risen and filled the sky with bright light and the water with even brighter sparkles. He glanced down at his phone and felt the familiar surge of dread in his gut. There was no putting it off any longer. He had to call Jarrod Harris and find out what the hell had gone on. He was no longer confident he could trust Steve's version of events.

With a sigh, he scrolled through his contacts and found Harris' number. He wasn't even sure the man would take his call. After all, Mac had fired him. To his relief, Jarrod answered on the third ring.

"Mac. What can I do for you?" The tone was short but polite. Mac got right to the point.

"I was wondering if you could tell me about what happened with that steel order?"

"I thought you'd already made your mind up about that? Didn't you speak to Steve?"

"Yes, but now I want to speak to you."

"Why?"

Mac gritted his teeth. "It doesn't matter why. Now, will you tell me what happened, or not?"

"I put that order in exactly like Steve told me to. They were his measurements. All I did was text them through."

"Are you sure you didn't confuse the numbers? Those measurements were wrong."

Harris made a sound of disgust in the back of his throat. "Of course I didn't confuse the numbers. What the hell do you take me for? I merely forwarded Steve's text to the supplier. There was no way the mistake came from me."

There was a sinking feeling in Mac's gut. His hand tightened around the phone. He drew in a breath and then eased it out and finally spoke again.

"Thanks for taking my call, Jarrod. I'm sorry I treated you so badly. If you still want a job, it's yours."

"That would be good, thanks. Work's scarce. I need the money." Jarrod's voice was gruff.

Mac was filled with guilt and made a mental note to give Harris a pay raise. "I'll see you in the morning, then," he said and then ended the call.

Mac tossed his phone down on the lounger and clenched his hands around the balcony rail. He couldn't believe Steve had lied to him. Again. His foreman was losing his grip. Something was definitely wrong. Whether it was the medication or lack thereof or something else, Mac needed to get to the bottom of it. Though Steve was his foreman, Mac no longer trusted anything he said. The situation was impossible. Not so long ago he'd considered taking him on as a partner. Now it was clear Steve would have to go.

The very thought filled him with dread. He looked forward to the conversation like he'd look forward to a root canal. Still, it needed to be done, and soon. Just not yet. Right now he had a date with Jessie and no one was going to interfere with that.

The late winter sunshine was warm enough that Jessie ditched her jacket the minute they reached the picnic spot. The botanical gardens were littered with people who likely had the same idea. It was a beautiful mid-August day. She looked at Mac, laden down with the picnic basket, and giggled. He gave her a wink. She felt like a teenager skipping school. It was just past midday on Wednesday afternoon. She couldn't remember the last time she'd taken time off work for her own pleasure. It felt wrong, but also exhilarating.

"This was such a good idea," she said to Mac.

He rolled his eyes, but a smile tugged at his lips. "And to think how hard a time you gave me when I first suggested it," he teased.

"It's all right for you," she replied. "You're self-employed. You keep your own hours. Unfortunately, I'm accountable to a boss."

"A boss who knows you work harder than any

other lawyer in the building," Mac finished. "What did he say when you asked for the afternoon off?"

"He said with the amount of hours I do each week, I deserve a day off every now and then," she admitted sheepishly. "It didn't hurt that I've already reached my monthly budget target and we're only three quarters of the way through."

"I wish my employees worked as hard as you. I'd put you on my payroll any day."

She smiled and lifted an eyebrow in silent query. "And what would I do?"

"Whatever I feel needs to be done at the time." His voice lowered to a husky growl, thick with innuendo. "I'm sure I could keep you busy."

A surge of heat rushed through her. Dammit, he only had to look at her and she was a mess of want and need. All she could see was Mac spread across his bed sheets, naked and aroused.

She hid her heated thoughts with a laugh and he joined in. The sun glinted off his tousled, beach-blond hair. Light twinkled in his clear green eyes. She was reminded just how beautiful he was. Inside and out, from top to bottom. There was no denying it. Mackenzie Callaway was a perfect specimen of a man.

She thought about his declaration of love. They hadn't talked about it and Jessie knew exactly why. At the time, she'd been shocked speechless. She'd eventually fallen asleep. When she'd woken the next morning, she took her cue from Mac who acted as if it hadn't happened. As if they'd done nothing more than spend a night of mutual pleasure in each other's arms. It was as if he'd forgotten he'd ever mentioned the 'L' word. So she followed suit.

That was hard because she'd known for some time that she still loved him, had always loved him. Twenty years and a handful of other boyfriends later hadn't changed that. *So why hadn't she told him how she felt? What held her back?*

She wished she knew.

Mac spread the red-and-blue tartan picnic blanket on a patch of green grass beneath the shade of a huge Moreton Bay fig tree. He set the picnic basket down not far away and then stretched out on the blanket with a sigh.

Jessie glanced across at him, surprised. "That sounds a bit heavy. Is anything wrong?"

Mac grimaced. "No, of course not. Everything's... fine."

Jessie sat down and scooted close. "You don't sound too convincing."

Mac looked up at her. "It's a beautiful day. I'm spending time with my favorite girl. I don't want to spoil it by talking about things in my life that are causing me grief."

Jessie's concern ratcheted up another notch. "What are you talking about? Has there been a development in the case?"

Mac sighed again and shook his head. "No. It has nothing to do with the police investigation."

"Then, what?"

He regarded her somberly. "Are you sure you want to know?"

The serious tone in his voice ramped up her anxiety. Still, she wanted to help him through whatever it was causing him concern.

"Of course. I'm here for you, Mac. Talk to me."

Mac pulled himself up into a sitting position and draped his hands over his knees. He stared off into the distance, as if trying to work out what to say. Finally, he spoke.

"It's Steve. I'm worried about him."

Jessie started in surprise. "Steve… Why?"

Mac told her about the recent goings on, including the delayed orders, wrong measurements, the rifle.

"It's so weird. I always knew he had issues. No one serves in Afghanistan without it leaving some effect on the psyche, but he's been getting treatment, taking meds and up until recently he was a model employee. The two of us have worked well together for a decade. Hell, recently I even thought about offering him a partnership in the business. Now it seems like he's doing his best to sabotage everything I do. I just don't understand it."

Jessie had stuck on the rifle in Steve's car and felt a stirring of disquiet. "Has he ever brought a gun to work before?"

"No, of course not. He told me he'd forgotten to take it out of his truck."

"Do you believe him?"

"Yes. I guess. Hell, I don't know. Something's changed. He just doesn't seem like the same guy I used to know. I'm worried he's gone off his medication and something's going on in his head – flashbacks or something. I don't know."

The frustration in Mac's voice tugged at her

heart. She understood how difficult it must be for Mac to have his foreman morph into someone he no longer recognized or trusted. And then she thought of what else had gone wrong in Mac's life recently and her heart skipped a beat.

"You don't think he had anything to do with Melissa's murder, do you?"

Mac's eyes widened in shock. "No way! Steve might be acting a little strange, but there's no way he's capable of doing something like that."

"None of us know what we're capable of until we're put to the test," she replied quietly.

Mac shook his head slowly back and forth, his expression still filled with disbelief. "Not Steve. No, I won't believe he killed Melissa. It's not possible."

"Why? Because you don't want it to be? How well did he know her?"

"I don't know. Not very well. He knew her, of course. She often came out to the job sites, especially toward the end of completion. It was her job to market them and find buyers. He saw her almost as often as I did during those times."

Jessie regarded him solemnly. Words bubbled up in her throat. She wondered how Mac would react to them.

"Do you think he could have been the man she was having an affair with?"

Mac reeled backwards like he'd been shot. He stared at her, aghast. "No way! No way in this world! Steve and I are not only work colleagues, we're friends. There's no way he'd do that to me."

"Okay, okay," Jessie murmured. "I'm sure you're right. Have you spoken to Steve about what's been happening?"

"No, but I'm going to. This can't go on."

"He needs help."

Mac sighed. "Yeah. Let's hope he's willing to accept that." Settling himself back down on the picnic rug, he stretched out and stacked his hands behind his head. The wide expanse of blue sky was dotted with fluffy white clouds.

"It's such a nice day. Let's not spoil it with any more talk of Steve. I'll deal with it, I promise. Right now, I just want to enjoy being with you," he told her.

Jessie regarded him solemnly. She wanted so much to tell him how she felt, how she'd always felt. Especially now, when he was feeling so low. Instead, she reached for his hand and squeezed it.

Mac closed his eyes on another quiet sigh.

Jessie slid her hand out of his and rummaged in the picnic basket. Not quite knowing what was behind Mac's impulsive suggestion that they both take the afternoon off, she'd been too nervous to eat breakfast and had left for the office early in order to get on top of things before she left for the day. Now it had gone past noon. Though the nerves still coiled in her stomach at the thought of spending a whole afternoon with Mac, her hunger couldn't be ignored any longer.

"What did you pack in here?" she murmured. "This basket's filled to the brim."

"All the things I thought you might like," Mac replied, his voice lazy with sleep.

She removed the cloth that covered the basket

and gasped in delight at what she found: three different cheeses, including her favorite Brie. Fig paste, quince jam, sea salt crackers. A plate of wafer-thin cucumber and egg sandwiches. And then there were the desserts – tiny handmade chocolates, each one different from the last. A bowl of juicy, ripe strawberries. A dish of clotted cream. Grapes and cherries and orange slices and right at the bottom were two glasses and a bottle of champagne. He'd thought of everything.

She glanced across at him and her heart swelled with tenderness. "When did you find time to do this? We only made the arrangements last night."

Mac opened one eye and looked at her. "That's for me to know and for you to find out," he teased. "I'll have you know, I'm *very* resourceful."

He eyed her knowingly and she blushed. The things he'd done to her during the night in his condo... It was as if he'd tried his best to make up for lost time.

Days later she was still a little sore from the rasp of his stubble on the more sensitive parts of her skin. Strawberries and fresh cream had been involved then, too. Seeing them in the basket was a vivid reminder of all that they'd shared and the uninhibited behavior she'd exhibited. Mac didn't seem to mind. She'd never been so uninhibited with any of her previous lovers.

But even with the men she'd been in steady relationships with, she'd never felt so free to express herself sexually the way she had with Mac. It was as if he'd pressed a button inside her that dissolved all of her inhibitions and turned her into a reckless, wanton ball of passion and need. She was seventeen again, embarking on sex for the first time. She was with the man she loved, giving him her everything. Just the thought of all they'd done to each other sent a wave of heat spreading across her cheeks.

Mac's expression grew even more knowing. His eyes darkened to a deep sea green. He shifted closer to where she sat. It was still officially winter, but the sun had the strength of spring. She'd chosen to wear a long-sleeved, magenta-colored knitted dress that fell to the top of her knees. She'd kicked off her high heels the moment they reached the grass and had carried them dangling from her fingers.

As if it were the most natural thing in the world, Mac reached out and languidly stroked her bare thigh where her dress had ridden up a couple inches.

She gasped from the light touch and her pulse immediately went into overdrive. His fingers were warm on her skin. All the while he watched her, a little smile played around his lips. She shook her head at him.

He knew exactly what he was doing. Driving her wild. Reminding her of all that they'd shared in his king-size bed with the magnificent Pacific Ocean as their backdrop.

His fingers moved in ever increasing circles as his hand made its way under her dress and further up her thigh. Excitement flooded through her the closer he got to the juncture between her thighs.

She wanted to squeeze them together in an effort to stem his progress and her aching need, but instead she remained as still as she could and tried to tell herself she could ignore it.

And then his hand slid between her thighs and his fingers stole inside her panties. A moment later, they were stroking her slick and heated flesh.

"It's only gone midday and already you're wet," he murmured. "What were you thinking about in your office while you were putting things in order for the day? I hope you were thinking about me."

His fingers continued to weave their magic. Jessie groaned. Her heart beat so hard and fast, she heard the rush of blood in her ears. As well, blood rushed to other regions and her clit now throbbed with need. Swollen and aching, she wanted nothing more than for him to satisfy her craving for him.

Though no one else was about, he moved even closer and shielded her body from view with his own. His fingers continued their wondrous stroking. She burned from the inside out. She'd never felt so wanton. They were in public, albeit concealed by the shadows cast by the branches of a centuries-old fig tree.

"It's all right, Jessie. Let yourself go. Nobody else can see. It's just you and me. Does that feel good?"

He ground his palm against her center and she swallowed back a moan. Desire built to a fever pitch. All she could think of was reaching the peak and crashing over the other side. Whimpers of need escaped her tightly closed lips as she moved against Mac's hand. His fingers stroked deep inside her, matching her rhythm.

And then she was there, at the pinnacle, gasping with relief. With her breath coming fast, the tension eased and she slowly drifted back to earth. She opened her eyes reluctantly, to find Mac grinning from ear to ear.

"Good?" His voice was husky, gravelly.

"Very good." She grinned.

He smiled back at her and his expression was filled with such tenderness and love it snatched her breath away. She opened her mouth to speak. "Mac, I—"

"It's okay, Jessie. I understand," he interrupted. "I don't expect you to feel the same way I do. You loved me once, but it's been twenty years. You moved on. All I hope is that someday you might come to love me again.

"I'm not a very patient man, but I promise you, when it comes to you, I will be. For years after I graduated high school, I searched for what we had. I dated too many women to count. None of them mattered. None of them touched my heart and soul like you did. We were only kids, but what we had was special. I know that now because, despite all the women I dated, slept with, lived with, none of them came close to you. So, take all the time you want. I can wait as long as you need as long as you're willing to move in that direction and give us a chance."

She smiled at him with all the love in her heart. "That's the thing, Mac. I don't need time to know how I feel about you. I... I've been in love with you most of my life. After high school, I forced myself to forget you. I dated other men. I had relationships."

His eyes darkened with possessiveness. His reaction pleased her. She liked knowing that he was jealous of the other men she'd had in her life, just like she was jealous of the other women who'd shared his.

"But it didn't seem to matter who the guy was, how nice he was, how rich he was, how much he made me laugh. He wasn't *you*. He wasn't Mac Callaway. You've been my one and only true love, then and now."

A smile as wide as the Grand Canyon, filled with incredulity, split across Mac's face. He stared at her with eyes that were huge with astonishment.

"Do you really mean that?" he whispered in disbelief.

She nodded and smiled. "Yes, I really mean that." Framing his face in her hands, she leaned forward and kissed him softly, tenderly on the mouth. She pulled back and stared into his beautiful green gaze.

"I love you, Mac Callaway. I always have. I always will."

Zane stretched his arms over his head and groaned. His back ached and his neck was sore. His butt was numb from sitting. He glanced at the clock on the far wall of the squad room. It was almost seven. Time to go home. It had been a long day and he was no closer to solving the riddle of who killed Melissa Sorenson.

They'd already eliminated Parker. That left Callaway and Demir. Zane had checked Demir's alibi. Joe DeMarco had verified much of what Demir had told them. He met Demir for dinner at Fat Tony's. They went their separate ways a little after eight. Demir didn't say where he was headed, but he turned in the direction of home. DeMarco headed off in the opposite direction and that had been that.

Still, there had been plenty of time for Demir to murder Sorenson. Demir had no alibi for later except to say he went home. Callaway had told them he and Sorenson argued a little after nine. Neighbors confirmed that they'd heard the couple arguing around that time. Callaway said he left his apartment shortly afterwards and didn't return until the early hours of the morning. By then, according to Callaway, Sorenson was gone.

Could Demir be Loverboy from the texts? Was he the missing link? Was that why he was so reticent to provide a fresh DNA sample? There could be all sorts of reasons why someone refused to provide a DNA sample that could eliminate them as a suspect to a crime, but one of the main ones the sample collection was refused was because they had something to hide. The fact that a mistake had been made that affected one of Demir's school friends so many years ago could explain his skittishness, but Callaway went through the same experience and suffered from no such reticence. It was more than interesting and further strengthened

Zane's resolve to look closer at Omer Demir.

If Callaway told the truth and his girlfriend had left the building somewhere between nine and one in the morning, there was plenty of time for her to meet up with her lover, Omer Demir, and for him to murder her. That's if Demir was her lover. So far, they had no evidence of that.

Zane frowned. He might not have anything yet to connect Demir to Sorenson, but he wasn't prepared to dismiss the man. There was something about him that didn't sit right. And that feeling he'd overlooked something was like a burr under Zane's skin. He wouldn't stop worrying at it until he'd managed to pull it free and into the light of day. Only then would he be at peace.

"What do you think about the Turk?" Willie asked, as if reading Zane's mind.

"Definitely suspicious, but so far we haven't found anything that proves he even knew Melissa, let alone caused her death. The only connection between them is Mackenzie Callaway."

Willie nodded. "There's plenty of circumstantial evidence linking Callaway to the crime, but..."

"Too much. He's an intelligent man. Leaving the body for weeks on his property when he had lots of time to move it before it was discovered... It just doesn't feel right to me. It's not likely, in my book, that he's guilty," Zane finished.

Willie nodded again. "I agree."

Zane sighed in relief. "I'm glad we're on the same page, that it's not just my gut telling me Callaway isn't our man."

"You're not alone, let me assure you. If I had to

guess, I'd put my money on Demir. I didn't like that arrogant prick one bit and that cravat shit he threw our way is just downright weird. And too coincidental..."

Zane clenched his jaw in frustration and ran his hands through his hair. "There must be some connection to Mac's ex!" He groaned. "We need to find out what it was."

"I've been thinking," Willie said. "A man as rich as Omer Demir must live in a pretty posh building."

"You're right. He told us he had a condo in the city."

"Exactly. And what do all those fancy condominiums have in common?"

A frisson of excitement went through Zane. His gut clenched the way it always did when he was on the verge of a breakthrough in a case. He stared at Willie with growing anticipation.

"All those fancy condominiums have top notch security systems, including CCTV cameras," Zane said quietly, as if to say it aloud would jinx the possibility.

Willie yelped and punched the air with his fist. "Go straight to the top of the class, Detective Sullivan."

Zane grinned. "You're a legend, Whitehouse. I'll call the building superintendent first thing in the morning to see if he has the tapes from the night of July sixth. With a bit of luck, we might have that footage before the week is out."

"Oh, yeah. Come to Papa, baby. We're right here waiting for you."

CHAPTER 18

A knock on the site office door snagged Mac's attention. He looked up from the paperwork spread across his desk and saw Steve standing in the opening. Determined to do what needed to be done, Mac steeled himself for the upcoming confrontation.

"Steve, thanks for dropping in. We need to talk."

Steve sat in the chair opposite him. The man's rough gray stubble had morphed into a beard. His eyes were bloodshot and there was an overall air of neglect surrounding him. Mac wondered how long the slide downhill had been going on. He'd been so busy and distracted with his own problems, he hadn't noticed. He felt badly about that.

"What's this about, Mac? I have contractors waiting for instructions out there. I need to get back."

"Sure, Steve. I understand. This won't take long." As succinctly as he could, Mac outlined his concerns and in particular, his shock that Steve had been doing all he could to sabotage their progress on this job. From the stunned look of surprise on Steve's face, Mac realized the man had been clueless that Mac had caught on. A few moments later, the surprise dissolved and was replaced with anger.

"You sanctimonious prick! How dare you sit there and judge me!" Steve spat.

Mac stared at him in shock. "What the hell are you talking about, Steve? *You* did this! I didn't. Now, I understand you had a tough time back in Afghanistan and anyone who's served their country like you have deserves the utmost gratitude and respect, but this can't go on, mate. You need help. A change of medication. Therapy. I don't know. Whatever it takes to get you well again. I'll cover all the costs. You need to take some time off and get yourself sorted out."

Steve's lip curled up in disgust. "Oh, yeah, typical Callaway response. Pull out your checkbook. That makes all the nasties go away, doesn't it? There's nothing like a bit of cash in the right hands for the authorities to look away."

Mac shook his head in confusion. "I don't have the faintest idea what you're talking about, Steve."

"Of course you do!" Steve cried. "Don't tell me you've forgotten Janice?"

"What does Janice have to do with anything?" Mac asked, astonished by the remark.

A vein popped out on Steve's forehead. His breath came fast. "She was my sister!" he shouted. "And you murdered her!"

Mac reeled back in shock. "No! I had no idea she was your sister. I-I'm sorry that happened to her. But it wasn't me, Steve. I only ever tried to help her. I had nothing to do with her rape and murder."

"Because your rich daddy paid off the police, that's why! They mixed up the DNA samples, put the wrong label on the bottle. Who the hell knows? I visited that poor bastard, Wes Parker, in jail. He told me it was you."

Once again, Mac was flooded with shock. The bombshells just kept coming. He shook his head and tried to clear the turmoil of thoughts that threatened to overwhelm him.

"I don't know why Wes told you that, Steve. I swear to you, it isn't true. Janice and I were friends. I helped her when things were...tough at home. That was all."

Tears of rage filled Steve's eyes. He pushed away and stood. At the same time, he reached into his back pocket and pulled out a gun. He waved it in front of Mac.

Mac's blood ran cold. It was one thing to try and deal with Steve's anger and pain while he was unarmed. It was quite another to do it in the face of a gun.

"What are you doing, Steve? Put the gun down. Please. There's no need for this."

"I should have paid that thug to beat you to death, that's what I should have done. Instead, he just roughed you up."

Mac stared at him. His fingers went instinctively to his still-tender bottom lip.

"Do you mean to say it was *you* behind that attack?"

"Yeah," Steve spat. "I was so furious. You were living your perfect life, getting away with murder, while my sister rots away in the ground. You killed her! And now I'm going to kill you!"

He lunged at Mac, but ended up catching his hip against the desk. It was all the distraction Mac needed. He hurled himself at Steve, taking care to tighten his fingers around the wrist that held the gun.

"Drop it," he demanded. When Steve refused to comply, Mac tightened his grip.

"Fuck! You're going to break my wrist!" Steve screamed.

"Drop the gun, Steve!"

With a cry of desolation, Steve released the weapon. It fell to the floor. To Mac's relief, the gun didn't discharge. As if all the fight had gone out of him, Steve's body folded in on itself. Mac released his hold on him and the broken man crumpled into a heap on the floor.

Mac bent down and picked up the gun and moved it well out of reach. His hand trembled with delayed shock. He couldn't believe what had just happened. Steve was far sicker than he'd thought and his problems even more complex. Saddened, he pulled out his phone and called the police.

Omer Demir was angry. In fact, he was more than angry. He was furious. He'd been that way ever since he'd had the visit from the cops. They'd asked him about Melissa, which was bad enough. What was worse were the memories they'd dredged up of Janice.

Another wave of pain and fury washed over him.

Janice. The light and love of his life. All that beautiful blond hair. Those long tanned limbs. A body just built for loving. She looked like the sweetest woman on earth. *How was he to know that underneath that veneer of stunning good looks was a woman with a soul filled with spitefulness and hate?*

It served her right to end up the way she had. Worm food.

And now the police had dropped by and dredged up that awful time all over again. What was even more alarming was that they hadn't seemed to believe his stock standard, well-rehearsed answers. The tall, good-looking one had definitely regarded him with suspicion.

What should he do?

His first instinct had been to run. He'd even half-packed a suitcase, found his passport and was online booking a plane ticket when he came to his senses. Running was the last thing he should do. Running made him look guilty. Police were inherently suspicious. It came with the job. If no evidence linking him to either crime surfaced, their suspicions would move elsewhere. Anywhere, but toward him. Preferably to Mac Callaway. After all, that had been the plan.

It had worked so well the first time – until it didn't. Mac Callaway was supposed to take the fall. Omer had left Janice in Mac's bed. Surely it wasn't too hard for the police to draw the only logical conclusion and put the man behind bars.

But it hadn't happened that way. Though Omer had been disappointed that Mac didn't get what he deserved, he was just as relieved he'd gotten away with the crime. Things hadn't worked out so well for Wes, but they'd worked out perfectly for him.

He'd left high school determined to destroy the man's life, the man responsible for what happened to Janice. Mac Callaway. One way or the other. First he'd tried to do it through business. It was no accident Omer owned most of the concrete suppliers in Sydney. It was one thing every builder needed, Mac Callaway included. It had been fun messing around with Mac's orders, causing immeasurable delays, but it hadn't kept the man out of business. It rubbed him the wrong way that Callaway had made *Forbes* magazine rich list, not once, but twice.

When they spoke last, the detective had taken great pleasure in shoving that bit of information in Omer's face.

The detective's manner seemed to say, *take that, you grubby little immigrant,*

Or maybe Omer was much too sensitive to slights he received from others. After all, he'd been the recipient of cruel jokes and innuendo since he'd arrived in this country with his parents so many years ago. Whenever he heard people talking about how multicultural Australia was and how they welcomed foreigners with open arms, he'd quietly scoff and jeer. Australians were welcoming all right, but only to those who were born here or those with lots of money.

Immigrants like him who came with an accent and who were awkward in manner and speech were shunned and teased and tormented. Just like Janice had done to him...

Well, he showed her.

In the end, he'd had the last laugh. She was dead and he was richer than he'd ever dreamed. Women clamored to be seen with him. Business rivals and politicians wanted to be his friend. All except Mac Callaway and those in the world he walked in.

His nemesis. Then and now. Some things never changed.

Omer's phone rang, interrupting the turmoil of his thoughts. He glanced at the screen and answered it.

"What is it?" he barked.

"That load of concrete for Callaway Construction—" his foreman began.

"What about it?"

"It's ready to load. Do you want me to put it on the truck?"

"No. He's not in a hurry for it. And he's having trouble with his cash flow at the moment," Omer lied. "Leave it another week."

He punched the end button on his phone and tossed the device back in his pocket with a curse. *Mac Callaway. Mac Callaway. Mac Callaway.*

The man just wouldn't go away. It was *his* fault the cops were looking at Omer, that they had even connected him with Callaway at all. It was time to up the ante and make Callaway pay once and for all.

As an idea formed in his mind, his lips opened in a smile. Yes, that's what he needed to do. Turn up the heat on Mac Callaway, hit him where it hurt, and do something that would ensure the police looked straight back at him. That way, Omer could go about his business as usual, and with a bit of luck, this time Mac Callaway might just end up in jail. Where he belonged.

—————————

Jessie tried hard to concentrate on the witness statement in front of her, but her mind kept straying to Mac. After playing hooky from work, they'd ended up at his condo. Stretched out in the sun on lounge chairs on his balcony, she'd learned all about erotic massage. First her and then him. No inch of their skin remained untouched.

There was something to be said for coconut-scented massage oil. It had a way of driving her wild. Or maybe it was just the touch of Mac's hands, smoothing their way over her skin? The way his fingers caressed each muscle, each bone, each sinew. His hands had been everywhere at once. The memory of their afternoon of lovemaking still had the power to fill her with heat.

She crossed her legs beneath her desk and tried to focus on other things. Like the witness statement.

Brian Jefferies was the fifteen-year-old son of her boss' best friend. Jessie didn't normally represent juveniles, but her boss had come to her three days earlier and asked her for a favor. The boy had been charged with supplying prohibited drugs to his fellow students at his very expensive private school. What was more, Jefferies had a record. This wasn't the first time the kid had come before the courts on similar charges. It was going to be difficult to keep him out of jail. But her boss had full confidence in her and he'd made it clear that a promotion might just be in the wings if she managed to pull it off.

Even with the alluring possibility of a partnership, Jessie had been reluctant to take on the case. She hated putting herself under that kind of pressure. There was so many variables she couldn't control. The fact that the boy had prior drug convictions was a huge strike against his chances of staying out of jail. It didn't matter who he was or how much money his parents were prepared to pay, the judge simply wouldn't care.

Still, the lure of a promotion was too much for her to resist. It was the first time her boss had even raised the possibility. She could only hope the black cloud Alistair had cast against their family name had finally started to lift. She might not want this case, but she needed it. What was more, she needed to win.

Her long-term career at Sydney Legal depended upon it. Her boss hadn't put it in so many words, but she could read between the lines. If she failed to keep the Jefferies boy out of jail, any future promotion to partner would be next to impossible. It was clear. Failure wasn't an option.

Great. Just great.

The phone at her elbow peeled, interrupting her dismal thoughts. With a sigh, she reached over and answered it.

"Jessie Wolfe."

"Jessie, it's Margaret. I have Mac Callaway on line four."

Jessie smiled. She couldn't help it. Just the mention of his name filled her with happiness. She reached over and answered the call.

"Mac, what a lovely surprise."

"Hi, Jessie."

His subdued tone caused her to frown. "Mac? Is there anything wrong?"

His heavy sigh on the other end of the phone only served to heighten her anxiety. In broken sentences, he told her about Steve.

"Oh, my God!" she cried, shocked. "Are you all right?"

"Yes. I'm fine. The police have been here. They've taken him away. I just...I just wanted you to know."

"Oh, Mac! I can't believe it! He's Janice's *brother*? How come we never knew that?"

"He's her step-brother and he's ten years older than she was. He was serving overseas in the military while we were at school. I guess that's why we didn't know about him."

Jessie shook her head slowly, still in shock. "Do the police think he had anything to do with Melissa's murder?"

"I don't think so. The detectives that attended were from Hornsby. I don't think they knew about Melissa. I'll have to talk to Detective Sullivan and let him know."

"Is there anything I can do?"

"No, it's fine. I'll call the detective now and fill him in."

"Okay, well, let me know how it goes."

"I will."

Jessie had no sooner ended her call to Mac when Margaret buzzed her again. "Jessie, I have Omer Demir on line two."

Jessie frowned. This day was getting even stranger. *Why would Omer be calling her again?* As far as she knew, they'd already discussed and resolved his problem. Besides, the legalities concerning security cameras and the filming of employees was hardly rocket science. He could've called any lawyer in the city to help him get the same information.

Still, there was no need for her to ignore his call. After all, they were friends from school. That meant something to her.

"Thanks, Margaret. I'll take the call."

She pressed the button for line two and spoke again. "Omer, it's Jessie. How are you doing?"

"Thanks for taking my call, Jessie. I'm sure you're way past busy and have better things to do."

"Don't be silly, Omer. I always have time to talk to an old friend."

"Yes, that's what we are, aren't we?" he replied, sounding pleased. "Old friends. In fact, you were one of my *only* friends," he admitted.

Jessie blinked in surprise. Though Omer tended to be a bit of a loner at high school, she didn't think he was without friends. He always gave the appearance of being happy and stable at school. Then again, the more she thought about it, she couldn't quite recall anyone specific that he used to hang out with. She was busy with her studies and doing her best to keep her mind off Mac Callaway. She'd been in love with Mac a long time before he actually noticed her.

"I'm sorry to hear that, Omer," she said quietly and she meant it. "But it looks like you've made up for lost time. You show up with remarkable regularity in the social pages and your Facebook friends are almost rabid."

"Don't tell you've been checking up on me, Jessie?" His voice was sly and full of innuendo. He also looked pleased.

Despite herself, Jessie blushed. She was quick to reassure him. "Not in a weird way, Omer. Please don't think that. After our meeting, I was curious. That's all. I guess I wanted to know a bit more about you, see what you'd done since high school. I must admit, I'm impressed. According to my research, you're the CEO of several companies, an industry leader, no less."

He chuckled softly. "Oh, Jessie, you're way too kind. Thank you, but you shouldn't believe everything you read. Some of those journalists go a little over the top."

"You're modest, Omer. It didn't seem that way to me," she replied with a smile. And it was true. She'd searched his name on the Internet and it had come up with several hits. Like she'd said, he seemed to have an active social life and more than enough friends.

"Well, I'm just glad things worked out for you," she added. "And I'm sorry your high school days were rough. I wish I'd known back then. I wish you'd said something."

"You were caught up in your own world, Jessie," he replied. "Mac Callaway was the only man who existed. Between him and your dedication to your studies, there was no time for anyone else."

Jessie was appalled. "Oh, Omer! I had no idea. I thought we were friends. I'm so sorry that you thought I didn't have time for you."

"It's all in the past now, Jessie," he said dismissively. "I'm glad for what we did have. We were good together, on the debating team. Weren't we?"

"You bet," she agreed. "We had some good times. I also recall we had a lot of wins."

He chuckled again. "That was mostly because of you. You had the gift of gab, even back then. It doesn't surprise me you became a lawyer. You always could think on your feet."

Jessie was filled with warmth at his compliment. It was true, she'd always been good persuading others to her side in an argument. It was an essential skill in the courtroom and one that had held her in good stead. A short silence fell between them and then she cleared her throat.

"It's lovely to hear from you, Omer, but I must admit, I have a heap of paperwork in front of me that needs my attention. Is there something I can do for you?"

"As a matter of fact, there is," he replied. "Remember when we talked the other week about security cameras and filming my employees?"

"Of course. I told you that, provided you make them aware of it, you're entitled to put surveillance cameras wherever you want. Within reason, of course," she added. "You're not allowed to film in the bathrooms."

Omer laughed. "As if I'd want to set one up in there."

She laughed with him. "Right. So, did you go ahead and set up the CCTV cameras?"

"Yes, I did. I hope it will put an end to the thievery."

"Good. I wish you luck. It's amazing how people change the choices they make when they know they're being caught on camera."

"Yes, I hope so. The thing is, I was wondering if you had time to attend my construction site and just let me know if there's anything you notice that's out of line. You mentioned the bathrooms, and of course I haven't put cameras there, but I want to make sure everything else is aboveboard. There are always people who look for ways to make a quick buck and when they know you have substantial means, it seems an easy route to bring a civil suit for any baseless reason. I don't want to give my employees a way out. I'd really appreciate it if you could come out here and take a look around, kind of give it your tick of approval."

Jessie paused. Brian Jefferies' hearing was in less than a week. She still had a lot of preparation to do. She'd already lost time by taking the afternoon off with Mac and after what had happened with Steve, Mac would probably need her again. Taking a field trip out of the office would set her back at least a couple hours, maybe more. She gnawed on her lip.

As if sensing her indecision, Omer spoke again. "Please, Jessie. It won't take long, I promise. I'm building a block of condominiums in Vaucluse, right near the water's edge. It won't take long to get here. If you like, I can come and collect you and bring you right back."

At the mention of Vaucluse, Jessie was immediately assailed with images of Mac. No doubt he was still at the construction site, but when he finished with the police, she might be able to persuade him to come into town and take the afternoon off. She couldn't imagine how shocked he must still be feeling about what had happened.

She glanced at her watch. It was almost lunchtime. It was possible she could meet Omer and then drop in and see Mac on her way back. Despite the work that waited for her, she wanted to be there for him if he needed her and reassure herself he was all right.

"Okay, why not?" she heard herself saying. "But it will work better if I meet you there."

"That's fine," Omer replied, his voice flooded with gratitude and relief. "Thank you, Jessie. I know how busy you are. I appreciate you taking time out for an old school friend."

"No problem, Omer. I'm happy to. I'll meet you there soon."

Omer gave her directions to his construction site and she jotted them down on a piece of paper. After telling Margaret she'd be out for a couple of hours, she collected her handbag and phone and left. She'd call Mac on the way. She hoped she could persuade him to go home.

It took her ten minutes to drive out of the parking garage and head toward the eastern suburbs. She'd punched the address Omer had given her into her GPS and was pleased to see it was less than a block away from Mac's condo. She dialed his number through her car kit and waited for him to answer.

"Hi, beautiful. What are you doing?"

His deep, husky voice washed over her like single malt whiskey. He sounded far less strained than when she'd last spoken to him and she sighed quietly in relief.

"Hey, you. I'm heading to Vaucluse. I was just wondering if you were free to leave your job site yet?"

"Yeah, I might be able to manage that. The police have left and I've sent everyone else home. What are you doing in Vaucluse?"

"I'm heading over to Omer Demir's construction site. He called and asked for some legal advice. He's building condos in your neighborhood."

Mac cursed quietly. "Yeah, he is. It isn't enough that every time I try and do something, he throws a wrench in the works. Now I have to put up with him working right down the road. I've started going home a different route just so I can avoid seeing him."

"Oh, Mac! That's too bad. I wish you two could sort out your differences."

"Yeah, me too. It just doesn't look like that's ever going to happen. It takes two to put something like this aside. Omer just isn't interested. He seems to take pleasure in the fact my developments are forced over budget and off schedule. I had a call from his foreman earlier. Apparently there's been a further delay on the concrete. It's just another one of his silly games."

"Surely he isn't that petty?" Jessie asked.

"It appears that way to me." Mac's tone was gruff with suppressed anger.

"Maybe I could say something to him? After all, we were friends back in high school. Besides, he just called to ask me a favor. It's the reason I'm headed over there now. One good turn deserves another, right? It's the perfect opportunity to ask him for a favor in return."

"You're welcome to try," Mac responded. "Who knows? You might just have the magic touch. Just don't get too friendly with him," he added. "He has a reputation around women, you know."

"Really? And why is that of concern to you?"

"Jessie..." Mac's tone held a warning.

Jessie laughed. "Relax, Mac. He might be rich and sinfully good looking, but I'm afraid he's just not my type. Too dark and brooding and arrogant. I prefer my men to be more the casual surfer type.

You know the kind. Bleach-blond hair and sexy green eyes and a good sense of humor to boot. To say nothing of the wicked way he can use his tongue..."

Her voice trailed off, almost breathless. Her nipples had pebbled against her blouse. She'd been only teasing, trying to lift his mood, but at the thought of what could happen when they spent time together, heat pooled between her legs.

Mac's voice was rough with desire. "Okay, I'm climbing into my pickup right now. Don't take too long with Omer. I need you. I can still taste you on my tongue, hear you whimper with need. And when you wrap your legs around my hips and beg me to fuck you... It drives me wild. I'll be waiting for you back home."

Her heart beat hard against her chest and her clit had swollen more with every husky word. She wished she was somewhere she could relieve the pressure that had built up between her legs. But she was stuck in traffic heading toward a job site to do a favor for another man.

A man who treated Mac with disdain.

Why was she even bothering with Omer? Then again, maybe there was something she could do to heal the rift. Maybe going to Omer when he needed her was exactly the best thing to do.

Anyway, it was too late now to change her plans. She was already halfway there. Might as well keep going and get on with it. *Who knows?* Maybe he and Mac would come out friends – and if not friends, at least not enemies any longer. It was worth a shot.

With a promise to get there as soon as she could, she ended the call and focused her attention on arriving at her destination. As she drove, she formulated a plan to get Omer and Mac back on the same side. It was the best thing for both of them; she was sure of it.

CHAPTER 19

Zane scratched his head and stifled a yawn and tried to remain focused on the CCTV footage that was displayed on the screen in front of him. He'd made the call to the building superintendent, but the man had been more than reluctant to play ball.

"No can do," the super replied when Zane had put in the request. "Standard procedure," the man added. "We guarantee our residents the utmost privacy. It's one of the things they pay for. Exclusivity and absolute privacy. Handing over CCTV footage of the comings and goings of the place to the police without a murmur doesn't exactly go along with that."

Zane had ground his teeth in frustration, but had reluctantly accepted the man's position. After all, he had no choice. He couldn't force someone to hand over their surveillance footage. Only the courts could do that.

In the end, they'd had to obtain a subpoena for the security footage. Twenty-four hours later, subpoena in hand, Zane had knocked on the superintendent's door. Within a short space of time, the man handed over the flash drives containing footage of the night in question. Zane had spent the past couple of hours going through them frame by frame, hoping to see something unusual.

He'd already seen several people enter and leave the building, including Omer Demir. At six-fifteen Omer exited the building and returned a little after eight... Just like he'd said. So that much of his story was true, at least...

Another hour of footage elapsed and then another hour after that. It was just past ten on the time recorder at the top right of the screen when something of interest caught Zane's eye. He sat forward in his seat and paused the footage. A woman of the same build as Melissa Sorensen and wearing a pair of jeans and a pale yellow blouse like hers, entered Omer's building.

The time was ten-thirteen.

Zane clicked on the fuzzy image and enlarged it. His breath caught in his throat. It certainly looked like Melissa Sorensen. The same long blond hair, knee-high leather boots. The only thing that was missing was the red silk scarf. As far as Zane could tell, her neck was bare.

He switched to the camera set up in the foyer that was directed toward the elevators. The lighting was better there. The woman turned momentarily to face the camera. His heart skipped a beat.

It was her. He was sure of it. One thing was now clear. On the night Melissa had argued with Mac

Callaway, she'd also visited Omer Demir's building. Zane would bet everything he had that she'd gone there to see Omer. At that time of night, she wasn't stopping by for a casual chat, either. From there it was easy to arrive at the conclusion that she knew Demir well and that he was more than likely the mystery man who she'd been sleeping with. It appeared Omer was in this up to his teeth. Zane would bet everything he had that the man was also the father of Melissa's unborn child.

Zane's mind raced a mile a minute as he considered everything he knew and didn't know. It all fit together so well. It was likely Demir's DNA sample that had been mixed up or replaced with Parker's twenty years earlier. And that pointed to the fact it was Demir who'd raped and murdered Janice Scott. It was Demir who should have gone to jail.

Demir went to school with Mac Callaway. Callaway knew Janice Scott. The dead girl had been found in his bed. Callaway was Demir's business rival. There was certainly no love lost there. It stood to reason that when Demir couldn't bring down Callaway through business, he'd upped the ante by going after Mac Callaway's girl. Melissa Sorenson.

With his heart pumping hard, Zane continued to watch the security footage right up until the very end. Omer emerged from his building at nine the next morning, dressed as he usually would for work. A five-thousand dollar suit. Expensive shoes polished to a high sheen. He stepped out of the elevator, crossed the foyer, looked neither left nor right but simply headed down the street. An hour later, he arrived back at his building, lugging a suitcase. Once again, Zane zoomed in on the detail and once again, his heart skipped a beat.

The Burberry suitcase. The same one Melissa Sorensen had been found in. The same one that matched other pieces of Melissa's luggage found in Mac Callaway's condo.

It was all so clear, now. Demir had set up Callaway to take the fall, going so far as to hide the body in the matching luggage. He must've strangled Melissa sometime after her arrival at his condo and in the footage, was now preparing to dispose of her body. At some point, he must have driven Melissa to Mac Callaway's jobsite in Hornsby. That was a masterstroke.

It was possible Melissa had even told Demir about her fight with her boyfriend. She'd turned up late on his doorstep, after all. She must have offered some kind of explanation.

Demir would have assumed their heated argument would have been overheard. In fact, Callaway's neighbors confirmed this. It gave the police a starting point and when the missing girlfriend turned up dead on Mac's job site, the circumstantial evidence couldn't be ignored.

It was only because the assumption of Callaway's guilt didn't feel right to Zane that he pushed for other explanations. If the case had been allocated to a pair of less experienced detectives or a detective who just wanted to bring the case to a speedy end, it was quite possible Omer Demir might've gotten away with the perfect crime. As it turned out, the case had fallen on Zane's desk.

Unlucky for Demir.

Zane glanced across the room to where his partner sat behind his desk. "Willie Whitehouse!" he hollered. "Get yourself over here!"

Willie took one look at Zane's face and didn't question his command. Instead, he pushed away from his desk and strode across the room. "What is it?"

"It's Demir. We've got him. It's all here on the CCTV footage."

"The bastard. I knew there was a reason I didn't like him."

Zane grimaced. "Yes. You and me both. But this is where it ends. He's been brought undone by the very security footage he pays a fortune for to keep him safe. Too bad for him."

"My heart bleeds," Willie replied with mock solemnity.

"Yeah, mine, too. Let's go and get him."

Zane reached for his jacket and Willie headed back to his desk to do the same. After letting their boss know where they were going and why, they exited the squad room. With adrenaline pouring through his bloodstream, Zane practically took the steps two at a time.

"I guess this means Callaway's off the hook," Willie commented.

"Yeah." Zane tossed the car keys to him. "You drive. I'll call him on our way over to Demir's place. For once I'll be the bearer of good news."

As Willie sped out of the parking lot with Zane in the passenger seat, Zane pulled out his phone and scrolled through his contacts until he found Mac Callaway's number. The phone rang out for so long, Zane was sure it was going to go to voicemail, but then Callaway answered.

"Mac Callaway." His voice was gruff and he sounded impatient.

"Mac, it's Detective Sullivan."

"Oh, good. I've been meaning to call you. We had an incident at the job site a couple of hours ago. My foreman, Steve Prendergast, had a little...episode. He pulled a gun. Don't worry, the police were called and he's now in custody."

Zane blinked. It was the last thing he expected Mac to say. And then the name registered in his brain.

"Steve Prendergast? As in Janice Scott's step-brother?"

"Yes. How did you know?" Mac's tone was filled with confusion and curiosity.

"It's a story for another day. Right now, I have some news," Zane replied.

"I see." Zane could hear the wariness in Callaway's tone and didn't blame him.

"It's good news this time," Zane hastened to reassure him. "We know who murdered Melissa Sorensen and that it wasn't you. You're cleared of all suspicion."

"I told you that a long time ago," Mac replied. "In fact, more than once. You didn't listen."

Zane dismissed Mac's anger. "I understand how you feel and I apologize but I had to do my job.

We had to look at this from every angle. The statistics show that most people who come to a violent end knew their offender. When you have time to calm down and think it through, I'm sure you'll understand."

"Maybe," came the noncommittal reply. "Who did it, anyway?" Mac added almost as an afterthought.

"It's Omer Demir. Your business rival. It was all recorded on CCTV."

Mac's tone was filled with incredulity. "*Demir?* You saw him murder Melissa?"

"No, not quite, but almost as good as. We have footage from his building showing Melissa went over there a little past ten the night of July sixth – the night of your argument. She goes into the building and never comes out. At least, not in the way she intended. We don't have all the details yet, but we're piecing it all togeth—"

"Fuck!" Mac interrupted. "Jessie..."

Zane's gut tightened at the panic in Mac's voice. "What are you talking about? What about Jessie?"

"She's with him. Jessie's with Omer Demir right now. She called me about twenty minutes ago. She's on her way over to his building site in Vaucluse."

Zane's heart skipped a beat. With a gargantuan effort, he forced himself to remain calm.

"Look, I'm sure this fellow's not about to commit another murder. He must know the heat's on him. My partner and I spoke to him a couple of days ago. He's well aware of our interest in him. He'd be foolish to do anything to Jessie."

"I don't give a fuck what you think!" Mac exploded. "This man's dangerous. He's already proven he'll stop at nothing to destroy me. He's even gone so far as to murder my ex-girlfriend." There was a slight pause and then Mac added, "What you don't know is that Jessie and I have been...seeing each other. In fact, we've fallen in love."

Zane frowned. "Does Demir know this?"

"No. I don't know," Mac admitted. "Maybe. Who knows what he knows?"

Zane blinked in surprise. "Okay, this changes things a little bit. We have to assume Demir knows. We'll head over there right away and make sure everything's all right. Do you have the address?"

Mac gave the address of Demir's project site in Vaucluse and Zane immediately relayed the details to Willie. With lights and siren blazing, they turned the squad car around and headed south to Vaucluse.

———

Mac's heartbeat went into overdrive at the thought that Jessie might be in danger. She'd gone to Omer's building site in good faith, even intending to help Mac with his problem with the concrete supplier who seemed intent on delaying Mac's project as long as he could. If he knew they were onto him and tried anything, she'd be taken completely unawares. His heart filled with dread at the thought of anything happening to her.

Please, God. Please, God. Please, God. Please keep her safe.

They'd only just found each other. He couldn't lose her again.

With his heart in his throat, he used the car kit to dial her number. It rang out and eventually went to voicemail.

"Jessie, it's Mac. Call me as soon as you get this and get the hell away from Demir."

He ended the call and sent up another silent prayer. Flicking on his indicator, he quickly changed lanes. It was fortunate that he was already more than halfway to Vaucluse. In just under fifteen minutes, he should be there. He prayed to God he wouldn't be too late...

Jessie parked outside the high chain wire fence that surrounded Omer's building site. More than half of the condominiums were completed. They created an impressive site. Though Jessie couldn't see the view from where she stood, she knew the building looked straight out to the ocean. They'd go for a pretty penny; there was no doubt about that. Omer had done more than well for himself. He'd come a long way from the shy and quiet boy she'd known in high school.

"Jessie! Thanks for coming."

She turned and caught sight of him striding

toward her. He wore a custom made designer suit in a dark charcoal color that fit him like a glove. His pristine white business shirt looked like it had just been pulled off the hanger and despite the humidity, even his designer tie was crisp and straight.

He pulled her into a friendly hug and immediately released her. She was still trying to come to terms with the contact when he grabbed her hand and dragged her toward the nearest condo.

"Come on. You need to see this. I'd like to know what you think."

Picking her way with care across the uneven dirt, she followed behind him. When she tried to extricate her hand, he only tightened his hold. In the end, she gave up. After all, they were old school friends. She guessed she could let him hold her hand if he wanted to.

"Where is everyone?" she asked, looking around. For a building site, it was strangely quiet.

"I gave them the afternoon off," Omer replied over his shoulder.

Jessie frowned momentarily and then shook off her confusion. Omer was the boss. If he wanted to give his staff the afternoon off, then so be it. She couldn't imagine his employees arguing with the decision.

He opened a large wooden door with inlaid glass panels that led into a wide foyer faced with marble. Though the interior wasn't quite finished, the space in the condo was amazing. The entryway opened up into an open concept kitchen and living room, both of which took advantage of the spectacular views of the Pacific Ocean.

"Wow!" she gasped. "How amazing! What I wouldn't give to live in a place like this."

He shot her a look of surprise. "Don't tell me your hotel suite just overlooks the city? I was sure a girl like you would splash out on a water view."

Jessie stared at him and her belly filled with disquiet. "How do you know where I live?" she asked and did her best to keep her tone casual.

"Of course I know where you live. I followed you home one night. It took less than thirty seconds for me to tease your room number out of the young girl behind the counter. I think she really believed me when I told her I had my own TV show."

He laughed and Jessie's disquiet deepened.

What was going on? Omer was acting strange – more than strange. He was acting downright weird.

"Where are the security cameras?" she asked, suddenly impatient to get away. "That's what I'm here for, right?"

"Right. But first let's take a tour. It's a great condo. It will sell for five or six million. A tidy sum, for sure."

With that, he led the way across the living room and down a marbled hall. Two bedrooms, each with their own high spec ensuite, were on Jessie's right, with another bedroom and laundry room on the left. All of the rooms had their own balconies, two of which took full advantage of the views. It was a spectacular apartment and worth every penny of its costly price tag. Of that she had no doubt.

"Pretty special, don't you think?" Omer grinned.

She sighed. "I won't argue with that. I'm already jealous of the people who get to live here. Who wouldn't want to wake up to that?" She indicated the view outside the window of the main bedroom. Even the ground floor apartments would have a view. She couldn't begin to imagine what Omer had paid for the land.

She turned to leave and discovered he'd moved up right behind her. He reached out and ran his fingers along the side of her face.

"So beautiful. Then again, you always were."

Jessie pulled back in shock. All through high school, he'd never once crossed the line. They'd been friends, members of the debating team together. Nothing more. Ever.

Stepping away, she shook her head. "I-I'm sorry, Omer. I'm confused. What are you doing? I thought I was here to inspect your CCTV cameras."

"Yes, of course. The security cameras. They're back down here." He turned and headed out the room and back down the hall toward the kitchen. She followed a few steps behind him, wary now.

Before he got to the end, he suddenly turned on his heel and in two quick strides was back beside her. This time, he pinned her against the wall.

"Omer!" she cried, her breath coming out in a frightened gasp. "Let go of me!"

He glared at her. The friendly, smiling countenance of a few minutes ago was gone. In its place was a look so dark and menacing, a shiver of fear arced down her spine. In a panic, she struggled to get herself free. His hands merely tightened painfully around her wrists. His body pressed against hers, pinning her in place.

"You were always so sweet, so beautiful, Jessie Wolfe. We got on well, didn't we? I thought so. But you only ever wanted to be friends. Why? Why couldn't you love me?"

Her mouth gaped in shock. *Who was this Omer, speaking such ridiculousness?* He certainly wasn't the same Omer she'd known in school.

"Omer, what are you talking about?" she asked, doing her best to keep her voice on an even keel. She instinctively knew if she showed any fear it wouldn't go well for her.

Omer stared at her in disbelief. "Don't tell me you didn't know I was in love with you?"

Jessie blinked and shook her head. "I'm sorry, Omer. I truly didn't. I thought...I thought we were friends."

"Of course we were friends! That's all you allowed me to be. That didn't stop me from yearning to be more."

She frowned in confusion. The pressure on her arms hadn't ceased. "I thought you were in love with Janice? Isn't that what you told me?"

"I only turned my sights toward Janice after you rejected me. All through high school I kept hoping and hoping you'd see me in a different light. We used to have such fun together when we debated or practiced debating. It was the highlight of my week. We'd talk and laugh and plot out arguments and all the time I was sure you'd see the real me." His eyes narrowed into another menacing glare.

"But you didn't. Not once. I was just Omer, the foreigner, another member of the debating team."

His hands tightened painfully around her wrists and he shoved her hard back against the wall. At the same time, he leaned forward in an attempt to kiss her. She turned her head and cried out.

"No! Omer! No! Don't do this! *Please!*"

Chapter 20

Mac was halfway across the dirt driveway which would become a large paved parking bay one day when he heard Jessie's cry. His blood ran cold. As stealthily as possible, he crept toward the building where the sound came from. Stepping with care around the construction debris, he moved on silent feet. The murmur of voices drew nearer.

Twisting the doorknob that was attached to an elaborate wooden front door, he eased the panel open and stepped inside. The marble flooring was high end. So were the light fixtures and the paint job on the walls was flawless. Omer had spared no expense.

The voices were much clearer now and Mac could easily make out Omer's deep rumble and Jessie's frightened response. Mac flattened himself against a wall and then eased around the corner.

He spotted them straightaway. They were about halfway down a long hallway. Omer had Jessie pinned against a wall. Mac's first instinct was to go tearing down there and rip Omer into shreds, but he paused and forced himself to take stock of the situation and formulate a plan. He had no idea if Omer were armed. The last thing he wanted was to bring Jessie any further harm. He drew in a deep breath and eased it out and with intent to gather his wits, counted to ten. Jessie began speaking again, oblivious to Mac's presence.

"Talk to me about Janice, Omer."

Jessie's quiet request was tinged with desperation. Mac guessed it was made in an effort to distract her tormentor. He prayed it would work as he strained to hear the police sirens.

Omer's lips curled up in disgust. "Janice Scott was a slut. She slept with every boy who smiled at her. But apparently she was too good for the likes of me."

Quickly, Mac's gaze scanned Omer's body. There was no telltale bulge in either of his pockets to indicate he might have a gun. The knowledge relaxed him just a bit and he eased his phone out of his pocket. Pressing the record button, he held it up in front of him toward the two people who were crowded against the wall.

"I'm sure she didn't think like that, Omer," Jessie quietly replied. Mac silently applauded her courage.

Omer's eyes flashed. "Of course she did! I don't know what I ever saw in her."

"What did she do to you, Omer?"

"What did she do to me? Ha! What did she *do* to me! She tore out my heart and ate it for breakfast, that's what!"

"How?"

"When I went to her, like you suggested, opening my heart, declaring my eternal love she laughed in my face. Poor Omer, the little immigrant boy no one could love. Well, I showed her."

Jessie frowned and Mac went still. "What do you mean?" Jessie asked.

"The night Janice died, I ran into her in a bar. She'd had a few drinks, but she wasn't drunk. I told her I loved her. You should've seen the shock and disgust that filled her face. And then she laughed as if it was the most hysterical thing she'd ever heard. As if the very thought of loving someone like me was something she couldn't comprehend.

"She told me I was out of luck. That she loved Mackenzie Callaway. Only, he didn't love her. That was the irony of it. Here I was in love with her, ready to offer her everything I had and she was in love with a man who didn't feel the same way.

"I left the bar, feeling more angry than I had at any other time in my life. For a while I didn't know what to do; I could barely even think. And then a plan came to me slowly."

"What did you do?" Jessie asked softly.

"I lay in wait for her outside the bar, hidden in the shadows. It was more than an hour later when she finally left. She stumbled to her car, the one her father had bought her, and headed for home. At least, that's where I thought she was headed.

"I followed her. But then she surprised me by turning off two streets before her house. She pulled up outside Mac's parents' house. I stopped my car half a block away and watched her walk inside like she owned the place. Mac's house was dark and quiet. I assumed nobody was home. A moment later, I saw a light come on in one of the back rooms. I crept up to the side of the house and listened, waiting to see if anyone was awake. The house remained silent."

He paused for a moment, as if remembering that night. Finally, he continued.

"I noticed the garage at the side of the house was empty. There was no one parked on the street. It looked to me like none of the Callaways were home. No one was there except for Janice.

"I saw an opportunity too good to turn down. It was like someone was watching me from above, dictating my every move. Someone who knew my pain and anger and who understood and wanted to help me out. I crept across the back porch and opened the sliding door. It was unlocked.

"Life was different back then in the suburbs. People felt safe in their homes at night. They didn't think so much about locking every door and window, even if they were out. Lucky for me.

"By then, Janice had switched off the light. I crept down the hallway and looked in all the rooms. Four bedrooms in total and only one of them was occupied. By the light of the moon, I saw her sprawled across Mac's bed. I could tell it was his room from the sporting trophies and medals that lined the walls and shelves." Omer grinned. "She didn't even know I was there until it was too late."

Listening to Omer's story, Mac barely dared to

breathe. He could see Jessie's eyes wide with fear and the horror of what was to come.

"What happened next?" she croaked.

Omer sighed. "You must understand, Jessie. I was still so angry. All I could hear was Janice's derisive laughter ringing in my ears. Her rejection had stung. I was hurting. If anything, her rejection was even worse than yours."

"I never rejected you, Omer!" Jessie protested. "I didn't even know how you felt!"

Omer shrugged. "Whatever. It still felt like a rejection to me. But not like Janice. She made it clear she couldn't even stand the thought of dating someone like me. A dirty foreigner."

"Did you... Did you rape her?" Jessie's voice broke.

Around the corner, Mac's fists clenched and his breathing almost came to a halt. He waited for Omer's response.

Omer chuckled and it was a chilling sound. The hairs stood to attention on the back of Mac's neck.

"She got what she deserved," Omer snarled. "I threw myself on her and pinned her to the bed. She was no match for my superior strength. Plus, I had surprise on my side and by that time, she was way past drunk. In the end, she didn't even struggle."

Jessie's face had gone pale and her eyes were wide with fear and disbelief. "So you were angry and you raped her. But why did you kill her? I don't understand."

"Of course I had to kill her! When I finally came to my senses and realized what I'd done, there was no other course of action. She knew who I was, what I'd done. My parents would never have been able to live with the shame. I loved her, but I had to kill her. I didn't want to do it, but I had no choice. Even so, it was Mackenzie Callaway's fault, every bit of it."

Jessie shook her head in confusion. "You're not making sense, Omer. How could it be Mac's fault?"

Omer's gaze narrowed into a menacing glare. "Of *course* it was Mac's fault! He was the one who drove me to it! If Janice hadn't been in love with him, I might've had a chance with her. Instead, she laughed in my face. No one could hold a candle to the almighty Mackenzie Callaway. He was a paragon of virtue that no other man could hope to match."

Mac watched as Omer sighed and his shoulders slumped with dejection, as if the memory of not being able to make the grade wearied him. His hold loosened slightly, but apparently not enough for Jessie to make her escape. Mac tensed, ready to leap forward if need be.

"You strangled her, didn't you?" It was a quiet statement of fact.

Omer nodded. "Yes. Like I said, I didn't have a choice. There was no doubt she'd go straight to the police and tell them everything and her father was mayor, for God's sake. My life would be over and Mac Callaway would go on his merry way. He had you pining for him, hanging on his every word. Then there was Janice, and every other girl in that high school who was in love with him. It wasn't fair.

Only *I* knew the truth about Mac Callaway and the façade he showed the world."

Jessie slowly shook her head, her expression now one of sympathy and sad resignation. "You're wrong, Omer. Mac Callaway never had a façade. He was always the real deal. He was good and kind and generous. He had a kind word for everyone. He'd help you out if you needed it. You didn't even have to ask. It was just the way he was. It's a shame you didn't see that. He might've been able to help you. Instead, you let your jealousy blind you. And look where it's gotten you?"

Omer shook his head from side to side in an increasingly aggressive way. "*No! No! No! No!* Jessie you have it all wrong. Mac Callaway's a fake! A fake! A *fake*! Why won't you believe me?"

Omer's face took on a red and purple hue. Veins popped out on his neck and forehead. Mac's fists clenched and he took a step in their direction and then pulled up short once again.

"It's okay, Omer. Calm down. Tell me about Melissa," Jessie said quietly, soothingly.

Mac tensed, but to his relief, the distraction appeared to work. Omer's tortured expression relaxed and he slowly smiled. Mac remained hidden, plastered against the wall.

"Melissa Sorenson. What a beauty. She fell for me hook, line and sinker. Too bad for her she was nothing more than an opportunity for payback."

"So you weren't in love with her?" Jessie asked.

Omer laughed. "Hell, no. She was an opportunity to set up Mac Callaway to take the fall. It hadn't worked with Janice. I killed her in his bed and left her there for everyone to see. Poor old Wes Parker, the loser. He has my father to thank for the fact he's spent the past twenty years in jail."

Jessie frowned. "What do you mean?"

Omer's laughter was devoid of humor. "That night, after it happened, I went home and broke down. I told my father everything. He was furious, but he promised me he would fix it. I didn't know what he meant until Wes was charged with Janice's rape and murder. Good old Dad paid someone to switch the DNA samples."

Mac swallowed a gasp of shock. Right from the outset, Wes had proclaimed his innocence and all this time he'd been right. It was unbelievable.

"I kept my mouth shut, of course," Omer continued. "But I was furious that Mac Callaway had gotten off scot free."

"Omer, Mac was innocent of any wrongdoing! He had nothing to do with Janice's death. You *know* that."

"I know nothing of the sort," he shouted. "As far as I'm concerned, Janice's rape and murder was all Mac Callaway's fault. He drove me to do what I did! Everywhere I turned, it was 'Mac this' and 'Mac that' and 'Mac's the greatest.' No one else came close. I was so furious at Janice, how she'd also fallen victim to his fake charms. It was that fury that pushed me over the edge. So you see how it was all Mac Callaway's fault."

Jessie shook her head in bewilderment. "You're delusional, Omer. There's no way I'll ever accept that Mac had anything to do with Janice's death."

Omer shrugged as if it was of no consequence. "What is done is done."

"So, what about Melissa? You said you saw her as an opportunity to strike back against Mac. Is that why you murdered her?"

Mac held his breath and waited for Omer's answer. He didn't have to wait long.

"For years, I dreamed of ways to destroy Mac Callaway's life, just as he'd destroyed mine by forcing me to kill the woman I loved. He graduated a year ahead of me, but I made inquiries and discovered he was studying business and marketing and property and I enrolled in exactly the same courses. He didn't even notice me and yet we walked the same halls. To him, I was a nobody, just like I had been to Janice.

"But finally I graduated and I set up a business of my own. It was no coincidence that I followed the same career path as Mac Callaway. Most people assumed my father was my inspiration." Omer's lips twisted into a grimace. "As if. My parents have never spoken to me since the debacle with Janice... They're *ashamed* of me... No, my decision to forge a career in the construction business had nothing to do with my parents and everything to do with my desire for revenge.

"For years, I'd done all I could to sabotage Mac Callaway's developments and to bring an end to his career, but he's proved far more resilient than I dreamed possible. No matter what I did or how long I did it, he always bounced back." Omer's lip curled up in a sneer.

"He even made *Forbes'* rich list two years in a row." Omer sighed.

"So then I looked to other ways I could interfere with Mackenzie Callaway's life. I wasn't having a lot of success on the business front, other than causing him a lot of frustration, so I looked to his personal life. There were a string of beautiful women in and out of his life, but no one special for many years until Melissa came along. She lasted longer than anyone, and I guessed this one must be serious. Serious enough that if he were to lose her, he'd probably be devastated."

"What did you do, Omer?" Jessie whispered.

Omer's smile was filled with cunning and a deep satisfaction. "I set out to steal her away from him, of course." He chuckled. "It was easier than I expected. It turned out little Melissa was restless. Apparently Mac wasn't quite as attentive as she wanted him to be. She was ready for marriage and babies, but he was taking his time with his proposal.

"When I came into her life, I showered her with attention and expensive gifts. She bore the full brunt of my charm. I wined and dined and flattered her. I bought her beautiful clothes. She loved every minute of the attention. What was more, she saw it as a way to make Mac jealous. So we used each other to our mutual satisfaction. It worked well for both of us.

"We saw each other for months and months before it all went bad. Sometimes we'd meet at

Mac's condo. It always gave me a kick to know I'd fucked his girlfriend in his bed. Other times, she'd meet me in the city. She worked in a building only three blocks away from where I lived. It was convenient. Mac mostly worked out in the suburbs. He had no idea it was going on. When the time was right, I was going to reveal all and sit back and watch the fallout."

Mac listened to Omer and his fury simmered just below the surface. He couldn't believe the extent of the man's vindictiveness. An innocent woman had been manipulated, a pawn in his sick game. Melissa might have gone willingly into his arms, but she had no idea how she was being used.

"How did you come to kill her?" Jessie asked softly.

Omer sighed with irritation. "My plan was working out perfectly. Melissa was eager to share my bed. I even considered keeping her permanently, proposing marriage to her, like she wanted. In fact, the night she and Mac argued, I did exactly that. I wasn't in love with her, like I'd been with Janice, but I liked her well enough. And knowing I'd stolen her off Mac permanently held a great deal of appeal. Unfortunately for her, she didn't feel the same way.

"She came to me that night all upset and angry. Mac had discovered our secret and he'd thrown her out. What was worse, she discovered she was pregnant and she wasn't sure which one of us was the father. She was beside herself with the thought it might be mine."

His eyes burned with fury. He moved even

closer to Jessie. Mac prepared to launch himself at the man. All the time, he made sure the phone was recording.

"Melissa's absolute disgust at the thought she might be carrying my child sent me over the edge," Omer continued. "She'd already told me about the fight she'd had with Mac and how she was surprised the neighbors hadn't called the police. From that moment on, a plan formed in my mind. I knew what I would do.

"I made a calculated guess the neighbors had already heard the fighting. If she disappeared, the suspicion would fall on Mac. I hadn't been able to set him up to take the rap for Janice, but Melissa was an altogether different proposition. Nobody knew we were seeing each other. I'd made sure we were discrete. If I texted her, it was always from a prepaid, untraceable phone. I knew then how easy it would be to make her disappear and blame it all on Mac."

"So you strangled her," Jessie stated.

Omer nodded. "Yes, I did. Just like I did with Janice. Only this time, I felt nothing but relief. There was no agonizing pain, no second guessing over what I'd done. As far as I was concerned, Melissa had it coming and it also gave me the means to destroy the man who'd ruined my life."

Omer's breath came fast and hard. It was like he'd run a marathon. But he didn't seem to notice as he continued.

"The next morning, I bought a suitcase. I made sure it matched a set I'd seen in Mac's condo when I'd met Melissa there one time. Fortunately, she was a small woman and she folded up just fine. A couple nights after I killed her, I drove out to Mac's construction site. I planned to leave her there as further evidence of Mac's involvement. I was prepared to break-in, but luck was with me that night. Someone had forgotten to lock the gate. I strode on in and hid Melissa's body – inside the suitcase – in an air conditioning vent. It was all so easy."

Jessie stared at him, aghast. Her eyes were huge in her face. "What about the scarf, Omer? According to the police report, both women were wearing one. I can't help but notice how often you wear intricately tied cravats. Was it your signature? Is that why you left the scarves behind?"

Omer smiled. "So clever of you to notice, Jessie. That pleases me so much. The first time, with Janice, I didn't plan it. She wore a scarf around her neck the night I murdered her. When I realized what I'd done, I was ashamed. I used the scarf to hide the evidence of my violence. With Melissa, it was different. I found a scarf in my apartment and tied it around her neck. It was bright red. I tied it in such a jaunty way. It was a bit of fun, a way of leaving my mark."

Jessie stared at him in horror, as if the full import of what he'd done finally hit home. Mac clenched his fists and gritted his teeth. He'd heard almost enough. Then Jessie started struggling in earnest and Omer's hands dropped from her wrists and went straight around her neck. Jessie gasped and struggled harder.

Fury ignited in Mac's gut and propelled him out of his hiding spot. In four long strides he closed the distance and grabbed Omer and pulled him off. The look of surprise and fear in Omer's eyes filled Mac with satisfaction, but he didn't have time to contemplate that. Jessie had her hands up to her neck and was gasping for breath.

"Are you all right?" he asked her.

She nodded in relief. "I am now."

"Get out of here, Jessie!" he urged her and prayed to God she'd do as he said. Then he saw her eyes widen in horror.

"Mac! Watch out!"

He twisted in time to see Omer swinging a ball pein hammer. Where he got it from, Mac had no idea. He wove to the side and narrowly missed being hit as Omer brought it down. Frustrated at missing his target, the madman brought the hammer up again.

"Jessie! Get out of here! Hurry! Run for your life!" Mac shouted, frantic to protect her.

He felt the air *swoosh* beside him and he moved, but not quickly enough. The hammer buried itself into his shoulder and he yelped at the searing pain. The sound of bone crunching made it all the more sickening. Knowing that Omer would keep coming until Mac was on the ground, he bent low and twisted and then drove his good shoulder forward.

He caught Omer in the ribs and they both tumbled to the ground. Despite the fall, Omer kept a firm grip on the hammer and continued to rain blows down on Mac's head. One after the other, Mac lost count. His arms came up as a shield. Gradually, as the blows increased, his consciousness faded.

"Mac! Get up!" Jessie screamed, but there was nothing he could do.

His legs were like jelly. His head was full of fog. The pain was more than he could imagine. And then there was the sound of a gunshot. He froze. There was a split second of silence before Jessie's screams once again filled the room.

Mac sighed. He was done. Everything faded to black.

Epilogue

The lights above Mac's bed were dim, but even so, their glow hurt his eyes as he squinted up at Jessie.

"Where am I?"

"Mac! Thank God you're awake! You had me so worried!"

He tried for a smile of reassurance, but it came out all wobbly. Jessie leaned over him and gently pushed the hair off his forehead.

"You scared me so much," she whispered. "I wasn't sure if you were dead. Omer kept hitting you with that hammer and then the police arrived and a gun went off and there was havoc all around... It was awful."

"They got there in the nick of time. What happened to Omer?"

"The detective's shot went wide, but luckily they were able to subdue him. He was arrested and taken to the police station. No doubt they're still questioning him."

"How long have I been here?"

"Since two. It's now going on for nine."

Mac blinked in surprise. "I've been here seven hours?"

Jessie nodded. "Give or take a few minutes."

"What did the doctors say about my injuries?"

"The main thing is, you're going to be okay," she reassured him. "You took several heavy blows to the head and shoulders and your collarbone snapped right through, but they've reset that and they're certain it will heal fine."

Mac glanced down at the sling across his chest. His shoulder hurt like hell. So did his head. It felt like a hundred-pound load of steel had been dropped on top of it. He guessed several serious blows from a hammer had done that.

Someone knocked on the door and he winced as the sound of it echoed like a cannon through his head. He squinted through the dimness. The door swung inward and Detective Sullivan entered. He smiled when he noticed Mac was awake.

"How are you doing?" he asked, slowly approaching the bed.

"I've felt better," Mac admitted with an attempt at a grin.

"I bet. You took a pounding from that hammer. I'm sorry it took us so long. We got caught up in a traffic snarl. We called for backup, but it cost us valuable time."

Mac shrugged and then grimaced as pain arced across his shoulder and chest. "Don't sweat it, Detective. You got there in time. I understand it was your bullet that put an end to Demir's frenzied attack. I'm very grateful for your quick response."

"So am I," Jessie piped up. She reached for Mac's hand and squeezed it and then brought it up to her face. Pressing her lips against it, she let him know without words just how glad she was that the police had arrived in time.

Sullivan acknowledged her comment with a nod and then returned his attention to Mac.

"We've managed to piece together most of what happened and Demir is being surprisingly cooperative, but there are a few things we need to clarify. Are you up to answering some questions?"

"Sure," Mac replied.

"Demir admitted to having an affair with Melissa, but he denied knowing anything about her death. We—"

"He's lying," Mac interrupted.

"Of course he is," Sullivan agreed. "We know that from the CCTV footage."

Mac struggled to sit up against the pillows. He bit down hard against the pain that stabbed through him, but managed to elevate himself a couple of inches.

"I've got something better than the CCTV footage," he managed between gritted teeth.

Sullivan's dark eyebrows rose in surprise. "Really?"

"Yes. While Omer was regaling Jessie with all that had happened since high school, I pulled out my phone. I recorded the whole conversation."

Sullivan's eyes widened in amazement. A moment later, his face split into a grin. "Please tell me you got a confession."

Mac nodded. "He confessed to both of them. Janice Scott and Melissa Sorenson."

Sullivan's expression filled with excitement. "Where's your phone?"

Mac looked down. He wore a hospital gown and nothing else. He gazed up at Jessie.

"I have it," she said to the detective.

Reaching into her handbag, she pulled out Mac's phone and gave it to Sullivan. He clutched at it and then dug around in his jacket pocket and pulled out a plastic evidence bag. He dropped the phone into it and sealed the bag.

"I'm sorry, Mac, but I'm going to have to keep this, at least until we can download the data. This should provide Demir with enough incentive to plead guilty, but you never know. It's great to have such good insurance." He winked.

Mac grinned. "Happy to help out where I can, Detective. I'm just relieved we finally have some answers. To everything." He paused and then added. "Has anyone been to see Wes Parker?"

Sullivan nodded. "Yes, I went out to the jail myself. He's understandably overwhelmed with the knowledge his protestations of innocence have finally been believed. I wasn't responsible for the original mess-up, but I still feel terrible about what happened and how much of his life has been stolen from him."

"Money won't ever compensate him for what he's lost, but let's hope the courts favor him with a generous settlement," Jessie murmured.

Sullivan nodded. "I agree. That would be the best outcome for everyone." He looked back at

Mac. "So, despite everything Demir threw at you, he failed at every point. Thanks for not holding a grudge against me. I went a bit hard on you early on, even when my gut told me you weren't the one. I just want to say I'm sorry for that."

Mac waved Sullivan's apology away. "There's no need for an apology, Detective. You were only doing your job."

Sullivan nodded again and soon after took his leave. Jessie squeezed Mac's hand again and he felt the warmth of it all the way inside. Her dark hair was tousled. There were shadows beneath her eyes. Her blouse was crumpled and her makeup was long gone. In all, she looked a wreck. The fact she'd been so worried about him filled him with tenderness and love. He loved her. He truly did.

"I love you," he murmured.

Her eyes welled up with tears. She moved even closer and kissed him on the lips. "I love you, too. I always have. I always will."

"Forever and ever. Amen."

Note To Readers

I do hope you have enjoyed reading Jessie and Mackenzie's story. If you've enjoyed this book, I would appreciate it if you could leave a review for The Perfect Crime at Goodreads and your favorite digital retailer. Every review increases visibility and helps other readers to find books they enjoy.

Malicious Love is the next book in The Sydney Legal Series.

Here's a sneak peek:

As a junior lawyer at the prestigious Sydney Legal, Meghan Chifley knows that if she works hard enough, one day she'll reap the rewards. In the meantime, she prays her family doesn't self-destruct. Always the peacemaker, lately it's become a fulltime job refereeing the battles between her father and her brother. To make things worse, her half-sister also has plenty to say and not all of it is nice. Meghan despairs her family will survive the pain they seem determined to inflict upon each other. Then her father is brutally murdered. Her world is turned upside down when she's forced to acknowledge his killer might very well be one of her siblings.

Detective Sergeant Zane Sullivan doesn't know what it's like to have a family. Put up for adoption within hours of his birth, he spent his childhood being passed from one uncaring foster home to another. He knows firsthand how badly family can treat each other and he's not at all surprised when the evidence points toward a family member being responsible for Grant Chifley's murder. The only question is, which one?

Steeling himself against the sad vulnerability and kindness he sees in Meghan Chifley's beautiful eyes, he holds himself at a distance. Hiding behind that appealing façade could very well be a cold-blooded killer. A man has been brutally murdered and Zane's determined to find the person responsible.

Is Meghan hiding a deadly secret, or is it someone else she's protecting? The answer will leave everyone gasping...

PROLOGUE

Sweat poured down Meghan Chifley's face. Her breath came fast and her forearms burned, but she didn't let up on the flurry of driving punches that connected with a satisfying *thwack* against the solid surface of the boxing bag that hung from the iron beam above her head. It was the kind of night she hated most. Unable to sleep, her head filled with the familiar torment and distress caused by her family, she found herself in the basement, taking her frustration and anger out on the boxing bag. Sometimes the punishment lasted for hours. More often than not, she'd collapse, exhausted, on the cold concrete floor and would finally find peace. At least for a little while.

One good thing – the only good thing – to come of such extreme physical exertion was the effect on her body. Slim and toned and muscled, without an ounce of fat, every time she caught a glimpse of herself naked in the mirror, she was reminded of the way Angela Jolie looked in a number of the action films she'd starred in. Not that Meghan had set out to become a warrior queen. If her family hadn't been so dysfunctional, so unable to get on, it wouldn't have come to this. She couldn't help but wonder if other families went through the regular turmoil hers did. Surely not.

The sound of her phone ringing interrupted her dismal thoughts. She blinked in surprise. It was past one in the morning. *Who would be calling so late?* Tearing off her boxing gloves, she strode over to where she'd left her phone on the workbench and checked the screen.

Cody.

Her heart sank. There was no good reason her twin brother was calling at this hour. She wondered what it was this time. She was determined not to give him any more money. She refused to support his drug habit, no matter how much she loved him. She answered the phone with a brusque hello.

"Meg, thank goodness you answered!"

She grimaced at the way he slurred his words. He was either drunk or high—or both. The speed at which her high-flying stock broker brother's life had spiraled out of control was terrifying.

"What is it, Cody?"

"I-I know it's late and I shouldn't have called you. No doubt you have some high profile court case to show up to in the morning. It's just that…"

His voice broke. A moment later, she heard him sob. Her heart clenched in an agony of indecision. *This was her brother!* Crying in such despair. He sounded…broken. She drew in a deep breath and let her impatience and irritation with him slide away.

"What is it, Cody?" she asked more gently this time.

"Meggie! I… I'm sorry! I'm so fucked up! I didn't mean to do it! He forced me! I didn't have a choice! Please, Meggie! *Please!* You've gotta believe me! I'm so sorry…"

Once again, he was overcome with a tumultuous bout of sobbing that tore at her heart. She forced herself to concentrate on what he'd said. A cold foreboding trickled through her veins.

"What are you talking about, Cody? Who forced you? You're not making sense!"

The call was abruptly terminated. In the dimness of the basement, she stared down at the phone in her hand and was filled with a mixture of confusion, fear and disbelief.

"Oh, Cody," she whispered, her raspy voice loud in the silence. "For the love of God, what have you *done?*"

CHAPTER 1

The bright morning sunshine that poured through her office window should have lifted Meghan's mood. Instead, she resisted the urge to scrub her fingers through her hair in frustration. The man who sat opposite her had tested her patience to the limit and she'd had just about enough. With a supreme effort, she gritted her teeth, drew in a calming breath and tried again.

"Mr Collins, you just don't seem to understand what I'm saying. Your father left his entire estate to be shared equally between you and your three siblings. Unless you can bring evidence to show cause as to why your siblings shouldn't get an equal share, I'm afraid there's nothing I can do about it."

"But they had nothing to do with my father! They didn't even live in the same city! Wesley lives in New York, for Pete's sake! He hasn't been back to Sydney for years! I'm the only one who ever visited our father! Why should they get the same as me? It isn't fair!"

Once again, Meghan called on her patience. "I'm not disputing your dedication to your father, but the thing is, he left his estate equally to his children, as is his right. No court will overrule that without good reason to do so and unfortunately, the kind of neglect you're referring to doesn't count."

The man continued to look belligerent and Meghan suppressed a sigh. Sometimes her job as an estate and probate attorney was like pushing a barrow of concrete uphill. The phone on her desk buzzed and she breathed a silent sigh of relief.

"Excuse me," she murmured and picked up the receiver.

"Meghan, I have a man by the name of Arjun Patel on line three. He says it's urgent."

Meghan frowned at her secretary's announcement. *Why would her father's gardener be calling her and why would it be urgent?* A shiver of apprehension trickled down her spine.

"Meghan? Are you still there?"

Meghan blinked. "Yes, ah... Sure, Dorothy. I'm still here."

"Would you like me to take a message?"

"No, it's fine. I'll take the call."

She shot the man who sat across from her an apologetic smile. "I'm sorry, Mr Collins. I need to take this call. I think we're just about done here anyway, aren't we?"

Looking none too happy, her disgruntled client pushed back his chair and stood. "Are you sure there's nothing I can do to challenge the will?" he asked.

"Other than the fact you spent more time with your father than your siblings, do you have any reason the court would move to overrule your father's last wishes with regard to his estate?"

The man's shoulders slumped on a dejected sigh. "No. But it isn't fair."

She looked at him sympathetically. "You're right. It's not. But that's the way it goes. Now, if you don't mind, I really need to take this call. I'll be in touch as soon as the final paperwork is ready for your signature."

Collins nodded and turned toward the exit. As soon as he'd left the room, she picked up the phone. Lingering concern still swirled in her belly.

"Arjun, it's Meghan. What can I do for you?"

"Meghan! Have you spoken to your father recently?"

She frowned. "I called him last week. He was buying herbs at his local market. He was cooking spaghetti sauce. Why?"

"It's just that I haven't seen him for a few days. Normally he takes his breakfast out by the pool. He's as regular as clockwork. Scrambled eggs, two pieces of toast, juice and coffee. He eats and reads the paper. Occasionally he'll call out to me and ask me about my day, but for the past three days he hasn't turned up. I wondered if he could be away."

Meghan's frown deepened. "No, not that I know of. I'm sure he would have told me if he was going away. Are you sure he's not home?"

"He might be home, but I haven't seen him. I've been over every step of the gardens, the pool and the boathouse. I even checked the garage. All four of his cars are there."

"Have you been up to the house?"

"No."

"Have you spoken to Mrs Abbott?" Meghan asked, referring to her father's housekeeper.

"No. Mrs Abbott's mother died. She's been away for a week. Your father's been there on his own."

"You're right. I remember he told me about that. The funeral's in the country. He told Mrs Abbott to take all the time she needed."

"Yes, he's always been good to his staff," Arjun replied. "I offered to get my cousin to come in and cover for the time Mrs Abbott was away, but he assured me he was quite capable of looking after himself, for a short while at least."

"I wonder where he could be?" she murmured. "Have you tried calling him?"

"Yes. Several times. The calls went through to his voicemail."

"I see. Well, I'll try him, too. If I don't get an answer, I'll come over and see what's going on. Is that all right?"

Arjun's voice flooded with relief. "Yes! Thank you, Meghan! That would be more than all right. I knew you were the best one to call."

She pondered that comment for a moment and then shrugged. It was true. Out of the three of her father's children, she was probably the closest to him and she definitely spent the most time with him. She knew the staff better than her brother and half-sister did, too. No doubt that was why Arjun felt comfortable about calling her.

"I'll let you know how I get on, okay?" she added.

Once again, the gardener's thanks were profuse and filled with relief. Meghan ended the call and then immediately fished out her cell phone from her handbag where she'd stowed it under her desk. Quickly, she dialed her father's number. The call rang out and eventually went through to voicemail, just like Arjun had said.

"Hi, Daddy, it's Meghan. Call me, okay?" With a sigh she tossed the phone down on her desk, perplexed. *Could he have gone away without telling her? But where would he go?* All of his motor vehicles were still in his garage, so if he went anywhere, it was in a cab. Could he have caught a plane somewhere? Surely he wouldn't take a trip out of town without telling her.

She sighed again. There was no help for it. She'd have to call around to his home and check on him. A stirring of misgiving filled her belly. *What if he'd tripped and fallen down the stairs? What if he was hurt?* Even now, he could be lying injured, bleeding, in pain with no one the wiser.

Trying hard to hold onto her panic, she collected her handbag and picked up her phone. Tossing it into her bag, she strode across her office and opened the door.

"Dorothy, I need to go out for a while."

Her secretary acknowledged her comment with a nod. "Of course. How long will you be gone?"

"An hour or so."

"So you'll be back in time for your eleven o'clock appointment?"

"Yes, I expect so."

"Good. Because they're new clients and I know for a fact the partners would be more than impressed if you manage to land them. They're the executors of a multimillion dollar estate. It will mean significant fees for the firm and would go some way to supporting your quest for promotion." Her secretary shot her a quick sideways glance. "I take it you're still angling for a partnership?"

"Of course. Isn't that the goal of every junior attorney?"

"I'm just looking out for you, Meghan."

"Yes, and I appreciate it, Dorothy. You know better than I do how these hallowed hallways work. I just have to duck out for a moment. It's a family emergency. I promise I won't be long."

"No problem. In case anyone asks, I'll cover for you while you're gone."

Meghan shot her a grateful look. The woman had been at Sydney Legal almost as long as the founding partners. There wasn't anything that happened in the place that Dorothy didn't know about.

Turning on her heel, she headed toward the bank of elevators and pressed the button. It arrived a few minutes later and as the doors slid open, she was thankful to discover it was empty. There were several legitimate reasons why she might be leaving the office at just after nine in the morning, but she preferred not to have to offer an explanation for her departure so soon after her arrival.

Striding out of the building, she made her way to the parking station where she'd left her car.

Often it was quicker and more convenient to catch a train into the city from her terrace house in the inner city suburb of Newtown, but today she'd taken her car and now she was grateful. Her father lived in an exclusive and ultra-expensive part of the eastern suburbs in a mansion that overlooked Sydney Harbour and though there was a public bus that serviced the area, it would be much faster to get there by car.

It was the same place where Meghan and her brother and half-sister had grown up. She'd had a privileged childhood, but despite her father's wealth, she liked to think she was a well-rounded individual who was prepared to work hard and do her bit to contribute to society. Just like Cody.

At the thought of her brother, she frowned. It had been three days since his bizarre late-night phone call. Though she'd called him back the next morning and several times after that, the calls had gone straight to his voicemail. She was almost certain he'd gone on a bender – cocaine was his drug of choice – and she wouldn't hear from him again until he'd come out from under his self-induced fog and decided to rejoin society. Sadly, it wouldn't be the first time. Everyone suffered from his absence. Well, maybe not everyone.

Meghan had called his estranged wife, Tanya, yesterday to ask if she'd heard from Cody. Tanya's response was brief and concise. She didn't give a flying toss where Meghan's brother was. The sooner he overdosed and removed his sorry ass from this world, the better as far as she was concerned. She had two kids to raise and she didn't need him and his drug-addicted presence in their lives. Period.

Tanya's bitter spray was well-deserved. Cody had gone from being a highly respected, incredibly talented stockbroker with a seven figure annual income to a man who could hardly get out of bed in the morning and who had turned to illegal drugs. It had affected his career, his marriage, his relationships. She couldn't deny it had changed the way she felt about him, but still, he was her brother, her *twin*. For all his flaws, she could never abandon him. She'd been worried about him ever since that strange phone call. And now there was something up with her dad. Maybe.

Her late model white Mazda CX-3 stood where she'd left it squeezed in between a large SUV and a pickup. Reversing out of the parking spot, she joined the stream of traffic headed east. Fortunately, peak hour was almost at an end and she made good time up New South Head Road. Less than thirty minutes after she left the office, she pulled up at the high wrought iron gates outside her father's impressive beachside mansion in the exclusive suburb of Point Piper.

Punching in the security code, she accelerated up the paved driveway, past the manicured lawns and symmetrical flower beds brimming with color and finally came to a halt outside the grand entryway that led into the house. Climbing out of the Mazda, she walked up the wide stone steps until she came to the front door. The handle turned beneath her fingers. That wasn't surprising.

Her father never locked the front door when he was home.

"Daddy? It's me. Where are you?"

Her voice echoed in the silence. She made her way across the highly glossed parquetry floor that lined the wide entryway and beyond and headed toward her father's study. The door was open and she made her way inside. The smell of his cologne immediately assailed her senses. Strong and pungent, it reminded her of all the times she'd sat in here reading or doing homework or texting her friends while he worked behind his grand cedar wood desk. He'd made his money from real estate and even at the age of sixty-two, he still continued to oversee the business, mostly from this every room. It held so many fond memories, but right now it was devoid of life.

"Daddy?" she called again as she crossed the wide hall and into the kitchen. "Where are you?" Once again, the house remained silent.

The kitchen was also empty. With a sound of frustration, she left the room and headed toward the staircase. Reminiscent of the resplendent staircase made famous in *Gone with the Wind*, as a dreamy-eyed teenager, she'd always found the whole idea of it so romantic. Now she barely noticed its grandeur. Hurrying now, she reached the top and turned left toward the wing her father lived in. It had been years since she'd been in his rooms. There had been countless nights after the death of her mother when she'd taken refuge in her father's bed, but that had been sixteen years ago. She couldn't remember the last time she'd been there.

"Daddy? Are you up here?"

No answer.

She frowned. *Surely he must be somewhere?* The front door had been unlocked, after all. If he'd gone away somewhere for more than a few hours, he would have secured it, like he usually did when he traveled.

The door to his bedroom was closed. A sudden surge of foreboding sent an icy shiver down her spine. Goosebumps sprung out on her skin. Turning the knob, she eased the door open and stepped into the room. A faint odor, not immediately recognizable, filled her nostrils. With dread weighing down her every step, she moved further into the room.

The king-sized bed with its huge carved wooden headboard was neatly made and empty. The room was spotless. Not even a single item of clothing was on the floor. She crossed over to the master bath. The smell got stronger. With her heart pounding, she forced herself to open the door.

Her piercing scream rent the silence. Shock held her immobile. Her father lay stretched out naked in the bathtub. His face was covered with a wash cloth. He could have been asleep except that his skin was completely bloodless and his body was grotesquely swollen. The smell of decomposition this close up was nauseating.

She held her hand up to her face as a rush of acrid vomit filled her mouth. Bending over, she emptied the contents of her stomach on the glossy pale gray marble tiles. Tears streamed from her eyes. When the retching had stopped, she stood up shakily and tried to get herself together.

"Daddy," she whimpered. "Oh, Daddy!"

Forcing herself closer, she reached out and took his hand. It was pale and cold and bloated. The underside that had been resting against the bathtub was a mottled dark purple where the blood had gathered and come to rest. And then she forced herself to look at the awful pattern that had been played out against his chest.

Stab wounds. Too many to count. They were dotted across his chest and abdomen in a pattern of unrestrained glee. A fresh wave of nausea rolled in her stomach and she braced herself against the unavoidable. To her relief, it was only dry retching. She'd already emptied out everything there was.

She had to call the police. Her father had been murdered. She was standing in the middle of a crime scene. She shouldn't have touched anything. What if she'd messed up vital evidence? Oh, God. Her father was dead.

The thoughts rushed through her mind in a kaleidoscope of increasing anxiousness. She was still deep in shock. *Who could have done this?* She shivered at the level of hate that seemed to permeate the room. This couldn't be happening. It was a nightmare from which she'd wake up. It had to be. The alternative was unthinkable.

Malicious Love will be released on
01 February, 2019 and is available for pre-order
from your favorite digital retailer.

About the Author

Chris Taylor grew up on a farm in north-west New South Wales, Australia. She always had a thirst for stories and recalls writing her first book at the ripe old age of eight. Always a lover of romance and happily-ever-afters, a career in criminal law sparked her interest in intrigue and suspense. For Chris to be able to combine romance with suspense in her books is a dream come true.

Chris is married to Linden and is the mother of five children. If not behind her computer, you can find her doing the school run, taxiing children to swimming lessons, football, ballet and cricket. In her spare time, Chris loves to read her favorite authors who include Richard North Patterson, Sandra Brown, Kathleen E Woodiwiss and Jude Devereaux.

You can find out more about Chris and sign up for her newsletter at her website:

http://www.christaylorauthor.com.au